| Performance Evaluation |

Major Tanya von Degurechaff

Counselor's notes on character and conduct:

Abundant loyalty and excellent fighting spirit.

Follows regulations to the letter.

Devoutly religious.

HAS A BAD TENDENCY TO TAKE MATTERS
INTO HER OWN HANDS.

COMPETENT BUT AS DIFFICULT TO
HANDLE AS A MAD DOG.

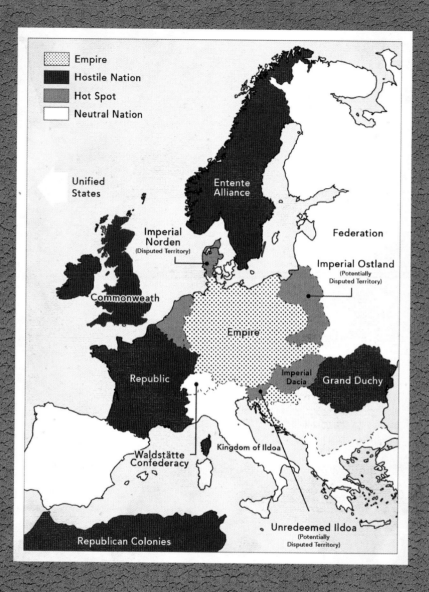

Empire
Hostile Nation
Hot Spot
Neutral Nation

Unified States

Entente Alliance

Imperial Norden
(Disputed Territory)

Federation

Imperial Ostland
(Potentially Disputed Territory)

Commonweath

Empire

Republic

Imperial Dacia

Grand Duchy

Waldstätte Confederacy

Kingdom of Ildoa

Unredeemed Ildoa
(Potentially Disputed Territory)

Republican Colonies

The Finest Hour

THE
SAGA of TANYA
THE EVIL

WE COMPLETELY MISSED OUR CHANCE TO END THIS WAR!

THE SAGA OF TANYA THE EVIL

The Finest Hour

〔3〕

Carlo Zen

Illustration by Shinobu Shinotsuki

YEN
ON
New York

The Saga of Tanya the Evil, Vol. 3

Carlo Zen

Translation by Emily Balistrieri
Cover art by Shinobu Shinotsuki

YOJO SENKI Vol. 3 The Finest Hour
©Carlo Zen 2014
First published in Japan in 2014 by KADOKAWA CORPORATION, Tokyo.
English translation rights arranged with KADOKAWA CORPORATION, Tokyo, through TUTTLE-MORI AGENCY, INC., Tokyo.

English translation © 2018 by Yen Press, LLC

Yen On
1290 Avenue of the Americas
New York, NY 10104

Visit us at yenpress.com
facebook.com/yenpress
twitter.com/yenpress
yenpress.tumblr.com
instagram.com/yenpress

First Yen On Edition: July 2018

Yen On is an imprint of Yen Press, LLC.
The Yen On name and logo are trademarks of Yen Press, LLC.

Library of Congress Cataloging-in-Publication Data
Names: Zen, Carlo, author. | Shinotsuki, Shinobu, illustrator. | Balistrieri, Emily, translator. | Steinbach, Kevin, translator.
Title: Saga of Tanya the evil / Carlo Zen ; illustration by Shinobu Shinotsuki ; translation by Emily Balistrieri, Kevin Steinbach
Other titles: Yōjo Senki. English
Description: First Yen On edition. | New York : Yen ON, 2017–
Identifiers: LCCN 2017044721 | ISBN 9780316512442 (v. 1 : pbk.) | ISBN 9780316512466 (v. 2 : pbk.) | ISBN 9780316512480 (v. 3 : pbk.)
Classification: LCC PL878.E6 Y6513 2017 | DDC 895.63/6—dc23
LC record available at https://lccn.loc.gov/2017044721

ISBNs: 978-0-316-51248-0 (paperback)
978-0-316-56057-3 (ebook)

2 4 6 8 10 9 7 5 3

LSC-C

Printed in the United States of America

THE SAGA OF TANYA THE EVIL

The Finest Hour

contents

One way or another, we'll find a path to victory.
If there isn't any to be found, we'll carve one ourselves.

Major General (at the time) von Zettour in
a personal conversation

In the gently streaming Arkansas sunlight, she raced over to her beloved grandma and presented a bag of bright red apples.

"Hey, Grandma, where should I put these apples the neighbors gave us?"

"Dear me, Mary, more apples? Carlos's wife must like you."

Smiling serenely, the old woman slowly began to rise from her easy chair. Her granddaughter was kind enough to offer a hand. Noticing her natural consideration, the elderly woman thanked God the girl had been raised to be kind and thoughtful.

The neighbors were proud of their harvest, and her granddaughter beamed like the sun after receiving a bag. Though the girl was staying with family, this was still a foreign country to her. Despite leaving her father behind to come live in a new and unknown place, she had won over even the most difficult people with that sunny smile.

She was a strong child, old enough that she wasn't oblivious to the events happening around her. She did everything she could to cheer up the whole household. The old woman was proud of her for that but, by the same token, found her circumstances so sad.

Thus, it was with mixed feelings that the grandmother eagerly stood and endeavored to keep the mood light by suggesting they bake an apple pie together. Her inability to do anything but worry about the miserable state of the conflict only fueled her frustration.

If only this cruel war would just end… The old woman sighed discreetly so Mary wouldn't notice and slowly headed for the kitchen. Catching a glimpse of her grieving daughter glued to the radio and newspaper in the sitting room, Mary's grandmother wiped tears from her eyes.

Ever since they had received notice about the death of her son-in-law Anson, the Entente Alliance soldier who had come to ask for her daughter's hand in marriage, Mary's mother had seemed listless, like her mind was elsewhere.

Anson had been a stubborn man, and the two of them had come to blows more than once, but for some reason in the end, they got along just fine. Now, the photograph of the happy couple merely served as a reminder that Anson was gone. The old woman could only lament her thoughtlessness in neglecting to put it away.

She knew that due to the physical distance between the Unified States and the Entente Alliance, as well as the immense confusion at the scene of the fighting, news wouldn't arrive very quickly. But at some point, she must have let her guard down. She was anxious for news of the war, but she never imagined that Anson would be killed.

And that was why she still kept recalling the day the death notice arrived and how stunned she had been.

A notice? For us?

It came on a tranquil, sunny day exactly like this one.

The old woman's daughter had finally started to smile again, seeming to have relaxed after returning to her hometown, while her granddaughter rushed around the foreign land giddy with curiosity. The old woman watched over them with a smile.

The bad news struck right as she was inviting the girls in for three o'clock tea.

Suddenly, a car flying the Entente Alliance flag pulled up, and an official from the embassy climbed out. When her daughter went to greet the man in her place, to spare her bad back, the old woman regretted that she didn't speak up and say, *"Let me go. I'd like to talk with a visitor now and then, too."*

If she had, she could have even taken the envelope he offered with a strained expression, his hands shaking, and hidden it away somewhere.

"Oh God! No!"

But instead, when she and Mary heard the screams and paused their tea preparations to rush for the doorway, they saw her daughter crumpled on the ground in tears and men in black whose faces said they couldn't bear to stand there any longer.

In retrospect, the old woman felt like a fool for blithely making tea at that moment.

Solemnly silent visitors in black? They were basically dressed for mourning, weren't they?

The reason for their visit should have been obvious.

DEATH NOTICE.

She hadn't even considered the possibility when she pulled the paper from her daughter's trembling hands, but the moment she read the single line printed on the front, time froze.

Her daughter still hadn't recovered from the shock.

Not only that, time is probably still frozen for her at exactly that moment.

After that, her daughter began listening obsessively to news broadcasts about the war, answering both Mary's encouragements and the old woman's consolations with the same hollow smile.

Tidying up the utensils in the kitchen, the old woman would think to herself.

How the war would surely end at some point. Apparently, from what she heard in the news, the Empire was retreating. She wasn't exactly sure what was going on, but…everyone whispered that the war seemed like it would end soon, so that's what she wished for. All she could do was hope. *If it's going to end, then I hope it ends soon.*

Perhaps the reason her daughter was tuning in to the broadcasts with a nearly religious devotion was that she hoped God would bring righteous judgment down on the Empire for taking her husband away.

Of course, revenge would only be empty and sad. At her age, the old woman knew that sorrows of the past could eventually be overcome. But for her daughter and granddaughter, the shock was still too great, so until the pain became dull and faded, she would endure it with them.

"All right, Mary, let's make this apple pie."

"Okay!"

Chapter I

Operations should be launched with a clear purpose and objective.

On that point, the General Staff praised Operation *Schrecken und Ehrfurcht* ("Shock and Awe") as a plan that embodied these ideals. Two major generals, Zettour and Rudersdorf, had drafted it.

The intentions of their proposal were plain and unambiguous.

By conducting radical but straightforward attacks that directly targeted enemy headquarters, it would be possible to knock out the opposing forces' chain of command, ultimately leading to the collapse of the enemy's lines.

That was it. One unit would be dispatched to complete one objective; it possessed the simple logic of *two plus two equals four.*

The reasoning behind it was obvious. A decapitated army cannot wage war.

Even a student at the academy would be able to grasp the intent immediately. After all, the strategy amounted to slicing off the enemy's head—neutralizing the command capabilities that were critical for a modern army.

However, the nature of the plan caused various staffers to raise serious doubts from the very beginning.

Naturally, the headquarters were considered incredibly important. Any army would establish their field command in friendly territory far beyond the reach of their enemies.

Common sense dictated that the Republic's headquarters on the Rhine front would be heavily defended. This foregone conclusion was confirmed with a reconnaissance in force at the cost of a great many lives.

Unless they could find a way past the enemy's dense interception screen and deal with any forces scrambled for defense, there was little hope of success. The majority of the General Staff had taken that into account and judged that if they were wholly prepared to dispassionately sustain losses in order to achieve a breakthrough, they would lose an entire brigade of aerial mages in the process.

So when the aim and execution of Operation *Schrecken und Ehrfurcht* were revealed, many staffers thought that anyone who would give such orders had to be crazy. There were even those who openly opposed the operation, claiming it was a joke that would accomplish nothing but recklessly send soldiers to their deaths.

Of course, none of the realists on staff objected to the operation's intended purpose. If it was possible to destroy the enemy chain of command by penetrating their lines and storming their headquarters, it didn't matter what sacrifices needed to be made. Assuming a reasonable chance of success, any number of casualties was acceptable.

Despite the appeal of undertaking bold ventures with no regard for the price, the staffers rejected the proposal due to the slim chances involved. Wagering their valuable troops on an operation with such a small probability of success was an unthinkable outrage under ordinary circumstances.

If chances were good, then sure, some losses could be ignored. Did it matter how high the returns would be if the likelihood of victory was impossibly low? Was this the operation they were pinning the success of the breakthrough on? If that was truly the case, every officer would have been forced to bitterly admit that they were done for.

Deep down, most officers on the General Staff privately believed that if it were possible to strike at the enemy headquarters directly, the Rhine front wouldn't have become a stalemate in the first place.

Such a meritless plan would normally be tossed in the waste bin and forgotten…but this particular proposal was drafted and jointly signed by none other than the generals Zettour and Rudersdorf.

At first, the staff were puzzled when they realized the two authorities on large-scale maneuver warfare seemed to be proposing the operation as a practical move. They reluctantly reviewed the document, and only upon an intensive reading did it dawn on them that the absurd plan was worthy of serious consideration.

In the end, loath as the other staffers were to admit it…they begrudgingly acknowledged that the operation might be possible. It all depended on committing the veteran 203rd Aerial Mage Battalion led by Major Tanya von Degurechaff, whose alias was in the process of shifting from the elegant "White Silver" to the more awe-striking and fearsome "Rusted Silver." They would also require supplemental acceleration devices that allowed the user to climb to altitudes where interception was impossible and gave them the speed to outrun any pursuers.

On paper, at least, the specs of the supplemental acceleration device, combined with the unit's accumulated achievements, made the proposal attractive enough to warrant discussion.

But even with all those cards assembled, the planners still hesitated— Zettour and Rudersdorf were suggesting, of all things, to dovetail *Schrecken und Ehrfurcht* ("Shock and Awe") with their next major plan, Operation Lock Pick. Claiming that there was no hope of pulling off Operation Lock Pick without the success of Operation *Schrecken und Ehrfurcht* invited particularly intense debate.

It was no small dispute. After all, having made their wager on Operation Lock Pick, the General Staff had already crossed the dangerous bridge of withdrawing troops from the Rhine front, a move that would normally be unthinkable. They were long past the Rubicon. It wasn't easy for them to maintain composure while listening to claims that their initial wager was now at the mercy of this gamble of an operation.

A fountain of objections erupted internally, and the debates that raged both in and out of conference rooms split the General Staff right in half. Calling the plan controversial didn't do it justice.

With officers grabbing one another by the lapels in fierce disagreement and cursing their peers as stubborn fools, the state of affairs was wild enough that it was more like a wrestling match than anything. It was plain to see how chaotic the internal strife had grown after multiple officers were officially reported to have "taken a tumble."

But in the end, the General Staff decided that the fundamental aim of attacking the enemy headquarters directly had a lot of promise. After all, even if they didn't manage to take it out completely, the attempt alone would still cause a great deal of confusion.

It might be a quixotic one-way charge, but the Republican Army would need to seriously take into account the threat of a capable aerial mage unit conducting a raid ever after, and that was huge.

They could expect this result even if the attack failed. In other words, if the Imperial Army carried out just a single decapitation strike, the Republicans would have to be constantly on guard against another.

They would have to station more of their precious few forces in the rear to guard the critical Rhine front headquarters.

It was a reasonable interpretation of the situation. Even in the sense of "trying is better than not," making a real effort didn't seem like a poor idea, either. At the very least, they would tie up additional enemy troops in the rear.

Some of the officers even added another thought in the back of their minds: *Major von Degurechaff might actually be able to wring out even better results.*

That said, no one could deny it was a risky operation. At worst, they would be sending their elite troops on a futile mission and could lose every single one. Of course, even if the attack force was wiped out, the threat would remain. It was a steep price to pay for a threat, though.

On top of that, the unit they planned to send in was the irreplaceable pet project that the General Staff kept close at hand—a quick response unit with a wealth of combat experience.

The 203rd Aerial Mage Battalion had been initially formed as an experiment, but it was currently serving as the General Staff's proverbial workhorse, consistently surpassing expectations on every battlefield. Its less flashy but nevertheless vital contributions in the field of testing new tactics and assessing new weapons couldn't be ignored, either.

This wasn't the sort of unit that could be duplicated overnight, and yet it was precisely thanks to their elite capabilities that anyone expected them to succeed. After struggling with that contradiction, the General Staff eventually settled on dispatching a company. That took into account both the amount of troops they were comfortable deploying and the number of troops necessary for success.

Once the size of the force was locked down, the Empire's intricate war machine became fully operational.

Twelve members of the 203rd Aerial Mage Battalion were promptly selected and transported to a launch base in the rear as the strike force that would utilize the supplemental acceleration device (code name V-1) to carry out the attack behind enemy lines.

The participants received technical briefings from the engineers as well as intelligence on enemy territory. All preparations for their combat mission were completed without delay.

However, the test run Major von Degurechaff petitioned for was denied due to secrecy concerns. It was an unavoidable decision, since the whole point of the operation was a sneak attack; from a counterespionage viewpoint, the General Staff couldn't allow it.

Of course, making an attempt with no practice was risky. The General Staff Office received many misgivings and doubts over this decision. Since the chances of success depended entirely on whether or not their unit could use the element of surprise, the mission's clandestine nature was emphasized to the point of suppressing any dissent. Ultimately, even Major von Degurechaff had to acknowledge the need for counterintelligence, though she did so reluctantly.

The team carried out piloting exercises in the hangar, but there were no actual launches with any equipment. In exchange, maintenance on the supplemental acceleration devices was performed with extra care at Major von Degurechaff's request.

The operation's itinerary was itemized in rigid detail, eventually settling into a plan to at least deal a blow to the enemy chain of command and temporarily take their communications down. Immediately following the raid on enemy headquarters, the strike force would head north where a friendly submarine or ship would retrieve them.

The General Staff debate ended with all participants more or less in agreement. The V-1 unit was given notice, and X-Day arrived on May 25.

"You can still see the shocking results today." (from the Commonwealth Army's War History Compilation Division's *History of the Rhine Front Volume 3*)

          MAY 25, UNIFIED YEAR 1925, IMPERIAL ARMY SECRET V-1
LAUNCH BASE

Major Tanya von Degurechaff stands resolutely on the runway at the airfield, watching the sun rise over the horizon with a gaze so unwholesome it could send even dead fish scattering as she utters a stunned *Guten Morgen* in her head.

The orders she received have instructed her to lead a select company in a direct attack on enemy headquarters to cut off the head of their army. In other words, decapitating their forces with a surgical strike.

As if the outrageous order itself isn't depressing enough, the method she needs to use is even worse.

Penetrating the enemy's defense by conventional means can't be done. Apparently, the brass understands that much. So for one reason or another, they've decided their only option is to adopt a radical approach, and what they came up with is a guided missile. The problem is that the guidance system is done on board and by hand.

To put it plainly, they're telling her to become a human rocket and charge in. If Tanya didn't have a reputation to worry about, she would be cradling her head right about now and shouting, *How did this happen?!*

Logically, Tanya understands that the operation she's about to carry out is not just a reckless gamble. There's no doubt that a reasonable chance of success exists. Once the plan was laid out in detail, the strategic practicality became clear.

The law of progress demands revolutionary advances fostered through vigilant skepticism of common sense as a potential for bias and consistent challenges to the paradigm. Given that, Tanya understands that from a military perspective, her moodiness could be considered irrational.

But from another rational viewpoint, waging war in the first place is a tremendous waste. Of course, there's no denying that the virtually meaningless exhaustion of every resource should be kept to a minimum. In a conflict, cutting costs wherever possible is necessary, logical.

All the data indicates that preservation measures must be taken. The numbers also suggest that it's necessary to secure an alternative source of supply to make up for inevitable losses. Unless the Empire seizes the Republic's assets in the terms for peace or something, Tanya's nation will collapse under the weight of its ever-increasing war expenditures. It's plain to see that the brass intends to wring reparations from the Republic.

In a debate, it's reasonable to employ statistical data to back up common sense or outwit it. Tanya can't deny that on moral or emotional grounds.

Of course, statistics lie. But they're the best kind of lies.

Statistically, no one expects someone with a savings account and life insurance to be a suicide bomber. If anything, a banker would actually like to maintain a long relationship with such a customer. Which is precisely why a practical, cunning terrorist could potentially duck surveillance by opening a savings account and purchasing life insurance.

In other words, anything can be good depending on how you use it.

Given all this, Tanya is fully aware how foolish it is to moodily declare, *That's impossible* or *It can't be done.* She is more than willing to undergo a healthy dose of introspection about her personal conclusions before disagreeing with others.

Nevertheless, she finds herself repeating the same unsolvable question to herself as she gazes with the eyes of a dead fish at the gigantic object in front of her: *How did this happen?*

What mad scientist had the ability to convince the army to approve of such an insane idea?

"A company will be launched via human-guided missiles, code name V-1." You'd have to be possessed to rationalize a plan like this to the point where Zettour and Rudersdorf would approve... It must have been *him.* Most Imperial Army engineers are constantly off in their own worlds, but Schugel is something else entirely.

Go to hell, Schugel, you piece of shit! Tanya feels like screaming when she recalls the man.

I should have killed him during those activation tests with a stray formula or a computation orb "accident." Even if he is a psychologically contaminated, pitiful puppet of Being X—or rather, because of that—someone should have killed him sooner, back when he still retained some human dignity.

The reason why I—or rather, why Tanya—gets carried away by her emotions and won't rest until she's shot Schugel to death any number of times in her mind is simple.

She's the commander of a battalion on the verge of falling apart due to the numerous casualties sustained in the course of rearguard duty, but the moment the unit finally made it back to a friendly base in the rear, they received a new operation along with newly developed equipment for it. She was so excited to see what kind of hospitality would be offered to them upon their return, but instead, events went in the exact opposite direction that she was hoping for, and worst of all, now they're being sent to a dangerous battlefield inside a sketchy weapon.

Major Tanya von Degurechaff knows herself well enough to realize she isn't the type to enjoy blasting off in a giant rocket.

Frankly, she's sick and tired of dangerous missions. And that's only natural, after being forced to carry out operation after ludicrous operation to help offset the risks simply because the plans are "theoretically possible."

As Heinrich's principles state, any accident that is liable to happen, will. There's no telling when one of these dangerous missions will end in a horrific mishap, and I don't want to keep going till I find out. No, I wouldn't mind being praised for my outstanding achievements and upgrading from my Silver Wings Assault Badge to a Silver Wings Assault Badge with Oak Leaves. Actually, I have been recommended for the Platinum Cross with Golden Swords, although informally, so at the very least, I can't deny that the risks are properly recognized.

Therein lies Tanya's agonizing internal conflict. A person of the modern world cannot forsake their duties without cause when they are held in such high esteem and receive medals for their contributions.

To do so would be a betrayal of contract and trust—the very things that make me who I am. Betraying your own dignity is essentially a form of suicide.

In a situation where an emergency evacuation is out of the question, Tanya's only practical choice is to loyally follow orders.

"I have to do it. If I have to do it, then I have to succeed." Standing on the runway glaring in the direction of the Republic, Tanya repeats those words like it's her duty.

She is so wrapped up in her own world that she doesn't notice someone has walked up next to her until they start speaking.

Unaware of the intense stare coming from nearby, she repeats herself, mustering her will and fighting spirit. "I have to do it. I just have to do it. I can't mess up this mission."

I'm going to live and hammer the righteousness of the market economy into that piece of trash Being X. Then I'll laugh as I shatter every last idol I can get my hands on. No matter what happens, I can't die before that.

"...Major von Degurechaff, sorry to interrupt you, but do you have a moment?"

Her conditioned reflexes clear all other thoughts from Tanya's head when she notices the voice.

"Ah, excuse me. Of course, Colonel von Lergen. What is it?"

Suddenly realizing she hasn't greeted him properly, Tanya takes a step back and extends her hand to the brim of her cap in a picture-perfect salute. As she thinks about ways to smooth over the situation, the gears of her brain go into overdrive, trying to remember if she has let something slip that she shouldn't have.

She only murmured two things on the runway. It's probably too much to ask for any eavesdroppers to think Tanya's feeling very motivated, but there shouldn't be much problem with talking to herself about needing to carry out her mission.

But that only means her muttering won't be taken badly on its own... It dawns on her in the next instant that, depending on the context, what she said could have grave consequences.

"No, you—ahh, er, rather, for you..."

"Huh?"

At the moment, Lieutenant Colonel von Lergen seems a bit bizarrely lost for words. This seems like the worst-case scenario. No matter how tightly the man clings to optimism, he's no fool.

One wrong move here and a report could be sent to the General Staff Office claiming her ability to carry out the operation is in doubt, revealing her motivation is lacking even if it doesn't go as far as to say she's disobeying orders. Lergen is undoubtedly someone who could submit such a report.

What will happen if Colonel von Lergen reports that he's skeptical about my will to fight?

All the discretion and freedom Tanya currently enjoys is granted on General von Zettour's say-so. If it comes to light that someone feels lukewarm—never mind outright critical—about a plan he and General von Rudersdorf put so much effort into, who knows what might happen.

"It's just rare to see you seeming so reluctant." Choosing his words with a bit of a wince on his face, he trains his gaze on Tanya and continues grumbling. "It's you we're talking about, so there must be some reason for your hesitation."

A vampire who's just been stabbed through the heart with a stake would probably feel like this.

"Ahh, I see… No, I was just wondering something."

"Wondering something?"

Tanya steels herself as she prepares to conduct damage control in hopes of minimizing the fallout. *This is an obstacle that must be overcome no matter what.* Furthermore, to cover up her lack of fighting spirit, she promptly decides to state how unfortunate it is that she can't lead an even bigger offensive.

Having come to both conclusions in the blink of an eye, Tanya von Degurechaff unhesitatingly furrows her brow to express regret. "Isn't it strange? All this gear and prep work…so much effort to maintain secrecy. The army is putting an astonishing amount of work into every area of this operation. That's why I wonder…" Appealing to Lergen for an answer with a glance, she asks, "Are we really carrying out this elaborately planned sneak attack for the sole purpose of causing confusion at the enemy headquarters?"

Rails have been laid on the runway to launch the supplemental acceleration devices. And resting on top of those tracks are the constructs themselves, hooked up to a mind-numbing number of boosters while workers fill the fuel tanks with an unbelievable amount of highly volatile liquid propellant.

Considering how much impact all this activity has on secrecy, Tanya can't be the only one who sensed a firm intention to go through with the operation by the time the rails were laid out and the rockets began fueling.

Which is precisely why she points a finger and asserts that it seems like a disproportionate amount of effort, even for hitting the enemy headquarters.

"I don't believe it's a mistake to assume that striking at the enemy headquarters will require a great deal of advance preparation."

Colonel von Lergen's gruff response is what she expected. Tanya doesn't object to the necessity of extensive preparations.

"You're correct, Colonel. But it almost feels as though…it should at least serve as the opening salvo of a greater battle."

Tanya suggests that they could pursue wider objectives while implying serious doubts regarding the cost-effectiveness of the current plan. Of course, she understands the technical reasons why it's difficult to cancel a launch once the rockets are filled with their highly volatile fuel. Nevertheless, she makes her point in earnest.

"Hmm, so you mean the plan as it is now won't accomplish much?"

"More that we're missing out on a chance to do something bigger. I'm not saying that attacking enemy headquarters will have no effect, but…"

Tanya casually evades the trap Colonel von Lergen set for her. Skepticism on this point could be seen as an attempt to shirk her duties by calling the effectiveness into question.

Yes, he must be testing her to see if she's using a plausible excuse to cover up the fact that she lacks the will to fight.

In response, Tanya boldly plays the unabashed patriot, highlighting that it would be a waste of an opportunity. She suggests that the mission should be paired with some other endeavor.

This strike is fundamentally different from hunting down a one-shot lighter carrying a certain admiral on an innocent inspection tour. As long as the target is immobile, we should be choosing the most advantageous timing.

"From my perspective, sir, it's like doing all this careful prep just to shoot off a couple fireworks. The cost performance is rather…"

But having said that much, Tanya gets a strange feeling and trails off. *Yes, this is very weird.*

"Major?"

Momentarily pushing Colonel von Lergen's questioning look out of her thoughts, she ruminates on the word that flitted across her mind and confirms the strange feeling.

The cost-effectiveness is suspiciously bad. Would they really invest so much to achieve this single objective?

Is this the sort of operation General von Zettour would propose with his coolheaded thoughts on attrition warfare? On top of that, the participation of General von Rudersdorf is also odd. This is an unorthodox operation that relies on cunning, so why is the bigwig maneuver warfare specialist from the General Staff involved?

"Ah, but...causing chaos at enemy headquarters...leading to a larger battle? No, they'd be put out of commission..."

That instant, multiple questions in Tanya's mind connect and lead her to the answer. Destroying the enemy headquarters would throw them into chaos. At that point, even a modern army devolves into little more than a mob. That is the General Staff's true objective. If General von Rudersdorf capitalizes on the confusion to make a move...he'll be able to break from the current trench warfare back into maneuver warfare.

A modern army, even when nestled in trenches, only exists thanks to its brain, the headquarters. If you look at how weakened the Red Army was after that idiot Stalin's purge, you can see there's no room for debate about what happens to an army that has lost its command structure.

And one more thing.

I don't know what it's like for a leader like that jerk Stalin, who seemed to think soldiers grew on trees, but in a normal nation under regular circumstances, probably the only country that could continue fighting after losing its regular army on the front is the American empire.

"...So it's all to encircle and annihilate them. In other words, we're trying to lure the Republican Army in."

Dare to allow the enemy to take a strategic location, then force a battle. It's the same art of war Bonaparte performed like a con man at Austerlitz. The Low Lands certainly are a key location. They're basically the Pratzen Heights.

It's impossible to ignore something so tempting dangling right before your eyes.

…Was the entire reorganization of the defensive lines done with the intention of baiting the enemy?

If that's the case…then this will be a mobile battle, but not just a mere breakthrough. It's a revolving door!

I've been wondering why they abandoned only the critical Low Land position and didn't continue reorganizing the rest of the line. Now it all makes sense.

"So…we're the switch for the revolving door?"

Those words trigger something.

"Major! Where did you hear that?!"

His face changes color as he snaps at Tanya. The fierceness in his eyes makes her smile in satisfaction as she thinks, *Aha, I see.*

"Oh, I just thought of it myself, but…from your reaction, I take it my hypothesis isn't far off?"

"…You really didn't hear it from General von Zettour?"

"No, but I've had an odd feeling this whole time, almost like a small bone was stuck in my throat."

Tanya knew something was off the moment she heard that the large-scale reorganization of the front was related to the situation with imperial supply lines, but then her unit was ordered to serve as the rear guard. It's not her fault she didn't have time to think more about it back then.

When the retreat went all according to plan, she felt incredibly relieved, so it took a little while to realize what was really happening.

After puzzling over the retreat for a few days, the Republican Army quickly proceeded to advance. Tanya heard from reconnaissance that the Republicans were marching along in high spirits, ready to destroy the Empire, but they were moving so slow that she was certain there would be plenty of time to reorganize the lines.

Assembling everything she knew about the situation, she was sure that she was missing something, though she couldn't articulate why it felt so strange.

Before, she wondered if it was really necessary to fall back so far just to reorganize. But now everything is clear. It was all preparation to swing the revolving door around.

In that case, I see why the mission has been kept so thoroughly classified and why a million arrangements have been made just for this one sortie. It's like we're the fireworks at the revolving door announcement ceremony.

"...All right, Major von Degurechaff. You must understand how much the General Staff is counting on this operation."

"Yes, sir, Colonel. I am fully aware."

We're serving as the vanguard of the General Staff's grand mobile operation that'll lay the groundwork for a massive encirclement. Of course, if we fail, the army will pretend nothing is wrong and reorganize the defensive lines accordingly. But seeing how far imperial lines have been pulled back, it's clear the higher-ups were extremely aware of how high the risks were when they decided to make this move. I can tell we have to succeed, no matter the cost.

"There is no greater honor for my battalion than to carry the hopes of the entire armed forces on our shoulders. Please leave everything to the 203rd Aerial Mage Battalion's select company. We *will* fulfill the General Staff's fervent wish with our martial prowess." Tanya makes her declaration while standing perfectly at attention with her head held high, the impeccable posture a product of her training. "I swear we will annihilate them. As for the General Staff, I humbly ask that they wait for our good news."

"You haven't changed one bit, Major von Degurechaff. All right, I wish you success. May God protect you."

Although Colonel von Lergen's expression indicates he's perplexed by the somewhat philosophical vow, he manages to smile awkwardly and extend his hand.

"May God protect the fatherland. Then again, as long as us soldiers are around, maybe we can handle it ourselves instead."

Tanya grasps the man's hand and smiles fearlessly. *Humans can handle God's work instead.* Though Lergen said it in a spur of the moment, it felt wonderful for her. She's practically falling in love with the turn of phrase.

We'll take God's place.

"May God protect the fatherland. Then again, as long as us soldiers are around, maybe we can handle it ourselves instead."

What a great way to put it!

The only problem with it is…I'll need to get rid of that damned Being X somehow. But even so, the wise and proper first step, atheism, will be taken.

I will save the fatherland in God's place. The enthusiasm that wells up inside her from the boast feels amazing. They're magic words that fill her with optimism and the willpower to be so accomplished that the very existence of God becomes unnecessary.

In theory, storming the enemy headquarters is a logical choice.

No, I would even venture to call it thoroughly rational. After all, committing significant forces to defend an important base in the rear while allotting troops to the front lines is an exceptional workload.

This goes without saying, but the fact that the Republican forces will have to implement countermeasures for the future, even if we literally deal no damage at all to their headquarters, means we can already expect the attack to have considerable effect.

Any soldier who hears their headquarters has come under attack would anticipate the coming trouble and bury their head in their hands. Nor has it been rare in wars of any place or era for heavy bombers to harass the bunker where the enemy commanders are holed up.

In this world, mages represent a unique branch of the military. They can serve as infantry or airborne troops that possess mobility on par with helicopters. Depending on how they're deployed, they can be quite handy for penetrating deep into enemy territory.

When we write a new page of history by displaying the quintessence of magic fighting power, if it's possible to put in a part about saving the fatherland in God's place, that would be the best publicity.

Tanya thinks to herself, *I'm just taking these lemons and making lemonade,* as she tries to turn a crisis into an opportunity, foreseeing the great promotional opportunity.

Granted, I'd be even happier to participate if this operation didn't entail being tied to a clump of explosives.

It's important to spell this out… I've been selected to be a part of the strike team that will insert into the field strapped to a V-1.

Even so, that was a day Major von Degurechaff felt exuberant after successfully finding a clear purpose to work toward.

Everyone who was present that day would pass down a wondrous story—a tale about how the Devil of the Rhine, Rusted Silver rushed toward the enemy headquarters in the highest of spirits.

Her quick, concise pre-sortie speech would be gossiped about in whispers long afterward. *"Gentlemen, may the gods protect the fatherland, but only if we soldiers are on paid vacation in Valhalla!"* Then, in front of her subordinates who howled with laughter, witnesses said she boasted, *"We will save the fatherland in God's place! Render unto Caesar the things that are Caesar's! Men, it is time for a war waged by humans. We go to win!"*

But history tends to pass down only one side of a story: Immediately after barking those words, she turned her back to everyone to climb nimbly up the ladder to board her V-1. On her face was a disappointed look that screamed, *Why me?*

Current altitude: 8,800 feet; speed: 991 knots.

The company made up of elites of the elite, selected from the 203rd, formally known as the 203rd Aerial Interception Mage Battalion, smashes through the sound barrier on their attack mission in three *Schwärme*.

For better or worse, the operation is smoothly under way with no mechanical trouble.

It's "under way," but really we're just being transported, grumbles Tanya in her head. Though there are a few things they can adjust, the V-1s Tanya and her company are riding are essentially rockets, not aircraft. There actually is a way to change direction, but even that's limited to a few millimeters, meaning it's only useful for slight course adjustments.

This makes piloting a V-1 extremely simple. After flipping the switch to turn on the engine, all that's left is to make minor corrections with the control stick.

There's almost nothing the mages on board can do once they launch. In fact, the only thing we have to do is maintain our protective films

and defensive shells. The stick is good for adjusting the angle of our approach and that's about it. If we need to perform emergency evasion for some reason, the only option available is a special function that provides more acceleration.

Ultimately, we're just being transported to the airspace above our destination with fuel tanks. In a way, we're like the early astronauts. A couple of people who're merely along for the ride.

Well, unlike the early astronauts, we can't expect an enthusiastic reception from bouquet-bearing colleagues upon a successful landing.

After all, we won't be arriving back on Earth where a support team is anxiously awaiting our return at the planned touchdown point but in a nest of dear escargots overflowing with hostility.

If we smile and cheerfully greet the startled Françoisians with a *Guten Tag*, we're bound to get lead bullets in return.

Which is why Tanya's unit visiting from the Empire will politely knock on the door first.

The plan is to detach from the V-1s, full of hydrazine and boron additives, then use them as door knockers to land the first blow.

Rocket shells traveling faster than sound will crash into their respective targets. It goes without saying that they carry quite a lot of energy with them. Our scientists have guaranteed that these are the best door knockers in all of human history; they'll jolt you awake no matter how deep your subterranean bunker is.

I'm sure our visit will be very surprising, what with us knocking so hard, but this is a gentlemanly two-part operation where our mage detachment will carry out our attack afterward.

In other words, whoever thought up this plan is awfully wicked. That's the best praise anyone can give an officer on the General Staff.

But as one of the people strapped to a rocket filled with doom, I want to cry. We don't even need to take fire like a one-shot lighter—an external explosion would be enough to do us in.

Well, this is the tragedy of war. We probably *should* cry. The fate awaiting both those of us forced to attack and the people we're hunting is to spill blood from our mouths in a fight to the death. By now, everyone on the battlefield is a victim—another tear-inducing tragedy of war.

Despite being a soldier forced to fight, Tanya von Degurechaff declares that peace is sacred.

It's much better for soldiers to putter around idly in a peaceful world. If soldiers are sweating and bleeding in earnest, it means the nation forgot to either wear its diaper or keep a guard dog.

Though this situation is spinning out of control, Major Tanya von Degurechaff sadly swallows her sighs and complaints as she reminds herself that she must push forward with her duty. *I'm currently a soldier, which means I must fulfill my military obligations. And in these modern times, a well-disciplined unit is not allowed to be late.*

To console herself, Tanya muses, *At least if history makes a note of this, it should also mention atheism on the battlefield.* This is a great chance for me to carve my beliefs into the history books.

If there's a chance to leave behind words that disparage God, then Tanya has no choice but to perform some outrageous promotional stunts today.

After all, there's no such thing as bad PR. Well, I guess the difference here is that instead of message boards lighting up in a flame war, it'll be organic matter going up in literal flames. Even if the varieties of flames are different, they achieve the same effect, so maybe I don't have to worry about it too much.

Time for work. Tanya checks the time and reviews her plans.

No, there's no time left to waste grumbling.

According to the schedule, it's almost time to prep for the strike, so Tanya switches gears and quickly confirms the steps she needs to take. Midcourse speed is normal. The afterburner settings for the terminal phase of the flight are also fine.

The empty fuel tank she was anxious might explode separates as it's supposed to.

With an eye on her navigation chart, Tanya gets a fairly accurate reading of her current position—which is quite critical—using her instruments. She's been concerned about miscalculations or being blown off course by the wind, but her approximate position is almost exactly as planned. Everything is within acceptable tolerances.

"01 to all units. We're now entering the final leg. Report in."

Receiving responses that there are no problems from her company via directional waves, Tanya suppresses a range of emotions and nods for the moment. There's a lot she wants to say, but at least the mechanics in charge of V-1 maintenance did their jobs right. She'll have to thank them for the way the machines didn't malfunction and suddenly come apart midflight.

Fearing the worst, she had secured enough tear-resistant, fireproof, automatic parachutes designed for extreme conditions that she had used back during her Elinium Arms days and outfitted the whole team. Fortune must be smiling on us since we didn't have to use them during the flight.

…No, destiny is something we humans grasp with our hands. It's decidedly not bestowed upon us by someone else's grace. *Luck* isn't really the right way to say it. This is a favorable outcome humans created themselves through careful maintenance and thorough confirmation.

"01 to all units. It's time. Measure your distance and calculate your angle of approach on the double."

A world in which success blossoms by the hands and efforts of humans… That is the ideal world. No matter how unproductive it is, praising humans for being so wonderful requires no pretense.

"05 to 01. Target located."

"09 to 01. Same. Target located."

"Splendid. All units, confirm that strike preparations are complete."

It's rare for war—or anything, really—to go according to plan, but it's far from impossible. If precautions are carefully taken ahead of time, the environment is forgiving, and inefficiency and recklessness are abhorred, then it can happen.

Isn't that spectacular? Hooray for efficiency! That's what I'm talking about.

"01 to all units. Transition into phase seven. I say again, transition into phase seven." Upon receiving confirmation from her men that preparations are complete, Tanya shifts to the next stage.

Phase seven, the strike order.

The moment she gives the signal, the members of the company separate from their V-1s and eject.

Due to the nature of the V-1's propulsion originating from the engine in the rear rather than a propeller out front, the mages are ejected forward before beginning their free fall.

Simultaneously, almost like a fun bonus, the empty fuel tanks and passenger-shielding elements begin to purge from the rocket; they'll function as camouflage.

Tanya and the other mages mingle with these jettisoned parts on their descent. Performing the first HALO drop[1] in recorded history is fairly risky business.

For additional stealth, we're challenging the limitations of HALO. Normally you would open the parachutes around 980 feet, but we're mages. We'll fall at the same speed as the rocket parts and decelerate right before two hundred fifty. By hiding this way, we dramatically reduce our chances of being discovered.

Still, that only means the probability of discovery is very low. The plan doesn't take our safety into account at all. It's a choice based purely on tactical necessity.

I won't be satisfied until I get back and force the person who thought this up to try it themselves.

"Men, may God protect you."

She meant to wish her troops luck but ended up saying something she didn't like one bit. Well, damn it.

If I'm praying for the protection of that infuriating deity, I must be really messed up in the head. Tanya's forced to lament this as another aspect of the tragedy and brutality of war. These conflicts spell nothing good for sound psyches.

And I wish so, so dearly for the creator of the Elinium Type 95, a particular mad scientist, to go straight to hell. It was a mistake to forgive him simply because he wasn't in his right mind. Tanya's so eager to see him go that she wouldn't mind doing it herself.

---

[1] **HALO drop** A type of parachute drop. If you consider a basic drop as descending to your destination with your parachute open, the HALO style has you jumping from outside of visual confirmation range (around ten thousand meters up) and opening the parachute around three hundred meters from the ground so your parachute isn't as conspicuous.

With all these thoughts in her mind, she adds another comment.

"Okay, gentlemen, let's put God out of a job!"

Really, my ambition is to become my own salvation, Tanya thinks to herself as she follows procedure to the letter and deploys her parachute at the prescribed altitude.

For a brief instant, the deceleration g's are absolutely unbearable. After that, I feel only gratitude for having such a small body until I encounter the shock of making landfall, which I just barely manage to distribute using the PLF technique. I complete the landing thanks to a mage's unique sturdiness and my protective film.

The day where I employ the emergency landing technique drilled into me during our computation orb aerial maneuvering course has finally come. What the hell. Tanya sighs, blowing off steam by mentally punching the guy who came up with this drop technique as she cuts herself free from her parachute.

Still, it seems that everyone in the unit has touched down without issue.

It makes me glad that we learned the five-point parachute landing fall properly.

I did wonder what was wrong with instructors who would willingly shove a child like me—even if only in appearance—out of a plane. But now I have to thank them from the bottom of my heart. I should send a note when I get back.

Having thought that far, Tanya winces. *The mission. I have to get through this first.* She reboots her mind.

Figuring it would be difficult to meet up upon landing, she instructed everyone to operate in *Rotten* with whoever was close by. *So who landed around here?* When Tanya scans the area, she sees Second Lieutenant Serebryakov running toward her. Apparently, my adjutant has landed safely. Of course, that's what Tanya expected from her tough buddy; they've been together since their time on the Rhine.

"09 to 01. Landing complete. No losses."

"01, roger. Report on the results of the supplemental acceleration device impacts."

This is a good sign. Tanya smiles. Happily, the unit seems to have maintained good order. First Lieutenant Weiss, who landed some distance away, promptly reports in that he has made contact with the rest of the company. Though the whole unit dropped separately, reorganization is going as smoothly as it possibly could—something that only a highly trained group can pull off.

"The door knockers hit almost all bull's-eyes. The only target we apparently missed is the ammunition dump."

But things can only go so smoothly.

To Tanya, a miss is a miss, but the warhead that was supposed to cause security at the enemy headquarters to descend into chaos after detonating their ammunition dump hasn't done its job. That's why Tanya doesn't reprove all the people who she can hear sucking their teeth over the radio. She only sighs, thinking to herself, *I told them to do at least one test run.*

Sadly, there's nothing else she can do. Or rather, she should probably be glad that they were transported via a barely tested clump of explosives and achieved most of the planned objectives so far without losing anyone.

That's why she hesitates for a brief moment, trying to think of the best way to proceed. The safe arrival of her eleven subordinates has been confirmed via a secure channel.

That's certainly good news, but since we failed to blow up the huge storehouse suspected to be an ammunition dump, the enemy probably isn't too confused. Still, the defenders probably haven't realized we're preparing to attack.

…In conclusion, we can still recover from this. Destroying that ammunition dump is still plenty possible.

"We have no choice, then. I'll work on taking out the ammunition dump. You guys, blow away any defenders. We don't have much time. Keep your eye on the schedule!"

"09, roger! Can I take two platoons?"

"01, sure. 07, 12, come with me."

"04 to 09. Form up in *Schwarm*."

"02 to 01. We're in *Schwarm*, too."

Satisfied with the swift assembly of the platoons, yet irritated at the poor V-1 impact results, Tanya finds herself a bit frustrated.

Her unit is in fine shape. They infiltrated enemy territory with no casualties and no organizational mishaps. It must be true that efficiency improves people's mood. Seeing a group that can capably carry out orders is a joy. The problem is the high likelihood that we haven't caused the chaos that this attack was predicated on.

My company may be in good form, but we aren't supposed to be going up against an enemy command post with its secure defenses intact.

"Be ready for the assault. I'll go after the ammo dump, but do everything else according to the plan."

"How should we divide up the objectives?"

"09, you take B and C. I'll do A."

Resigned to the high potential of taking terrible losses, Tanya chooses to carry out the raids, as if she has any other choice.

According to the data they received beforehand, there are three possible locations for the main Republican Army headquarters facilities. They were counting on the chaos for a chance to identify their target properly—a V-1 was supposed to have blown up the Republican Rhine Army Group's ammunition dump.

...Maybe I asked for too much.

Because the people who equipped us are engineers through and through, they gave us flying objects that use leftover boron additive to light afterburners and actually accelerate into the ground instead of coasting. Would there ever be any manufacturing line problems if every industrial product functioned exactly according to the manual?

Anyone who believes machines work completely according to design either has no idea what it's like in the field or is a designer in a lab who turns a blind eye.

Certainly, according to its specs, the V-1 has a speed of one thousand knots during its terminal phase. And in reality, Tanya can guarantee they were going at least that fast. It was no lie when the engineers assured her that a direct hit with that much kinetic energy would smash even a pillbox to smithereens.

But the engineers and designers forgot one critical thing. Yes, it's physically possible for a V-1 to obliterate anything that isn't an underground shelter fortified to paranoia levels in case of nuclear war. And given those things don't exist in this world yet, that means V-1s can destroy practically any hardened position.

But Tanya thinks of another important condition. These results are only possible if the V-1 lands a direct hit. Put another way, if it doesn't score that hit, it's just throwing away energy.

...Wasting so much of that extreme destructive potential is so pointless it's distressing.

This issue must be due to the engineering crew's disregard for cost-effectiveness. Something that scatters like a cluster bomb would have worked better. *If I get to return to base, I'll berate those asses in the Imperial Army Technical Arsenal.*

"No sign of enemy mana signals."

"Not detecting any here, either."

"Okay, let's do this."

Still, for now it's time to focus on the operation. Our first move means everything.

Success depends on us attacking before the enemy can respond. From the lack of enemy signals, it seems they're concentrating entirely on dealing with the aftermath of the rockets.

...Well, that just makes sense.

Tanya almost feels for the enemy on that point. No one's going to be thinking about a direct assault. A sane person wouldn't expect humans to be hitching a ride on long-range shells or rockets.

In other words, in a sense, their first move will be somewhat easy. Sure, there are probably guards around the headquarters. But if the numbers are even, well, her subordinates are war crazy and have earned the title of veterans even from an objective standpoint. They'll be able to eliminate them.

"01 to all units. Watch the clock. Ten minutes in is the most we can hope to get before Republican reinforcements show up."

From the sounds we can catch and what else we can make of the situation, the Republicans don't seem to understand what's going on at all. At least, instead of scrambling, they're prioritizing damage control. Well, they're trying to figure out how to handle their first time being attacked by long-range rockets. They're so busy puzzling over the impacts, they haven't realized that attackers have snuck in.

Otherwise, there's no explanation for the lack of mana signals.

"03 to 01. I've succeeded in intercepting a signal. It's uncoded."

Tanya is sure of it when she hears the report from her man making observations and tuning into the waves. The Republican Army really has no idea we're here.

"That's a good sign. Push in with your mana signals suppressed. After the attack on the headquarters, withdraw at full speed. We'll shoot two rendezvous beacons ten minutes after we leave."

"Roger."

Suppressing a sigh, she clutches her weapon and flies toward the enemy headquarters with the others. If only her buddy Lieutenant Serebryakov had messed up landing, Tanya could have loudly claimed she couldn't abandon someone who'd been under her since the Rhine Battle and pretend to search for her while sending in the rest of the unit.

No, I should use my legitimate sabotage card (as a laborer) for later.

Now, the correct thing to do is be happy that my partner has been improving so tangibly since the Rhine Battle or thereabouts. I should appreciate any increase in human capital.

"All right, we're going in."

The second lieutenant following behind her looks so dependable when she nods that Tanya's conviction deepens that humans are great beings capable of growth and development. Meanwhile, she suppresses her mana signal as much as possible and charges.

Her subordinates follow behind her.

And what Tanya finds when she arrives is enemy soldiers caught utterly off guard, gaping at them.

Maybe the problem is that it's a rear base. The officers here clearly have no idea how to get a handle on this kind of confusion. Not that I can blame them.

Tanya smiles as she sweeps them with the submachine gun she "found," thinking how user-friendly it is as she cleans up the Republican soldiers while continuing her advance.

I feel slightly uneasy about the fact that many of them aren't carrying weapons, but in the end, assuming people at the base are combatants and shooting them won't be an international legal issue.

So I just have to calmly eliminate the enemy. *The word* enemy *is so convenient in that it requires no discussion,* Tanya thinks as she looks over at her subordinates, and her face inadvertently relaxes into a smile.

Promptly shooting in response to the four words *It's the enemy! Fire!* is the apex of military discipline. Operant conditioning is truly great for improving effectiveness in combat.

"Lieutenant, how's it look over there?"

"Clear! No problems."

Upon receiving exactly the answer she wanted from Lieutenant Serebryakov, who was keeping an eye on their back, Tanya grins with pleasure. *Wonderful.*

For a unit charging forward, finding no sign whatsoever of any of those fearsome enemies who pursue from behind is unexpected good news. I'm surprised, but it appears that the General Staff's prediction that the Republican Army headquarters would be heavily defended was way off.

"A failure of rationalists. They couldn't believe the enemy would be that stupid. Well, I should be careful myself."

The rationalists who work on the General Staff consider the headquarters as the cornerstone of the command structure and something that should be guarded with one's life no matter the cost. According to the Imperial Army's common sense, the Republican Rhine Army Group headquarters should be defended like a fortress. Hence, why the generals Rudersdorf and Zettour embarked on this sneak-attack plan that entails bending over backward to launch aerial mages in V-1s.

And…Tanya had barged in here nervous about what might be waiting for them, but now that she takes a look, it seems like an awfully slack rear base.

In other words, the Republicans assumed that this place wouldn't become a battlefield. From the looks of it…there aren't very many experienced NCOs around, either.

So we can be a bit bolder.

A civilian financial institution has better security than this. Managing badges for entry and IC tags is actually quite effective, and the guards are more prepared.

"What can I say…? I guess once in a while it's not bad to be foolhardy."

This is the kind of thing that makes me want to slump forward and grumble. The eat-or-be-eaten determination found in civilian financial institution guards is a natural result of necessity. In a way, everything works according to the market principle.

In that sense, this is pretty much what happens with a conscript army. You can't very well expect guards to take their duties seriously when they're clinging to the wishful thought that enemies won't appear in the rear.

"Major, look."

"…Is it a trap? I don't see how. Are we in the wrong place? Four seems like awfully few to be guarding an ammo dump."

When you encounter the unexpected, you inherently can't predict what will happen. My intention was to blow up the enemy ammunition dump to cause chaos, but…there are only four guys in front of the warehouse that appears to be the target. Not only that, but they look like MPs, and they're smoking and chatting without a care in the world.

What military policeman would smoke right in front of an ammunition dump? It's hard to imagine those sticklers for regulation breaking rules in the disciplinarian heaven of the rear. In other words, circumstantial evidence indicates that none of these buildings are anything remotely like an ammunition dump. For Tanya's platoon, it means they've been approaching the wrong target. All pain, no gain.

"Remember, they could be using optical camouflage. Any irregularities in the refraction ratio?"

"No. No suspicious signals, either… Those guys are probably it, Major."

"…Intelligence sure did a bang-up job this time. Well, we have no choice, Lieutenant. Let's blow this thing to pieces and head back to make Weiss's life easier."

"Understood, Major." Lieutenant Serebryakov nods.

Tanya whispers that they'll take it out in a single attack as she loads several formula rounds into her submachine gun.

To be extra safe, I double-check before attacking, but the number of enemy guards really is so low that it's equal to our forces. And they're regular old infantry. The only notable thing is that there are awfully few of them.

I see, so it's not the ammunition dump. This is just some storage facility. In that sense, it's easy to understand why no one's coming after us. From the way those four are equipped, they're MPs. In other words, they're standing guard there purely as a formality.

"Is this really the Republican Rhine Army Group headquarters? It's hard to believe given how lax the security is."

"Ahh, Major, umm, well…"

"If you have something to say, Lieutenant Serebryakov, go ahead and say it. I'm not so narrow-minded that I would refuse to listen to a subordinate's valid advice."

"Yes, Major. Perhaps…the enemy soldiers are only concentrated at the more critical facilities…?"

Lieutenant Serebryakov meekly offers her suggestion. But it's a point Tanya can agree with. If the Republicans aren't the least bit concerned if this place gets approached, then surely they can't understand why anyone would target it. If I myself consider how many troops to station at an unimportant position versus a critical one, the outcome is self-evident.

"That's very possible, but what a pain."

Tanya sighs as the weight of her near future presses down on her.

If there aren't any enemy soldiers around here not because they're incompetent but because this area just isn't very important…? It means that Weiss's unit could be up against far more resistance than expected.

In that case, we might be unable to achieve our objectives, endure endless counterattacks, and miss our rendezvous with the submarine.

None of that is good.

"Okay, Lieutenant. All the more reason to hurry."

It's the worst possible future.

No, it's a horrible outcome that we must do everything in our power to avoid. I'm not interested in getting shot down over the sea *or* roaming around forever.

"We'll eliminate them. Let's go. We clean these guys up right quick and then get back to help the others."

So Major Tanya von Degurechaff makes up her mind.

As long as we're here, we have to do what we came for.

What's done is done, as they say. I meant to leave the dangerous act of storming in for my subordinates and act as their support, but considering the possibility of someone catching up to us from behind, maybe charging into the tiger's den isn't so bad.

That said, I can't ignore the objective right in front of me: This is the designated point. Tanya's only choice is to take rapid action.

Don't laugh at my bureaucratic mind-set. Even if I blow this worthless facility up, it's not going to count as any sort of achievement. For that, I'd like to unleash a treasury's worth of curses on Intelligence for apparently seizing on and passing along false information. At the moment, though, those gripes will do me no good.

So there's no point in talking about it now.

Since I have orders to destroy this place, it'll be insubordination if I don't. Tanya would like nothing better than to scream, *Eat shit!* However, as a disciplined cog of a modern nation, the notion of a right to refuse doesn't exist for her.

When it comes down to it, as long as Tanya has orders, it doesn't matter what else happens. She has to blast that nondescript concrete building to bits.

And if she has to eliminate these four measly guards to do it, she doesn't feel so much as a shred of guilt.

In the end, she may be the one shooting the gun, but what makes her open fire is the state's will. It's the country's power that wields the war machine. Guns don't shoot people. People shoot guns—and it's the army, on the state's orders, that gives them those orders.

So pulling the trigger launches lead bullets from the barrel as it always does, which leads to the utterly natural result of four fallen lumps of protein that used to be alive.

"Clear!"

Chapter **I**

Nodding in response, Tanya follows the rest of the platoon to back them up as they kick through the gate the MPs had been guarding, beginning their raid. Her subordinates advance with superb skill. They go in vigilantly despite the worthlessness of the target, which is reassuring.

Tanya covers their charge with her own. She's prepared for a gunfight, and it should be easy to maneuver with her submachine gun indoors.

She's already attached to the gun she swiped from that Entente Alliance officer, which she didn't expect at all. It suits her body size better than her rifle, although she's not as keen to admit to that benefit.

Anyhow, Tanya and her crew should have been triumphant once they stormed the place, but instead they're struck by disappointment. Still confused, and with nothing else to do, they shift their attention inside the building to search for a target.

As expected, in a way, the building is vacant with almost no signs of use.

Or really just empty.

It seems like it's being kept clean, but there's next to nothing in it. When Tanya sighs and says they should at least look through the records, she steps into the area that seems to have been used as an office. All the memos stuck to the wall and the calendar are relics from almost a year ago.

On top of that, the cabinets and safes that should be securely locked have been left wide open. Tanya and her troops ransack the place, but everything they find indicates that this location was abandoned. Apparently, the area was closed off long ago because it was too far from the main base.

I suppose this is just a total failure on Intelligence's part.

No, it's not like I personally wanted the winning ticket, so I'm not sad there aren't any enemies here. I just thought that if we could blow up the ammunition dump...we could wreak some havoc, so I'm a little bit disappointed.

"'Better luck next time,' then, huh? Oh, well. It's a waste, but our orders are to blow this place up. Let's blast it."

"Understood. Then just in case, I'll stand guard."

"Okay, Lieutenant Serebryakov. Let Lieutenant Weiss know that this one was a dud, so it won't do anything to help him. We're getting this over with and heading to the next objective."

"Roger."

"All right, I'll secure our retreat... Hold up, a mana signal?!"

At that moment, Tanya's guard could be described as out of focus—a rare occurrence. The situation was entirely different from the harsh battle of fierce resistance she had been expecting. Contrary to Tanya's fears that the enemy was using every available second to prepare themselves, taking care of the guards was such a leisurely endeavor that it threw off her instincts. That was why despite being keenly farseeing, she missed what was right under her nose.

At that moment, Tanya is caught off guard.

But conversely, that's all that happens.

Suddenly the wall opens, someone leaps out, and once her brain processes this information, she makes her call right there. It's not "someone." This is enemy territory, so she doesn't need any other information to judge the situation.

The moment she identifies the person as an enemy, she internalizes the information that an assailant has appeared. Then, the instant the enemy casts a hostile look her way, she responds with nearly mechanical precision.

She slams interference formulas into her bullets and fires immediately. Her submachine gun bangs out the results in a battle to subdue the room.

Luckily, the enemy mage who popped out, anticipating an advantage with the element of surprise, is only putting up a weak protective film. That's why Tanya's able to get past it with just 9 mm rounds and penetration formulas, sinking multiple shots into the defenseless human's flesh and easily rendering her target helpless.

"Engage! Clear the room!"

The other three promptly take up their guns against the enemy mage who has lurched forward and collapsed from the shock of the gunshots.

I'm a mage, too, so I know how they work. Mages are tougher than they look, and it's too optimistic to think you can down one with just a handful of bullets.

A live mage is like a hand grenade with the safety pin removed. Until they've stopped breathing, you can't relax. If they have even the tiniest chance, they're liable to blow themselves up as a last resort.

Sometimes mages die too late, but they can never die too early. And because Tanya pounded that lesson into her subordinates, they swiftly deprive the enemy mage of the chance to counterattack.

After finishing the sudden encounter battle, Tanya and her troops immediately turn their barrels on the hidden door the mage appeared from and set about inspecting it.

For a moment, the worry that more soldiers might pop out grates on her nerves. But the space is so quiet all they can hear is their own slight movements and the accompanying rustling of their gear, much less any footsteps. No sign of any changes.

"...I didn't expect it to be this deep!" Having kicked aside the corpse of the enemy mage, her subordinate inspecting the door delivers the report with a click of his tongue.

The door was concealed in an awfully clever way. It appears to lead underground. And it seems like it goes quite far down.

"How deep is it?"

"Take a look, ma'am."

"Let me see."

Even Tanya gasps when she looks into the endless-seeming tunnel. A muzzle light can't even reach the bottom.

The stairway goes unusually deep. Even if this building suffered a direct hit in a bombing or shelling, this basement would probably go unscathed. It might even be able to withstand 280 mm railway gun shells. And from the way the entrance is hidden, it seems like they really took a lot of care when constructing it.

If that mage hadn't burst through, we would never have known there was anything here. Considering how elaborate the setup is, I can't help but sense the maniacal preparation unique to Intelligence agents.

Perhaps Intelligence was right, and my feeling that there was nothing here was wrong? Tanya revises her mental evaluation of the team.

Of course, I still have no idea how they managed to mistake it as an ammunition dump, so I still count it as their error overall. I don't mean to say Intelligence is completely incompetent, but they make enough mistakes that you can't count on their intel when you need to.

That said, the enemy has screwed up, but we have not.

This gives us a major advantage. It goes without saying that whether you get to make the first move or not will affect the outcome in a big way. In any competition—in the struggle for survival as well, not only war—the one who messes up should get screwed. Surely that's a law of nature.

"Maybe we're onto something after all, Lieutenant."

"But it doesn't really seem like..." Lieutenant Serebryakov swallows what was probably the words *an ammunition dump*, but she's right.

Of course, Tanya has zero intention of declaring this place an ammunition dump, herself, so she nods. "Yes, but it is something. Otherwise, why would they have gone to the trouble of concealing it so well? Hey, how's the directional mic? Can you hear anything?"

"Sounds from multiple sources. Probably voices."

Bingo! Tanya wants to shout with glee at how the enemy chalks up another error for us, but she looks at her adjutant with a satisfied smirk that says, *Do you know what this means?*

No matter who is down there, if they're hidden like that, they must be making secret plans. This is a juicy target.

She doesn't have to say anything more for Lieutenant Serebryakov and the others to understand.

"Can you make out the conversation?"

"It's rather difficult. They're pretty far away...and from the sound of the echoes, it's a bit of a labyrinth."

Everyone is enthusiastically listening in, but unfortunately the sounds we're working so hard to pick up through the echoes contain too much noise to be a clue.

...We can't make out the words, but we can hear them.

And using the sounds in place of a sonar signal, we can tell they are quite far down. Tanya quickly weighs the risks and decides it's too dangerous to rush in. Nothing ventured, nothing gained, but there is no reason to bend over backward at the moment for this particular gain.

Even if expecting a trap is overthinking it, on the off chance their enemies get desperate and self-destruct, there'll be nowhere to run. Tanya is sure it would be a mistake to think the guys holed up in this basement are going to act according to common sense.

I have to be prepared for the worst-case scenario: a group of mages resigned to their deaths, unleashing huge formulas and wiping out my teammates and me as well. Diving into a subterranean nest of enemy mages for a fight in an enclosed space is a total nightmare.

But—there Tanya has a strange feeling—*it can't be.* But when she triple-checks, sure enough, she detects almost no mana signal. Of course, it's possible they're just too far down to pick up, but...

"Lieutenant, I'm not getting any mana signals. Are you?"

"No, ma'am."

She even has Lieutenant Serebryakov check, but the result is the same.

...Does this mean that they aren't prepped for a rapid response? Or could it be the place is packed with non-magic personnel only? Either way, it seems fine to conclude that there aren't any mages with defensive shells and protective films up.

Which means...we can take it exceedingly easy. There's even a move that is usually ineffective on mages that would work great in this situation.

It's something she learned in Norden. While it may be possible to neutralize poison gas with one's protective film, mages are still living things. Their talents still don't enable them to shield themselves against poison before realizing it's there.

So.

"...I'd like to take prisoners, but we don't have time. We have no choice. Eliminate them."

"We're going to charge?"

"Oh, right, you weren't in Norden. There's a bit of a technique we can use. It's pretty handy to know, so I'll teach you," Tanya says in a low voice, giving her promising subordinate a bit of advice with a smile, like a good boss. "Listen, Lieutenant. Carbon monoxide is quite effective in closed spaces like this. Or, if you're prioritizing speed, make hydrogen and throw a match into it."

"...But is just a simple explosion enough to...? Oh, the oxygen?"

"Exactly. Oxygen reacts more readily than you would think. You really need to be careful not to asphyxiate in an enclosed, underground environment like this."

Being underground means all the oxygen in the space burns up in a single explosion. People have a surprising tendency to forget about asphyxiation, but it's treacherous.

Actually, in an enclosed space, the blast alone is threat enough.

Even if you have multiple escape routes, the explosion and bad air balance will get you before you can use them. If we create hydrogen first and then launch a combustion-type explosive vaporization formula, it will rob them of all their oxygen—perfect. I wasn't expecting much out of this storehouse, but we should actually be able to get some halfway decent results.

"We're going to burn up the oxygen. Ready formulas. On my count."

We repress the formulas' manifestation as much as we can while we're constructing them. We don't want to let the enemy notice us. Initiating the formulas as potentials to the extent possible and casting them at the last second makes them particularly effective sneak attacks and entails very few drawbacks.

Of course, I can't deny it's a total pain to cast like that, and for that reason, it's not a technique used very often in actual combat. Initiating formulas the usual way is much preferred, considering the time and effort required to repress them.

But the technique is stealthy and thus optimal for sneak attacks. It's a shame it doesn't get used much during encounter battles or high-maneuver warfare due to the effort involved; even mages find it extremely difficult to protect against formulas that manifest only just prior to taking effect.

In any case, mages at a location in the rear like this probably only have textbook-level coping skills. I can't imagine they're proficient in countering the sly attack methods found in trench and unconventional war.

"Three, two, one, now!"

She casts and projects her formula in time with her shout.

Venting a strong mana signal, she prepares her next formula as heat rages down to the farthest reaches of the basement.

As veterans trained for high-maneuver warfare, rapid firing and quick casting are the 203rd Aerial Mage Battalion's specialties. They aim to maximize the effect by skillfully casting a swift series of napalm-type combustion formulas.

The enemies on the receiving end have only two choices: Get blown away or get burned. They aren't terribly different, and the outcomes are practically identical.

And once the job is done, the correct thing to do is skedaddle. They say only foolish birds foul the nest when they leave, but we'll be burning it. Tanya unleashes one last napalm formula just in case as she leads her subordinates out of there.

Because, as noted more than once, she has no time.

The time limit rings in the back of her head like an alarm. The schedule is so crazy because the General Staff overestimated the enemy's response.

We have a mere ten minutes, down to the second. That makes the schedule to attack the headquarters extremely tight.

And the ten-minute limit was set based on an estimate of how much time we would have. If we take any longer, locally deployed enemy troops will show up to handle things. At that point, our prospects of securing a retreat become dismal.

No matter how lax security is at the headquarters, I don't want to cling to the optimistic fantasy that nearby combat troops are the same way, and then end up surrounded.

That's why we have no time to lose. We fire everything we've got as a parting gift and then zoom out of the building. Surely the Republican Army has figured out that we're attacking by now.

They cover one another in *Rotten* as a precaution against pursuit while moving inside the facilities, but Tanya finds it irritating to lose time even for that.

"Major, Lieutenant Weiss says location C wasn't it, either."

"Got it. Shit. We can't expect counter efforts to be terribly disrupted. Tell him to take care of B at all costs, and we'll figure out a way to tackle A."

"Understood."

And then, though it's a bit late, the enemy begins their counterattack. If only they could have behaved for a few more minutes!

Fortunately, unlike on the front lines with the trenches and no-man's-land, these rear facilities have no lack of flammables. Tanya takes note of how the enemy soldiers are using buildings for cover, not dirt, and makes up her mind. *Let's believe in our defensive shells and protective films and burn this place to the ground!*

"Attention! I want three rounds of explosive vaporization formulas! Your target is 360 degrees around us!"

"We'll be roasted alive!"

Lieutenant Serebryakov's comment, and the look of utter shock on her face, is half-correct. Casting an explosive vaporization formula while surrounded by buildings like this is a bit like setting yourself on fire.

"But the enemy soldiers will be roasted first! Do it!" Tanya screams back at her with a defiant grin.

It must have been those words that finally reminded them of their situation. Lieutenant Serebryakov begins constructing a formula right after me with no overthinking.

It's a simple truth that mages are less flammable than infantry. Hooray for being flame retardant.

The formulas, indiscriminately scattered in every direction on Tanya's order, scorch the entire area.

The fire is spreading a bit quickly, but the panicking Republican soldiers are fortunately too busy to pay attention to us, so I'd call this good work.

Since it would be stupid to roast in her own fire, Tanya takes advantage of the lack of resistance to continue advancing.

Flying out of the flames that have already begun lapping at the surrounding buildings, she races away with her troops in tow.

At a glance, it probably looks like we're fleeing the fire. For the Republican soldiers, this is home; there probably aren't many people with the balls to shoot someone escaping a fire on sight.

Of course, we are actually half fleeing, so our acting approaches reality, thinks Tanya, wincing.

In any case, as far as she can tell from how disordered it is, the Republican Army wasn't expecting their attack in the slightest.

Really, we'd been expecting enemies ready for organized combat, but when we got in, it was a total crapshoot with the occasional brave guy putting up a valiant resistance at his own discretion. Frankly, they're only taking up the fight in a haphazard—and extremely disorganized—way.

If this were the Rhine lines, the artillery would be raining shells down on wherever the enemy thought we were lurking. But I guess that's not how they roll at this rear base? Maybe it's a cultural difference.

"01 to all units. Objective A is destroyed. Time's up. Report in with your status."

"The attack on objective B was successful. That was the spot."

Hmm, so apparently B was the headquarters. C must have been some kind of storage facility. Anyhow, if we managed to smash their headquarters, we can expect some confusion. Luckily, even if neighboring troops are scrambled, they won't be able to tell which way we went.

"Understood. We withdraw. Leave at full speed. Head north. Beacons up after ten."

I guess we don't need to worry about playing it safe; we can just move out and have the submarine pick us up. Anyhow, I'll need to report our achievements to the General Staff once we're out of here.

Sheesh, I'm clearly doing work way beyond my pay grade. They'd better have a nice juicy bonus ready for me next round. Agh, and I have to recommend my subordinates for decorations, too.

》》》   MAY 25, UNIFIED YEAR 1925, THE COMMONWEALTH, WHITEHALL   《《《

The birth of an unopposed superpower on the continent could absolutely not be allowed. Having to face such a continent was the Commonwealth's geopolitical nightmare.

That was the foundation of the Commonwealth's foreign policy.

Which was why ever since the Empire had appeared as the latest blooming power, it had become a headache for these men. Outwardly, they were understanding when it came to the self-determination of nations, but inwardly, countries that were too powerful made them anxious.

And in fact, this man was taking it quite seriously. No, he was probably the one taking it the most seriously in all the Commonwealth—as a challenge to the destiny of the glorious Commonwealth as God's chosen nation.

So when the massive Empire began snapping at the other powers to break through their loose encirclement, he imagined the worst possible scenario, which made him quake with anger.

They were too dangerous. And when military personnel in the Commonwealth saw that the Empire was deftly fending off even the Republic's assault (practically a sneak attack at that), they came to him in shock to have a frank discussion about what to do.

Up to that point was fine.

But are you daft? he roared in his head as he plunged his cigar angrily into the ashtray. He exhaled smoke, mentally berating the numbskull gentlemen and their ridiculous burgeoning euphoria with every curse he could think of. He could only despair at the way every face he could see was relaxing into a cheerful smile.

The other day, the Imperial Army had retreated, abandoning the Low Lands to reorganize its lines. And now even his friends were commenting, as if they were certain the outcome of the war was self-evident. There were even idiots concerned about fashionable society, saying that if the war would just hurry up and end, they could rekindle relationships with old friends in the Empire.

To him, it was simply unbelievable. Even the sharpest critics and skeptics were questioning the Empire's ability to continue fighting in the newspapers, claiming its armed forces were quite vulnerable.

Thus, he deplored everyone else's relieved sighs.

And it wasn't uncommon for the key figures in the Commonwealth to be the target of his lamentations and contempt. Meanwhile, their sighs echoed off the walls of Whitehall, expressing relief that the balance of power would be restored.

The noble gentlemen sitting around playing cards, talking about how the war must surely be nearing its end, were evidence of how relaxed the Commonwealth had gotten. Was it a reaction against the dreadful prospect of a dominant Empire taking over the continent? A smooth advance for the Empire meant the collapse of their plan to balance power. The idea of the maritime nation facing the continental power alone had recalled the nobles' worst nightmares.

But yes—"had." Now that was all spoken of in past tense. Despite endeavoring to control themselves, everyone was grinning and chatting. The resonant laughter was erupting from their delighted anticipation of a bright future free of national security nightmares.

Thus, men like him, who made noise about the continued threat the Empire posed, were kept, albeit indirectly, at arm's length. *"Oh, come now, you're not really interested in debating a problem that's already solved, are you?"* came the gentle, roundabout reproofs. It was clear to see that the rampant euphoria and accompanying optimism had reached even the politicians, who should have been Machiavellist. *What a bunch of happy fools!*

Hence, impatient and seething with irritation, he was forced to attend another cabinet meeting.

"Well, gentlemen, it seems our friend the Republic will get this done for us."

Until just a few days ago, the prime minister had been clad in bespoke misery tailored from his anguish and suffering. But today he was leaning back in his chair puffing a cigar.

Even if he wasn't hiding his contentment, he did show self-restraint in his expression. Still, it was clear to all the cabinet members with one glance at his cheerfully relaxed face and unusually crisp suit that he was in a good mood. They could all tell from his calm visage and the lack of dark circles under his eyes that he had slept well.

That thoroughly aggravated this man's already touchy feelings. He was forced to bemoan that, regardless of how this prime minister dealt with domestic problems, his political ability vis-à-vis foreign affairs couldn't be relied on.

It was up to this man to protect the country God had chosen.

No matter what. He looked gloomily around at the complacent faces of the cabinet members in disbelief.

"Well, it's still a ways off, but…soon we'll be able to spend our weekends reuniting with old acquaintances at cafés in the Republic. I may love my country, but I miss wine."

"Indeed. It's been hard to go without the subtle flavor of those galettes."

Most of the cabinet ministers nodded at the murmured comment from the elderly minister sitting opposite the PM, showing that they all felt the return to normalcy was near. Only one man found their optimism difficult to fathom.

To the others, however, it was a foregone conclusion: The bothersome war would soon end. When that happened, the ferries would resume running between the Commonwealth and the Republic, which was why they could have these easygoing conversations about sipping wine over galettes on the Republican coast.

To put it in extreme terms, all these cabinet ministers were tasting the sweet happiness of freedom from anxiety. Hence the wherewithal to smile wryly at their country's poor food culture.

Of course, no one went so far as to say the war was actually over. As relaxed as everyone looked, besides this one man, they hadn't forgotten that the Imperial Army still existed. It hadn't been wiped out yet.

But once it lost the industrial base necessary to continue fighting the war, its fate was as good as sealed. "No matter how strong its soldiers are, they won't be able to change the outcome," the ministers commented as if they knew.

"In light of that, gentlemen, and focusing on what happens postwar, our plan should be to intervene. Restoring the balance of power will come with a pile of challenges."

The prime minister and everyone else indicated that since they knew the outcome of the war, they could turn to the next issue. To them, the problem was the shape world order would take once the Empire fell.

"Our friends have borne nearly all the burden. We can't very well just enjoy the fruits of their labor. We should help them out a little."

"We still have the problem of the Federation as well as the loan from the Unified States. Couldn't we just take our improved national security situation as an opportunity to limit military expenditures?"

Some even preemptively celebrated victory, saying it was time to clarify the Commonwealth's position and that now was a chance to make an easy profit.

"It's still a bit too soon for that. Shouldn't we use our uninvolved position to arrange the peace talks?"

"I agree. We should order each agency to conduct a preliminary survey about a peace treaty. We should also have the fleet suggest to the Empire via a demonstration that unless they reach a swift peace, they'll make an enemy of us."

Even the people with fairly grounded opinions talked as if the war would end soon.

"If we hit them with the Royal Navy? Yes, indeed. Surely even the Empire would abandon their reckless resistance if it came down to picking a fight with the world's strongest maritime force and the world's most distinguished land army."

"Yes, they're a sickening bunch of rationalists, they are. If they were able to understand what our intervention would mean, perhaps they would sign a peace treaty before we even had to join the fight."

That is laughably optimistic.

At that point, the man finally had no choice but to chime in, and the urge drove him to his feet.

"Lord Marlborough? Did you have something?"

"Excuse the interruption, Prime Minister, but shouldn't we try to get our feet on the ground? I never thought the day would come that I would have to say, *Lauso la mare e tente'n terro* ('Praise the sea, but keep your feet firmly planted on the ground') to you gentlemen."

"Lord Marlborough, it's a bit strange to ask you this, considering the navy is your jurisdiction, but our navy possesses not medieval galleys but capital ships up to super dreadnought–class, does it not?"

He understood the sarcastic fellow was reaching for a contextual meaning different from what he intended. So the man, Marlborough, brought his cigar back to his mouth, took a drag, and argued confidently back. "Chancellor Loluyd, I beg your pardon, but if you would kindly take the simple meaning and not get distracted by the context. We can only strike a decisive blow against the Empire with our land army. They're a land nation, so threatening their sea lanes will not cause critical damage."

"Lord Marlborough, I admit that what you're saying is correct. But even so, the Empire is in the process of losing their western industrial region. How will they fight a war once that occurs?"

Sadly, his ideas were only capable of attracting agreement from a purely military viewpoint. As Loluyd sarcastically pointed out, in the event that the Empire lost the western industrial region, which contained the nation's largest manufacturing base, it would lose much of its footing for continuing the war.

Once that happens, surely the Empire will lay down its sword. Even if it wasn't stated explicitly, Marlborough could hear it.

"If you'll allow me to speak in my capacity as Chancellor of the Exchequer, both the Empire and the Republic have virtually obliterated their finances. Just imagine them spending at the same levels for a few more months. They'll end up in the red following the end of hostilities and be stuck paying back loans for forty years."

He spoke of what should perhaps be called the biggest illusion of all: financial limitations. *No matter what happens, the Empire and all the rest of the countries participating in the war will go broke.* Reaching for his tea with a "Nonsense!" Loluyd must have felt, with a little bit of Commonwealth austerity, that it would be stupid to join a war in which everyone was running their finances into the red.

"Well, but we're going to end up joining anyhow, so it would be annoying to do so too late. For now, get ready to send the fleet out. Let's also order the army to prepare for an expedition."

Marlborough couldn't understand everyone's leisurely attitude; they didn't seem to grasp the gravity of the situation or how great the glory was that awaited. Permission for "preparations," as if that were the prudent move? From his point of view, it would be too late.

"Excuse me—if it's an order, I'll instruct the fleet to be ready, but do you really think the Empire will shamefully retreat and swallow a peace treaty? Don't tell me you gentlemen all seriously believe that!"

And that's why, as his bulldoggish face flushed with anger, Marlborough shouted at the top of his lungs. He wanted to scream at them, *Quit joking around!* At the same time, he knew that his worst-case prediction wouldn't be funny at all.

The cold looks he was getting proved that they were sharing the same thought. *Prepare to deploy? You must be kidding.*

"If anything, what comes after that will be the hardest part. Shouldn't we be talking about postwar reconstruction? Where is the money to rebuild the Entente Alliance and Dacia going to come from? I'd like you to think of our gold reserve balance. No matter how City we may be, I'm not sure we can pay all those reconstruction fees."

"On the other hand, we don't want to get overrun by the anarchist Reds. This is such a headache. We need to take into account what the Federation is up to."

From the Chancellor of the Exchequer and the home secretary's exchange, it sounded like everything was decided; they all but said no further debate was necessary.

Of course, they had their points. They gave much more weight to the issue of how to deal with the postwar situation because they had sincere concerns how obliterated finances and economic confusion in a country would give tremendous leeway to the communists for their schemes.

"...Lord Marlborough, did you have something else?" The prime minister's somewhat irritated tone of voice made his thoughts clear: *This issue is closed, so why are you still prattling on about it?*

"Of course, consulting one another about postwar matters is all well and good, but I'd like you to remember that all of that will only come after we finish up what you gentlemen seem to think is a small matter. Now I hope we can begin drawing up a plan for dispatching troops?"

"If we're dispatching troops, we should keep the Imperial Navy in mind. In other words, the navy should send escorts alongside the land units. To put it another way, the plan is up to you, Lord Marlborough. You may draw it up as you like."

The prime minister, sounding fed up with the whole conversation, readily gave the permission, telling the First Lord he could do as he wished with his authority. His mind was otherwise occupied with intentions to solve domestic issues, especially the serious one to the north, so he felt conflicted about having his time taken up with foreign affairs.

To be frank, the predominant mood of the room was one of annoyance at the First Lord, who seemed so eager to stick their nose into war and root around for glory.

"That said, Lord Marlborough, I realize it's not your jurisdiction, but do you know how many infantry units we have available to send overseas? Seven divisions, plus a division of cavalry. We can't deploy Local Defense Volunteers overseas. What are you even planning to do with that few troops anyway?"

"They can die with the Republicans, can't they?"

The prime minister made that remark with exasperation befitting the leader of a nation with its hands tied, and he was momentarily shocked by the Duke of Marlborough's resolute reply.

Die with the Republicans...? You're saying that's a reason to send young people to the battlefield?

About the same time, however, the cabinet meeting understood the political implications. If Commonwealth soldiers formed ranks with Republican soldiers, and if at the end of their march, boots in step, they fell—if even one man from the Commonwealth fell—in an imperial attack, the Commonwealth wouldn't be able to back down.

"Forgive me, Your Grace, but why must we bleed for the Republic? Why not let the Republican peasants till the stability of the continent and then respectfully reap their harvest?"

"It's not as if I necessarily agree with the home secretary, but I'm not going to jump into a fire I am capable of putting out."

And so the cabinet members furrow their brows in thought, pondering why anyone would doubt that staying out of such absurdity would best serve the Commonwealth's interests.

"So the biggest illusion is right after all? The war is already so huge that it's not worth the cost. It would be a waste of money. Did you look at the financials of the warring countries that the Chancellor of the Exchequer put together?"

Ridiculous! They can't keep up these irrational expenditures forever. Why should we have to waste money like that? They had doubts backed up by numbers; in a way, they were right.

"Chancellor, are you certain there's no mistake?"

"Yes. The warring countries are already relying on domestic bonds and foreign loans. The Unified States, in particular, is underwriting the war in great part; their influence is rapidly expanding. The Empire and the Republic are no exception—they don't have enough even after coming up with provisional measures that throw most of their national budget into the military."

"Well. So between reparations and whatnot, the Empire will be put out of commission. Perhaps we should be more worried about political stability in the Republic?"

The opinion indicated that they were convinced the warring countries were already facing those troubles. In other words, the war would naturally end soon. No nation had enough energy to maintain such excessive consumption forever.

And so, as God's chosen country refused to act, Marlborough, with no outlet for his frustration, was compelled to construct a deployment plan "just in case."

But...

Marlborough's plans would change when a furious man from the admiralty flew into his office and told him that all the assumptions the Commonwealth had made were crumbling at their very foundations.

All right, gentlemen. Time to add our page
to the history of the art of war!

Major General von Rudersdorf (at the time)
about Operation Lock Pick

That day, the change in the war situation accompanying the dramatic shift in the lines was enough to slightly frighten the people in the Imperial Army Supreme High Command meeting. To anyone who saw how the pale-faced government officials were silently staring down the General Staff officers, it was readily apparent that the discussion would be stormy.

The reason for the gathering was the situation in the Low Lands resulting from the Imperial Army's surprisingly large-scale retreat.

Thus, when Major General von Zettour from the Service Corps entered the room, he gathered a lot of attention. Everyone expected him to have a good explanation and was eager to hear it.

"Very well, I'll explain our strategy. Currently, our army has succeeded in performing a major reorganization of the front lines by fighting a retreat to a designated defensive position."

But they were disappointed to find their expectations betrayed as Zettour matter-of-factly explained that the operation was going according to plan.

This is the general said to be most knowledgeable about logistics and organization in the rear in the whole army, but this is the best he can do? The civil servants and politicians glared at him accusingly. *So you succeeded in retreating. And?*

But Zettour himself was unfazed. He leisurely wet his palate by savoring his coffee to the last drop, with a smile that seemed to say, *What fine beans.*

Not only that, but he reached for the cigar case and began examining the selection one by one to make his choice.

"Yes," he grudgingly continued before putting a cigar in his mouth. "The General Staff feels we are in a position to say that the only forces that pose a threat to the Empire are the Republicans. As such, I would like to report on various developments regarding our maritime strength."

Despite the dissatisfied glares that said, *Isn't there something else you should tell us?* Zettour nonchalantly closed the topic of the land war. Then, with everyone else looking on speechlessly, he abruptly launched into a calm report on their sea strategy from a diplomatic perspective.

"There have been no major changes to the strength of our fleet. According to the latest reports, the Entente Alliance fleet is being detained by the Commonwealth, but they're actually being protected. We have no reports that any of the personnel on board have actually been captured."

This was all known information that had been previously discussed in this setting. Zettour continued, paying no mind to the incredulity in all the eyes on him.

"In any case, at least the serious seaborne threats are limited to the navies of the Commonwealth and Republic."

He continued his seemingly endless speech with a "Therefore..."

That, combined with his unbelievable composure in the face of the crisis, made them more and more impatient.

His composure in this crisis was acceptable. That could be explained if they accepted that he was a soldier with nerves of steel. But it was shocking to hear an officer of the Service Corps speaking as if he didn't understand the gravity of the situation.

Had the army, the General Staff, failed to notice the crisis under their noses due to their purely military perspective? The attendees of the meeting had to wonder. They had no idea what the General Staff's understanding of the situation was. Zettour's attitude was incredibly concerning.

"May I say a word from the Ministry of Finance?"

"Go ahead."

"Thank you. As we have been warning for some time, and you are no doubt aware, we're already almost entirely reliant on domestic bonds for war funds. I must caution you that prolonging the war could invite economic problems—financial issues—on a scale that would be difficult to ignore."

When Zettour nodded benevolently, yielding to the finance ministry official, the man maintained formal manners, but everyone gasped at the directness of his statement.

That's an awfully serious warning for the finance ministry to give! Or rather, *Is the situation so bad as all that?*

"General von Zettour, does the General Staff have anything to say on this point?"

"In response to your comment, allow me to say that I'm aware of the hard work and sacrifice taking place on the home front to maintain the front lines. We are tremendously grateful to the home front for its support, and we are fully engaged in our most pressing objective, the obliteration of the Republican Army."

But the response they received from the General Staff's representative was so easygoing and unsubstantial that it was hard to see it as anything but equivocation.

The look on his face spoke volumes.

Zettour pronounced each word carefully in a low voice and made clear that his response was at an end. Afterward, he took his seat and returned to perusing the cigar selection with undisguised confusion on his face at everyone's expectant stares.

We don't doubt your understanding of the home front's situation, but the structured stiffness of your reply makes us wonder if you grasp the severity of it. Though they knew it was rude, the frowning attendees were nonetheless compelled to ask what the hell was going on.

"I don't want to mince words. The Ministry of the Interior points out that not only have we just lost the Low Lands industrial region but the enemy has the western industrial region within range of its heavy artillery. If the army can't resolve this crisis, our industrial production power will be obliterated. What does the army think about that?"

No, this is intolerable.

The official from the Ministry of the Interior projected that sentiment with his entire body. After calming down with a couple deep breaths,

he delivered his words slowly, as if tasting each one, and all the civil servants present nodded in heartfelt agreement. The Low Lands industrial region—well, the western industrial region—was truly the Empire's manufacturing base and, hence, its key to continuing the war.

"The Foreign Office understands that we need to consult with the army regarding what steps to take. As for our understanding that we may have to take some unfortunate political measures, we'd like you to indicate what is appropriate."

"The Ministry of Finance hesitates to say it flatly, but…"

I can't believe you would brazenly do something as foolish as to reorganize the lines and open up the Low Lands industrial region to crisis. His whispered voice hesitated to say it, but the mood of the meeting veered distinctly toward the negative. Yet the man at the middle of the maelstrom, Zettour, didn't seem the least bit ruffled. In fact, he seemed completely relaxed, sipping his coffee over the cigar case, completely absorbed in making his selection. "Should I go with this Double Corona? No, I should think a bit more."

After all the exhortations and frank opinions, he finally requested permission to respond, in a tone that said he found it tiresome. It served to stoke everyone's anger.

"I've heard the same concerns at court. I wish to apologize here on behalf of the army for worrying His Imperial Majesty. But I have every confidence we will achieve a breakthrough soon."

The result, however, was that he made a move that was either bold or out of touch and launched into an extended apology to the imperial court.

Everyone was thoroughly irritated at losing so much time to this unproductive exchange, but someone whispered that they had to hand it to him, in a way, for his impressively thick skin. He had even ordered a second cup of coffee.

Then Zettour suddenly seemed to be conscious of the time and took an easygoing look at his pocket watch, which brought the entire room's patience to its limit.

"…Must be almost time."

When he mentioned this in an untroubled tone, everyone stared as if to see whether he would start preparing his things to leave.

"Time?"

The participants of the meeting glared at him with eyes that said, *Don't expect to get off easy if we don't like your answer*, but Zettour ignored them and looked toward the door.

As though someone had appealed to the heavens, the door to the huge conference room came under attack from a violent knocking, causing a stir among all the participants besides one.

"Very sorry to interrupt your conference!"

But when the curious gazes of everyone in the meeting landed on the newly arrived soldier, he, unlike Zettour, backed up several steps and looked to one of the men in the room for help.

"Oh, you have the code?"

That's all that was said.

But one sentence, one question, from the man who had been making endless ordinary conversation was enough to jolt the fellow back into reality, and he unfolded a sheet of paper he retrieved from his pocket, ready to announce its contents to the conference room.

"Sir, telegram received! 'We are the Reich, crown of the world!' I repeat, 'We are the Reich, crown of the world!'"

"Very good... Now then, everyone, I'll explain. As of this moment, the first phase of Operation Rot-Gelb, Operation Shock and Awe, is complete, and we've simultaneously launched the next phase, Operation Lock Pick."

What the officer had read, in a ringing baritone voice, was a verse from the national anthem.

Everyone in the meeting was so bewildered to hear the lyrics in this setting that when Zettour nimbly jumped up, doing a one-eighty from his previously sluggish demeanor, and not even requesting permission to speak from the chairman like he had before, they just stared at him in disbelief as if they had been tricked.

"We're currently still confirming, but according to the code from the unit who sent the telegram, we've succeeded in destroying the Republican Rhine Army Group headquarters and rendering them completely helpless."

"What did he just say?"

Someone's whisper said it all.

"The Republican Rhine Army Group HQ is destroyed?"

When someone repeated the report in a daze, they finally began to understand what a huge thing that was.

We blew away the enemy...the enemy army's...their general headquarters?

"The main objective of Operation Lock Pick is to obliterate the Republican Rhine Army Group units ahead of our defensive line. The General Staff believes the units deployed in that area are the Republic's main forces, so we're effectively working toward the complete destruction of the Republican field army."

And in response to their doubt, Zettour promptly chimed in as if his previous languor had been a ruse.

"Our army has already destroyed the enemy's chain of command as phase one. Please look forward to future reports."

>>> THE SAME DAY, THE GENERAL STAFF OFFICE, OPERATIONS DIVISION <<<

"Open sesame."

That day at the General Staff Office, members of every section were on edge yet unable to suppress their excitement. Still, they bustled about doing their duty to prepare for what would come next.

The entire General Staff was enveloped in the atmosphere of exhilaration and nerves that preceded a major operation, but Operations had erupted into back-patting upon hearing news of Operation Shock and Awe's success.

The unexpected plan to blow up the Republican Rhine Army Group headquarters, the results that caused everyone to marvel at how perfectly it had been pulled off—it was all thanks to the 203rd Aerial Mage Battalion's skillful performance.

So to Major General von Rudersdorf, who read the success telegram with a grin, things were off to a great start. Pessimists had said, "Well, at the very least we'll throw their headquarters into confusion...," but here was the pleasant outcome of expecting what he knew he could from that rascal.

Zettour, you rascal. What a pet you've pulled out of your pocket for us. Even Rudersdorf was so delighted that for a brief moment, he wanted to forget about appearances, hit the beer hall, and roar, *Cheers!*

Thanks to the Service Corps' efficient procurement of the necessary equipment and personnel for Operation Shock and Awe, Operation Lock Pick was proceeding almost completely according to plan.

Which was why Rudersdorf wondered what was making his brother-in-arms so worried when he was called out of a meeting for an emergency or some such.

"Just received an important message from the Foreign Office. We got an official notice from the Commonwealth via the embassy."

"An ultimatum?"

"No, more like the opposite. Apparently, they've taken the bizarre position that 'the time for international cooperation to restore peace has come!'"

He gave an "ohh" of understanding. Rudersdorf could understand the awkwardness of receiving an offer for peace talks right as they were preparing for a major offensive.

"They want to facilitate peace? So things have gotten delicate...?"

"Exactly. And their request is extremely problematic. Supposedly they want us to respond to their peace offering, but the condition they've given is restitutio in integrum.[2] And apparently, they're demanding an answer within a week."

But the condition Major General von Zettour mentioned was so unexpected, even Rudersdorf was surprised. *Restore the situation to the way it was prewar?*

"Restitutio in integrum? I don't want to say this, but that means all our hard work will have been for nothing. They've got to be kidding! Peace under those terms is out of the question. If we were going to agree to that, why would we have not once but twice eradicated threats in our

---

[2] **restitutio in integrum** A diplomatic idiom that means "restoration to the original state." Specifically, it calls for a return to the pre-conflict status quo, so in this case it would mean reverting to prewar state lines and diplomatic conventions.

region? I never want to see the borders established by the Treaty of Londinium ever again."

Rudersdorf was a bit puzzled by the strange timing of this notice from the Commonwealth, but the terms erased his confusion, and he gave his answer roughly.

So they're telling us to reset our national security environment to the way it was before the conflict started?

He understood that their request was based on the balance of power theory. In other words, the proposal was only what the Commonwealth wanted for itself.

Of course, Rudersdorf understood the reason of it, as a diplomatic motion in the name of the country's own interest. But even bias has its limits. His look said, *There's no possibility that they wrote this as a joke?*

But the other man wore an equally perplexed expression.

Which was when Rudersdorf finally realized, *Ahh, that's why he had such a strange look on his face.* After all, they were being offered a tone-deaf diplomatic proposal written in an absurdly self-serving tone. It was no wonder he was confused.

"Yes, but if we ignore them, we risk an intervention. It seems that part of the Commonwealth's fleet has already begun maneuvers. I'm currently inquiring with the High Seas Fleet as to their movements..."

But behind his puzzled expression was a struggle to understand the motive behind the Commonwealth's message.

He had no idea what the Commonwealth authorities were thinking. The notice was dripping with egotism that made it seem like the writers were going out of their way to display what a self-serving nation they represented. But the Empire didn't know what kind of thinking went into the draft.

For the Empire, it would be hard to swallow a request to return everything to the way it was before the war. The only possible reply was a no; in short, if the proposal was made with the expectation of refusal, it meant the Commonwealth wanted an excuse to attack the Empire.

But then...why not just send an ultimatum?

Or rather, would those miserly fellows really come stick their necks into a continental war where there was nothing in it for them? No one was sure about that point. That plus the intel that part of their fleet was on the move despite their strange posture made the Commonwealth's goals more or less impossible to fathom.

Those inconsistencies gave Zettour pause, and he couldn't find a way to explain the situation well, even to himself.

"At least for now, we haven't confirmed the mobilization of any land troops. So maybe it's just diplomatic posturing? There hasn't been an ultimatum, right?"

"No, we haven't received anything like that. No sign of mobilization, either. What is the Commonwealth after, making a proposal like this?"

"Could the root lie in their domestic situation? If you think of it as a way to get around parliament and evade the demands of their internal politics, it starts to make sense."

"That seemed to be the consensus in the meeting of the Supreme High Command, too. Anyhow, nothing good will come of worrying about it. We just need to do our duty... So the die is cast, huh? No, I suppose we crossed the Rubicon the moment we made the Low Lands bait."

But in the end, even if they were confused, both Zettour and Rudersdorf knew the Empire didn't have many options left at that point. In which case, their job was to simply choose the best one for the current situation.

They understood the folly of getting distracted by external noise and losing sight of their duty. They were soldiers and officers of the Imperial Army General Staff. Their job was to push ahead, so there was nothing else they needed to do.

"That's right. Hesitation would be the Reich's downfall. We can only press on."

In order to catch the Republican Army in their revolving door,[3] they had carried out a reorganization of the lines despite significant opposition. The bait was something the enemy couldn't resist. Hence why they flourished the red cape of the western industrial region in front of the enraged bull of the Republic to lure it to the killing grounds.

---

[3] **revolving door**   One way to lure and exterminate an enemy. For details, see the diagrams at the back of the book.

If they didn't slay the bull with one strike, they would be the ones to get gored to death.

"Even if the Commonwealth joins the war, how many divisions does it have in the first place? Probably less than ten it can deploy, right?"

According to Rudersdorf's thinking, it couldn't have much effect on the Rhine front even if it did come to intervene, so he didn't see anything to worry about.

"All we have is estimates, but seven or eight divisions, plus a division or two of cavalry. Plus a few brigades. Oh, and they also have some degree of air force capable of striking land targets."

"If that's all, frankly, they aren't much of a threat. If they attack, all we have to do is call a police officer and have them arrested on suspicion of violating immigration law."

Honestly, in numerical terms, the Principality of Dacia's army posed a bigger threat. The Commonwealth was an island nation. It was hard for the Empire to get to them, but the opposite was also true.

If such a country wanted to interfere, it would have to transport troops by sea. Suppose those troops did come that long way on the water—the scale of the Commonwealth's standing army was simply not big enough to be a serious threat.

Even a generous estimate of their available troops gave them ten divisions. The Commonwealth's infantry units could operate as a threat only on the tactical level. On the Rhine front, where well over a hundred divisions were clashing, ten wasn't nothing, but...it was still only ten.

That wasn't enough to be a threat on the operational level, much less the strategic level.

"Certainly, in the case of the land army, that's true, but the power gap between our navies is indisputable. It would be a headache if they put a blockade on us."

"Whoa, whoa, are you serious, Zettour? If they could just keep a blockade going, that would be a surprise. I don't know how long you want to keep fighting this war, but I want to end it. I'm sick of getting complaints about ersatz coffee."

In truth, the Commonwealth was still a troublesome power. There was no way to attack them without getting past the Royal Navy they were so proud of. Of course, the Imperial Navy was ashamed of it, but although it could fight as well as or better than the Republican Navy, the outcome of a battle against the Commonwealth's navy would be a toss-up at best, even if it brought all its warships to bear on the Commonwealth's navy—even just the home fleet. If the Commonwealth pulled ships from its channel fleet or the forces it had dispatched to other locations, that would be enough to make the Imperial Navy inferior.

On the other hand…

That was it.

Without a finishing move, they could stare each other down as much as they wanted, but they would arrive at nothing but an endless stalemate.

"Let's get it over with."

"Yes, I'd certainly like to end the war sooner rather than later. So… you want to go through with that plan?"

"Exactly. Which is why I need to ask you about the logistics… Zettour, can't you do something to make that advance possible?"

Rudersdorf, the one who had mustered all of his know-how to draft the plan for the operation, was confident that glory and victory were within the Imperial Army's grasp. To him, the war against the Republic was like a footrace, and all that was left was to run unhindered through the tape at the finish line.

The question was whether they could keep their strength up long enough to make it.

"General von Rudersdorf, I had some of my staff make an estimate. East of the Rhine lines I can promise whatever you need, but if we're going as far as Parisii, we'll have to overcome the significant obstacle of distance. I can't guarantee you more than eight shells a day."

"That's awfully stingy."

"Furthermore, that number includes only shells under 155 mm, and we can just barely maintain that amount for a short period of time under optimal conditions. Our supply lines are nearing their limits."

"No heavy artillery and only eight shells per gun? You've got to be kidding me."

The number Zettour gave was so outrageous that Rudersdorf glared at him, paying no heed to the staffers in the area looking their way in shock.

There's no way to fight a war with that allotment of shells.

The words were on the tip of his tongue.

"If we can't use enemy railroads, then we're forced to rely on horses and trucks. I explained the circumstances already. We've requisitioned everything we can from our regional army groups and the two occupied territories, but it's nowhere near enough."

"I understand how hard the Service Corps is working, but getting hit with numerical reality is harsh. Under these circumstances...we could be done for if it turns into an artillery battle. If we can't get at least forty-four shells per gun per day..."

"There aren't enough horses. We're also hopelessly low on hay. Even if we wanted to get it on the ground, it's not the right season. Neither is there enough time to have field engineers lay narrow-gauge rail in no-man's-land. We'll be running our horses into the ground to get even those eight shells and food to the front lines."

Rudersdorf abruptly swallowed his next words. Zettour was the one telling him this, and that fact left him no choice but silence—because he knew that if Zettour was saying it couldn't be done, the depths of human ingenuity had already been plumbed.

If the job was left up to anyone else, they probably wouldn't be able to deliver even half of what Zettour had promised.

"My friend, I'll be frank. I agree with your plan for the operation as such. I don't intend to withhold any support I can give. I did my very best, and my very best is that number. Please understand that this is the limit of what we are capable of."

"All right. Then how long can we operate under those terms?"

Thus, accepting the extreme unpleasantness of their harsh reality, Rudersdorf asked where the line was. If that slim amount of supplies could be provided for a short amount of time, then how long, exactly?

"Two weeks. If we don't get too worn down, then maybe another two weeks from there, but after that everyone should pray to God in whatever way they believe in."

Rudersdorf thought the time limit was harsh, but he did manage to find one ray of hopeful light in it.

If they could succeed in taking out the enemy's main forces...

If they ripped up the enemy's ability to fight back by the roots, they would be having the ceremony to occupy Parisii's palace before the next month was out.

"In other words, I need you to understand that if we get bogged down in trench warfare, our supply lines will become paralyzed. Our army is specialized for mobility along interior lines." Zettour's grievances clearly indicated areas the Imperial Army needed to improve. "Providing logistical support for operations that go beyond our organizational plan—such as sending troops onto foreign soil—is a nightmare. If you could manage to pull horse fodder and railways out of thin air, we might be able to do the impossible. As it is, though, we're just barely managing to make penguins fly, so please understand."

"Fine. We'll make an unstoppable advance. You sure talk like a textbook, though. But when push comes to shove, you can provide the minimum supplies for the advancing troops, right?"

The only direction to go was forward.

And he believed that the Service Corps, that Zettour, could get them the minimum—the bare minimum—of what they needed to do so.

"Only to Parisii. I'm not an alchemist. Don't go assuming I can create an endless supply of gold. Also, the hard truth is that the route is too slim to deliver shells. If you can't lure in and annihilate the Republican Army's main forces, you'll have to give up on Parisii. Please keep that in mind as an officer of the General Staff."

"Of course. Still...isn't there anything you can do about heavy artillery?"

Rudersdorf found himself asking the favor even though he knew it was taking advantage of their friendship. *Even just a little bit, please.*

"Don't be ridiculous! You were the one who said to assume enemy railroads would be basically destroyed! How are we supposed to transport heavy artillery shells and guns with no trains? I'm repeating myself, but the horses are already worked to the bone. If we work them any harder, the rate of attrition will be insupportable. The army doesn't have any logistical leeway; in fact, the eight shells I can get you, I can only get because we're commandeering farm horses and fodder stockpiles from civilians. And furthermore," Zettour glared at Rudersdorf, annoyed, as he went on in a low voice, "practically all our heavy artillery is camouflaged in place in the Low Lands! So no more crying for the moon!"

Having personally requested the concentrated placement of those guns, Rudersdorf couldn't very well ask his friend to somehow come up with more.

"I know, I know. Ahh, I guess there's nothing we can do. We'll have to work on improving artillery mobility."

"You mean the mechanized artillery idea? Yeah, with the trench war we've had to be focused on existing guns. This'll be a good opportunity. Let's talk to Kluku Weapons."

Rudersdorf and Zettour agreed that the mobility issues with not only the heavy artillery, but artillery in general, had become worrisome when considering an advance.

In trench warfare, guns with limited mobility could withstand a degree of counterbattery fire by holing up inside their positions and bunkers. But in a field battle, it was extremely difficult to rapidly change their positions. The current reality was that their firepower was often late to critical engagements.

If the guns couldn't advance after the army broke through the trenches, the infantry had to fight without artillery support. Even if they provided mage or air force support, they couldn't expect the same level of firepower as from the big guns.

Still, Zettour repeated, "But don't forget. This is all only if the revolving door goes around like it's supposed to."

So Rudersdorf nodded confidently. "Leave it to me. Open sesame!"

Those were magic words.

Rudersdorf was secretly very pleased with his very appropriate key phrase for Operation Lock Pick. They would literally blow up the trenches where they had been piling up corpses in vain, as neither side could break through. They would pry open the Republic's stubborn defenses.

"…I see you still have devastatingly bad taste in catchphrases."

"It's way better than getting all pedantic, isn't it? Above all, it's easy to understand." Rudersdorf did worry about the fact that those outside Operations didn't seem to care for it much. Still, he thumped his chest with his fist to say, *You can count on me.* "Well, 'renaissance' isn't bad, either. This is ancient wisdom."

Tunneling had been used to break castle walls in the ages before there were cannons. Now was the time to employ that knowledge once again. *Let's teach those arrogant Republicans not to scoff at ancient ideas.* Just the thought of it made Rudersdorf happy.

"...What's most important is the principle of the revolving door. Now, which side will history put the weight on?"

"Both—it'll be a historically huge encirclement. Now then, gentlemen, let's end this war."

The Low Lands had become a vacuum when they let the Imperial Army withdraw. While the left wing of the Republic's Eastern Army Group advanced to push their front lines up, the units of the right wing were still facing off against the left wing of the Imperial Army, and they were all sick of the deadlock.

As far as they could tell, all the radio and official reports covered was the pursuit of the enemy on the Low Lands front. Meanwhile, their daily lives were filled with the monotony of quiet lines.

In the forward-most trench, they were anxious about little scuffles in no-man's-land and snipers. In the reserve trench a ways back, soldiers sulked about the unchanging menu, engaging in futile arguments with the logistics man. And even their frontline HQ was envious of the fortune of the Low Land troops; its officers, beset by irritation and embarrassing impatience, sat around in meetings with nothing to say. No one was having a very good time of it.

To make matters worse, it was being whispered that the Commonwealth was intervening, mediating, or possibly even joining the war as an ally, and they heard that the battle to annihilate the Empire was nearly at hand. It didn't feel very good to be so far from the action at a time like that.

In such an atmosphere, it wasn't rare to see a certain mid-ranking officer wearing a particularly grouchy frown, standing firmly with a cigarette gripped so tightly between his teeth it seemed like he would chomp it to pieces.

The officer, Lieutenant Colonel Vianto, gave off an aura of fury he couldn't hide, projecting the fight of a bulldog from every part of his body. He wasn't allowed an outlet for that energy, for some incomprehensible reason, and it had him seething with anger.

He fiercely protested the assignment of the few mages who narrowly escaped from Arene to the colonies for "reorganization," but he was blocked by red tape, which made him furious just thinking about it, and the higher-ups, who evaded taking indirect responsibility for the tragedy in Arene.

I swear these assholes have no goddamn clue!

Vianto was so mad the bitterness of the cigarette he had crushed in his mouth didn't even register to him. Seized by violent emotion, he drove his fist into the wall. His fist was charged with a formula he had cast unconsciously, leaving distinct cracks in the wall, but he was still fuming.

That was how much he resented his current situation.

…The operation in Arene to damage the Empire's rear had threatened the Imperial Army's logistics. That was true. So he could understand why the brass talked about the Imperial Army's retreat as an outcome of that.

But…

They were supposed to *pursue* the enemy once they retreated. If they had gone after the Empire's forces, surely they could have achieved something, perhaps even something as fanciful as an imperial surrender.

But instead, the enemy got away, and Republican troops moved in to take the land left behind like beggars accepting pity, which the brass then proclaimed as a victory. On top of that, when Vianto realized the significance of his mages being transferred, he had the urge to punch out higher-ups by the dozens.

Those sons of bitches! he screamed in his head. They were silencing anyone who had been involved in the uprising at Arene or doing everything in their power to transfer them away from the front lines—all to cover up the fact that their prediction had been too optimistic. *Pathetic!*

Service in the rear or a post at some colony is probably in my near future, too, he thought with an exhausted sigh.

He had written a mountain of petitions in protest. *This is what I get for fulfilling my mission? It's absurd! I can't go on like this.*

Sadly, the only people he could complain to were the generals at the frontline HQ he belonged to. In other words, they would just let him vent until he ran out of steam.

Eat shit.

It was so stupid, he couldn't stand it.

"Fuck!"

He hurled his cigarette to the ground, then used a booted foot to grind the butt out with the rage of someone avenging his mother, before requesting permission to fly from airspace control.

He couldn't just stand there smoldering.

If I don't somehow stay on the front lines until we defeat the Empire and knock those assholes out of the sky, I can't say a proper good-bye to my dead men and the people we failed to protect.

He could hardly bear the boiling pressure inside him as the two sides stared one another down.

Worst of all, due to the various difficulties that add friction to any advance, they didn't have a clear picture of the advancing units' situation, which was unsettling. He knew from experience that the communication lines of an advancing army faced an unending parade of obstacles.

Once you got a ways away from the railroads, communication grew more difficult. Then the phone lines the field engineers finally managed to roll out would end up severed in every possible way—whether on purpose or not—from getting blown up by enemy shells to run over by friendly cavalry or trucks.

The enemy, being the enemy, would emit jamming signals at full power, so allies would increase their output as well, but that only created all manner of confusion. For instance, it became more difficult to pick up other units' signals.

So Vianto thought he would go see for himself what was going on.

Luckily, perhaps, his excuse that he was special ops going to get a handle on enemy movements worked—they needed the intel and flight permission was surprisingly easy to get.

Since he was going anyhow, and they didn't have regular contact with the front lines, he was asked to perform unofficial officer reconnaissance and messenger duties. On top of that—surely out of genuine good will, but still—he got saddled with a trunk filled with all sorts of alcohol and tobacco scraped together by everyone from the staff officers to the NCOs with a "Please give this to the officers suffering on the front lines."

At this rate, thought Vianto, laden with a mountain of notes, *I'm no different from a messenger pigeon or a cigarette dog*, but he knew the significance of the things he'd been trusted with.

There was emotion behind the requests, and knowledge that these items were needed on the forward-most lines.

This way of spending his time was a zillion times more meaningful than wasting it on the bureaucrats and their stupid regulations.

More than anything, Vianto personally knew how comforting it would be for the officers struggling on the front to receive tidings and luxury items from the rear. Thus, even though he knew flying with a heavy load meant a whole new level of exhaustion was in his future, he didn't turn down a single request.

"This is Vianto. Call sign Whiskey Dog. Requesting permission to take off from CP."

When he was granted permission to fly, they asked for his call sign, so like those before him, he jokingly referred to himself as a delivery dog that was planning to shuttle cigarettes and whiskey to the front lines.

"Whiskey Dog, this is CP. All Rhine airspace controllers have been notified. Multiple signaling stations have replied, and all state that they're hoping you arrive as soon as possible. We've also received enthusiastic welcomes from each unit in the Low Lands…"

"Ha-ha-ha! Then I'd better not worry them by being late. Okay, I'm off!"

Though his exchange with CP included laughter, each word told him how hard it was for the soldiers out there. Vianto knew from experience how easily logistics for an advancing army could get screwed up. All the more reason he just had to get his delivery through. With a wry grin, he told himself he couldn't be late.

"CP, roger! Have a good trip!"

"Whiskey Dog, roger! I know you told me to get there on time!"

"Got it. I'm betting on you, Colonel! If I lose, you owe me a drink!"

"Okay, you can count on me."

With that solemn assurance, Vianto took off. Although he ascended a bit more cautiously than usual, with so many bottles of alcohol, the process was the same one he had repeated a number of times. Focusing on the point he wanted to manipulate via the computation orb, he deployed a formula that would only interfere as much as necessary. After that, he gave in to the floating sensation and let the propulsion carry him upward.

Which was why, when he managed to get safely into the air, there was nothing particularly special about it to him. It was a normal takeoff.

Until the following moment.

Without warning, he was struck by a flash and the thundering roar of an explosion. Sent spinning like a leaf tossed on white rapids, he lost all sense of direction and couldn't even tell if he was upright or not.

Between the enormous shock waves and the blast resonating in his stomach, it was all Vianto's disoriented brain could do to keep him in the air.

But the shock only lasted a moment.

A few seconds later, when his senses had calmed down enough to function, he was glad to find them telling him there was nothing wrong with his body.

Relieved, he sighed.

It was then that his brain finally wondered what in the world that explosion had been.

He started. Once his cognitive faculties were recovered enough for him to look around, the sight of thick black smoke in the direction of the front lines and *above him* froze his brain.

He had been in the process of taking off, but he was still up in the air.

Yet, here was smoke he had to look up to see? Multiple plumes? Hanging over the front lines?

Noise, shock, and smoke.

The first possibility that occurred to him was that the ammunition dump had suffered a hit and exploded. It would have to be a huge amount of powder going at once or something similar...

"...More than one?"

But as he voiced that fact, he was forced to admit that his guess was decidedly off.

There were multiple sources of black smoke.

And as far as he could tell, they were *at even intervals.*

Once he understood the significance of the fact that they were man-made explosions, he realized what had happened.

Man-made explosions?

On the Rhine front, man-made explosions could only mean combat action. *So did the ammo dumps get caught up in it?*

But then he realized his understanding was flawed. *Even if all the ammunition dumps on the front blew at once, there's no way they would make such neatly spaced plumes of smoke.*

When he realized that, it dawned on him through not logic but his gut, via experience, that the situation was far worse than he imagined.

This was an imperial attack. *Then that means...* He quickly tried to see what the scene beneath the smoke looked like. What he saw via the observation formula he initiated made him gasp.

There were supposed to be trenches on this side of no-man's-land. Defensive positions three trenches deep with artillery installations and multiple pillboxes to provide protected firing positions. They should have been right there.

But what he saw was a big lonely wasteland covered in rubble and a cloud of dirt.

All their defensive positions had been wiped off the map.

They had all literally vanished.

"CP to Whiskey Dog, what's going on? What was that explosion?"

"...Gone."

Chapter **II**

Vianto spoke almost without realizing it.

"Huh? Colonel? Sorry, please say it again."

It's all gone.

He shouted, his voice shaking, "It's blasted to bits! The entire front was blown up! The lines are gone!"

"Gone? Colonel, you'll have to excuse me, but that's not..."

The CP still hadn't grasped the situation. Annoyed by the radio operator's laidback attitude, Vianto focused via his observation formula on a moving group, and in the next moment, he was practically straining his vocal cords screaming a warning to all units.

"Ngh! Enemy spotted! A composite group of armored units and mechanized infantry! The scale is... They're everywhere..."

"What?!"

For a moment, CP was speechless.

"W-warn the front lines!" the radio operator added as if he'd finally remembered.

At that moment, the normal instructions, the need to warn the lines, made Vianto feel strangely off somehow.

Why do I feel weird? he asked himself. *Ohh.* A wry grin spread across his exhausted face.

I don't need to send a warning anymore. There's no one left to warn.

"Whiskey Dog to CP. I question the necessity of that."

"Sir?" The tone of voice said, *What are you talking about?*

Ahh, he still doesn't get it, thought Vianto as he said, "No, right now, I'm on the forward-most line. The front lines have been wiped out."

"...Colonel?"

"I saw it. The frontline trenches—our front lines—were all blown sky high. Everything. They're a huge crater now!"

This is the forward-most line. Our army's defensive lines are being pried open at this very moment, on an unprecedented scale. And Vianto had experienced Arene. There was no escaping the chill that ran down his spine.

"I'm coming down! Call HQ! Hurry! There's no time to lose!"

Once the imperial military machine is up and running, it's not an easy feat to stop it. He learned that in Arene.

Those guys don't miss a thing. They're borderline psychotic perfectionists. Their devotion to their war machine must transcend even the fabled raison d'état.

"Urgent to Rhine Army Group HQ! If you don't send every last mobile and strategic reserve unit here, we won't be able to plug this hole! Hurry!"

He conveyed the crisis in a panic over the wireless as he landed. When he rushed into the command area, distress was written all over the face of the officer waiting for him.

"Lieutenant General Michalis, 10th Division. Colonel, go to the army group headquarters immediately! You've got to warn the others!"

"I beg your pardon, sir, but why?!" *Why go to the trouble of sending a messenger?* But the division commander interrupted.

"Colonel, we've lost all methods of communication, wired or otherwise! Nothing connects!"

No communications...? That means...

"...What?!"

That means no one received my warning!

As he processed the news in a daze, he had hardly any choice but to despair... With even the reserve trench obliterated, did frontline command have even a single division to work with? Whatever they had, they would have to use it to defend a front an entire army had been protecting.

They *needed* reinforcements as soon as possible.

"Colonel, the enemy is headed this way, right?"

What the hell? thought Vianto as he nodded despondently and continued his report.

HQ doesn't know what's going on. So they haven't sent reinforcements. They probably haven't even realized the enemy is about to break through.

"The explanation is simple. In order to take us out, those imperial bastards are not only jamming but they went so far as to cut our wires in the rear. That's borderline paranoid, but it sure was effective as hell."

"Ngh. Understood. I'll fly to the army group headquarters immediately!"

They were detestably familiar with how thorough the Empire was, and yet here they were. But there was no time to wallow in frustration.

Chapter **II**

Someone had to sound the alarm. And the fastest in this situation would be a magic officer messenger.

"It's scribbles, but I wrote you a note. I'm counting on you—please alert HQ! At this rate, the front will... Even Horatius[4] couldn't defend the bridge on his own. Reinforcements—we need reinforcements now!"

The moment Vianto understood everything, he cast away the backpack full of bottles and notes he was still carrying. Feeling much lighter, he took the envelope from the commander, wrapped it in cloth, put it away in his breast pocket. Then he shook the commander's hand and made a vow.

"I *will* deliver this message."

There was nothing else he needed to say.

As he rushed out of frontline command and deployed a flight formula, his chest was bursting with violent emotion. He couldn't bear leaving fellow soldiers like that, essentially running away, but his sense of duty told him: *Alert the others to this crisis!*

The members of the 10th Division...were prepared to die. Just like Horatius, they would protect the fatherland as gatekeepers. *That's why, no matter what it takes, I have to call reinforcements while they buy time.* If he was too late, the service of those heroes would be all for naught. *I've got to fly.*

Thus, though he was still bewildered, Vianto shouted warnings and orders to intercept as he wove his way through the jumble of soldiers, and as soon as he was up, he flew desperately toward the rear headquarters with all the speed he had.

But before he could get enough altitude, he had to take erratic evasive maneuvers.

The optical sniping formulas raining down on him couldn't have come from more than a company's worth of mages. But the scale of the attack was nothing compared to the reality that imperial mages had penetrated this far into their territory—a curse escaped him.

---

[4] **Horatius** From the Roman legend, "Horatius at the Bridge." The story goes that Horatius and his friends blocked the enemy trying to enter the city while having others take the bridge down.

Or should he have been amazed at their skill? *They're so good at war it makes me sick.*

"Ngh! Shit, you rotten potato bastards!" he spat as he deployed a series of optical deception formulas not to repulse the enemy but to help him get away.

At the same time, he needed to avoid pursuit, so though his consciousness was threatening to fade, he willed it to stay bound to this world and whipped his agonized lungs, ascending to 8,500.

Immediately after that, the enemies who seemed like they would follow him fired several explosion-type formulas, undisciplined, perhaps as a diversion, and then turned around, abandoning him.

There was some distance between them now, but surely wiping out everyone at the HQ facilities was a higher priority for enemy command than taking Vianto out. The inhuman rationalism of their disgustingly clear sense of purpose sent a chill up his spine.

What it meant was that...the friendly HQ that had just sent him out would come under fire.

The relief of escaping pursuit clashed with the shame of sacrificing his fellow soldiers to escape—his current circumstances were infuriating; there was nothing he could do.

"I'm sorry... Shit! Why...why did this happen?"

His clenched fists trembled with anger as he choked out his fury at an oxygen-poor altitude. Really, this was the situation his kind were meant to prevent, and that realization gave birth to outrage toward the enemy mage unit freely attacking their frontline command post. *So why am I leaving the ground troops as lures and running away?*

It was so pathetic and humiliating.

A tsunami of indescribable emotions was welling up inside him, but he repressed even that and focused completely on flying with all his might toward the rear—because it was his mission, in order to avert the collapse of the front, even if he had to sacrifice everything to complete it.

"...HQ, come in. HQ? Ahh, shit, it won't connect. What are the air defense controllers doing right when I need them?"

Chapter **II**

Which was why, spurred by impatience, he furiously continued calling the Rhine Army Group headquarters even though they weren't answering. Of course, he knew what the situation was. He realized it must have been utter chaos.

But Vianto couldn't help but feel some contempt. *How could they have let imperial mages penetrate so far into our territory without so much as warning us? Are the air defense controllers taking a nap or what?*

The only emotion he could summon was disgust. Especially because once initial interception was delayed, enemy contact would be disorganized.

"...Calling Rhine Army Group Headquarters. Rhine Army Group Headquarters, come in! I say again, Rhine Army Group Headquarters. Rhine Army Group Headquarters, please respond!"

Are the waves just not reaching them because I'm still a ways away? Irritated at the thought, he continued calling via his computation orb, but the lack of response was getting frustrating.

Why does this have to happen now? All he could do was fly on, burning up with impatience.

"Agh, damn it! Did the radio operator fall asleep? It's kind of a bad time!"

So he continued unleashing his rage at HQ as he flew near the limit of combat speed. Then he saw it.

"...What is this?"

Cratered land. The headquarters facilities smoking, in flames.

It was the cluster of facilities that had been known as Rhine Army Group HQ.

The soldiers running to and fro on the ground performing rescues and fighting fires were clad in Republican uniforms.

So this was where the Rhine Army Group headquarters was.

This was the place.

This place giving off black smoke, plunged into a crucible of unsalvageable confusion, *this* place was...?

"This is HQ? Of all the..."

The interior of a submarine is, albeit by necessity, terribly cramped. For that reason, most inexperienced passengers end up grumbling about how they keep bonking this or that part of their body against something.

That's what normally happens.

"Excuse me, Captain Treizel, you called?"

The one who passed nimbly through the hatch without even ducking was the aerial mage battalion commander Major Tanya von Degurechaff.

She was the only one the crew wouldn't get to tease about bumping down the passages in confusion, at least not for a while.

Why? Because she had an exceptional body, in a way. Even sailors of the shortest stature would need to stoop to move around inside the sub, but her height clearly presented no issue.

...And even if someone wanted to go out of their way to comment on it, anyone with a lick of sense would think twice upon seeing the many service ribbons she wore as proof of her brilliant achievements.

"How's the ride, Major?"

"It's been quite tranquil, sir, thank you. And the food is so delicious that I can't hold back tears of gratitude."

As they exchanged leisurely greetings, Major von Degurechaff saluted in the naval style with a precisely bent elbow.

The captain suddenly wondered if he should be impressed or repulsed, but he responded with an army-style return salute.

It was his boat, but he could still show a passenger respect.

In fact, he wanted to show respect to her—after all, the little lady getting a lift was an old hand, casually sporting service ribbons for every sort of medal given to those serving in the field, not the least of which was the Silver Wings Assault Badge.

"I thought mages were treated as magic army members and given high-calorie diets?"

"I don't mean to be contrary, Captain Treizel, but most of what we're given is blocks of nutritional supplements. Even things like canned fruit and white sausage are rare..."

Chapter **II**

And she handled the flattery between combat unit commanders in different fields with aplomb. Even just the commanding officers having a cordial relationship could make it easier to avoid quarrels in a small community, so the exchange was compelled by necessity.

Still, he was happy to hear Degurechaff grumble about how great the food was on the submarine.

Having a chef who could make use of the tiny onboard kitchen and limited utensils, but who also did their best to be creative, was something for a submarine crew to be proud of, even more than other naval units.

"It's a perk you only get on a sub, where it's very hard to find anything else to enjoy."

"Even so, isn't it awfully elaborate?"

"You can tell? Ah, maybe your young tongue is more sensitive to the difference. All right, I'll let you in on it... We actually poached an outstanding cook from Fleet Command! Still, more than anything, I'm glad the taste is to your liking. There really isn't much else to look forward to. It may be cramped in here, but I hope you'll enjoy mealtimes."

Long patrols, endless routine. Yes, to a submarine crew, patrol duty essentially meant each day would be no different from the last. Until an enemy ship was spotted, they could only earnestly endure the idle hours. *And the result of that,* the captain grumbled in his head, *is that when the torpedoes we were recently issued were discovered to have defects, the submarine captains took their anger out on the Technology Department instead of enemy ships.*

Hence, for some time, Treizel and the other submarine captains had been getting particularly good treatment when it came to food in an attempt to mollify them. The outstanding cook was one instance.

"When the state is so understanding, it usually means there's something else going on."

"I'm not sure that suspicion is warranted. Come now, Major!"

The two of them grinned. Commanders knew that if high command happened to show some consideration, it meant they had their reasons.

"Oh, please extend my thanks to the sub that pulled that feint for us off the coast of Norden."

"Hmm? You were up in those waters?"

"Yes, the submarine provided a *splendid distraction*. I was touched by the Technology Department's minute thoughtfulness in issuing 'diversionary blast torpedoes.'"

"Ha-ha-ha! We were so thankful to the developers that we invited them to a party on board in appreciation of their work."

"What a beautiful friendship. I'm envious." Though Degurechaff was joking around more than usual, her tone contained some slight resignation.

The captain replied with the smile of someone in on a secret and added one other thing. "Yes, it's just as you say. Oh dear, oh dear, I almost forgot."

"Sir?"

"We received a message just a bit ago... Operation Lock Pick is under way."

"Excuse me while I take a look."

The smirky vibe of their conversation up to that point was gone. Degurechaff took the telegram and ran her eyes intently over it, nodded once, reread it, and then smiled in satisfaction.

"Wonderful. Now the revolving door will work."

It must have been subconscious, but with her eyes alight like those of a predator cornering its prey, she looked insane.

Ahh, so that's why. That's why this young girl was given an alias—White Silver.

"Cut off the rear and encircle them for a perfect annihilation. This will be the ideal mobile encirclement battle—one that ends in obliteration. What truly, *truly* wonderful news. With this, the fate of the Rhine front is decided." She exhaled. "This is just great."

It was the sigh of a beast that had its prey right where it wanted it. But if she didn't have that mentality, there was no way she would have been given an elite aerial mage battalion at such a young age.

"Yes, I'm a bit jealous. The General Staff told us to keep patrolling, but they ordered you to go immediately to participate in the decisive battle in the Low Lands."

"Huh?"

"We're currently heading east, quite a ways off the patrol line. We'll surface before dawn fully prepared for you to take off."

Chosen specifically by the General Staff to return, sent on a special operation ahead of Operation Lock Pick—it seemed she and her unit were "exceptional" in all sorts of ways.

"Thank you, Captain. Allow me to wish you everlasting luck in battle."

"We've all been very honored to assist you. I wish you luck as well."

Thus, as an imperial soldier, Treizel was proud that his boat had been able to lend a hand to such a unit. Everyone did the job they were meant to do.

As such, Degurechaff was a fellow soldier he could be proud of, which was why he extended his hand in utmost seriousness to wish her well.

Even if her hand was as small as his daughter's, this was a handshake with a fellow soldier.

Upon leaving Captain Treizel, Tanya is relating the good news to her subordinates, who are clustered in the space the crew managed to find for them next to the forward torpedo tubes.

"Attention, Company! Our battalion commander has instructions for us!"

"Thanks, Lieutenant. All right, gentlemen. You can listen as you are. We're mooching a lift on this sub, so we should be more worried about causing trouble for the crew... Anyhow, I just heard from Captain Treizel that Operation Lock Pick is under way!"

Her subordinates are hearing this for the first time, and from the tone of her voice, they gather it's something quite important, so they brace themselves to learn what it could mean.

Their eyes ask, *What's Operation Lock Pick?*

"It's one of the main offensives planned for the Rhine front. And, gentlemen, it's going well. According to the report, the leading group blasted through the enemy trench line. The main forces of the Republican Army are completely cut off in the Low Lands."

Cheers go up.

To veterans of the Rhine, a major operation, along with the expected changes in the state of the war it would entail, mean the victory they've been dreaming of.

So many imperial soldiers sank into the muck to put them on a road to victory, and breaking the trench lines and tying down the enemy is what will take them there.

"Troops, it's a complete encirclement. The main enemy forces are like a rat in a trap."

"Complete encirclement" sounds to everyone like their long-cherished wish for victory. After all, a surrounded, isolated army can no longer be called an army.

Unable to hide their excitement, her men whisper among themselves. They're so bubbly that normally Tanya would be confused—*Are these really the select elites of the 203rd Aerial Mage Battalion?*

But today, she will generously affirm their behavior.

Victory. It's such a spellbinding fruit.

"This ship will participate in a mission to blockade the coast. We, on the other hand, will sortie before dawn tomorrow. We'll participate in the annihilation battle in the Low Lands and then return to base. The field trip lasts until we make it home. My brothers-in-arms, I won't forgive you if you race off to Valhalla without joining the victory banquet!"

That's why, though she's giving them a warning, her tone is spirited. In order to taste the sweet nectar of victory, it's important to tighten the helmet straps even after a win.

"All right, gentlemen, before we go to war, let's fill our stomachs. Captain Treizel and the crew have kindly furnished us with what little provisions they can. Drink as you like up until the twelve-hours preflight regulation cutoff. That is all!"

Then she clinks glasses in hasty cheers with her nearest men. She celebrates imperial victory with canned food and instant coffee, and once the troops pull in some off-duty sailors and start drinking, she rises. "It's probably hard for you guys to let loose with me around," she says to Lieutenant Weiss, then withdraws.

In this way, Tanya escapes the drinking party as a considerate superior officer and retires to the only captain's quarters on board, which Captain Treizel was extraordinarily kind enough to yield to her. Now she can think at her leisure.

The topic is the upcoming war situation and how she should comport herself.

The initial phase of Operation Lock Pick is a total success. As a result, the scales are tilted heavily in the Empire's direction. Under these circumstances, the Republic is almost certain to drop out of the fight. What's more, as long as we don't get Dunkirked,[5] we should be able to end the war.

In other words, de facto victory is right in front of us. Supremacy in battle—yes, victory. So Tanya understands that the end of the war, peace, and promotion—that wonderful future—hangs on the outcome of these operations.

That truth gives her renewed hope. After all, humans are capable of working awfully hard when presented with a purpose. Right purpose, right method, fair compensation. It's actually quite a lovely labor cycle; I'm inspired.

And there's next to no worry of being Dunkirked.

After all, submarines, among other units, will be blockading the seaboard. And perhaps most importantly, the Imperial Army thoroughly demolished the proper Low Lands sea access point when they withdrew. On top of that, the underwater mines originally deployed to protect the port facilities are thick.

Escaping by sea this way is impossible. So the Republican Army is literally a rat in a trap.

Ahh, splendid!

That satisfaction uproots her nagging hunch that they were in for a sorrowful defeat and tosses it out the window. It's more than enough to compensate for her pent-up anxiety and exhaustion. And with the strings of tension loosened, Tanya, who also has a cozy bed for the first

---

[5] **Dunkirked** You let your enemy get away, and on top of that, they come back, mount a counter operation, and eventually defeat you. A textbook example of that scenario.

time in long while, gives herself readily over to sleep and is able to get a good rest.

In this way, while her partied-out subordinates struggle to wedge their long bodies into the cramped crew beds in the torpedo tube room, Tanya enjoys her peaceful nap.

Then, having relished every last wink of her unbelievably comfortable sleep, she stretches her back in anticipation of a great morning, inquires as to the boat's whereabouts from the duty officer on the bridge, and nods in satisfaction.

"Ahh, Major, you're awake?"

"Oh, morning, Lieutenant Weiss. Were there any idiots trying to pull pranks on Lieutenant Serebryakov while she slept?"

"Rest easy, ma'am. The boat hasn't sunk, so I think perhaps not."

"Ha-ha-ha!"

Chatting with Lieutenant Weiss and the duty officer, who apparently had been discussing the weather, Tanya is even able to experience the joy of a quiet morning aboard the submarine for a moment.

"She's on a perpetual battlefield like you, Major. If any numbskulls had attacked her while she was sleeping, I'm sure the hull would have been breached."

"I'll agree to disagree. We can't start the morning off with a pointless debate. What's our situation?"

The ability to have trivial conversations can't be underestimated. Especially in extreme circumstances, soldiers who can't crack a smile will be useless before long. On that point, Tanya is impressed by the sense that life goes on even in the belly of this submarine, *proof of humanity's greatness*, but she remembers their important duties and obligations and cuts the frivolous conversation short.

"I woke everyone up. They must be sober by now. I'm sure they're in better shape than during our endurance training."

"Very good. If anyone collapses due to a hangover, we'll have to throw them into the sea to ice their head."

As she is getting the unit's status from Lieutenant Weiss and thanking him for saving her time, a naval officer addresses her.

"Excuse me, Major von Degurechaff. I have a message from Captain Treizel. We're almost at the appointed coordinates."

"Thanks. I hate to make you run back and forth, but I'd appreciate it if you'd tell him I'll have my unit up on deck right away. Also, do you think I could get a weather report and a sea chart?"

It's time to wish a fond farewell to comfortably cruising the ocean, great food, and bottomless coffee. But what is there to be upset about? If we just finish this war, we can reclaim daily life in a flash.

We're going to end the war. In that case, there's another benefit to one final push. Meaningful work means happiness.

So Tanya merrily lines up her subordinates on the narrow deck of the submarine. Though a company's worth of personnel is a tight fit, it feels positively spacious compared to the sub's interior. Surely it's human nature to feel relieved.

Upon giving the orders to perform a quick equipment check, Tanya notices Captain Treizel, who must have come out of his way to see them off, in the bridge lookout position.

"You're off, then?" he says, descending with a hand extended.

The two commanders shake hands as the etiquette goes, and Tanya expresses her gratitude.

"Yes. Thanks for everything, Captain Treizel."

"Thank *you*. It was an honor to assist such brave soldiers as yourselves. It's cliché to say, but I hope you stay safe out there."

"Thank you! On behalf of my unit, I hope that you and your men will be victorious."

With that, they salute each other. Tanya nods at her troops, and they take off.

"Wave your caps! Caps!"

Hearing Captain Treizel's order at their backs and receiving a modest yet heartfelt send-off from the crew, the company is on their way.

Their destination is the good old Low Lands. The flight goes extremely smoothly, and they arrive at the designated airspace. Then Tanya calls Rhine Control as she is accustomed to doing.

"This is Fairy 01 to Rhine Control. I say again, this is Fairy 01 to Rhine Control. Please respond."

And the controller answers as usual. "Fairy 01, this is Rhine Control, call sign Hotel 09. You're loud and clear. Go ahead."

"Hotel 09, this is Fairy 01. You're also clear. I can hear fine."

"Hotel 09, roger. You guys have done a bang-up job. There's a whole army of people who want to treat you—I guarantee you'll be drinking for free for the rest of your lives."

"Fairy 01, roger. The only problem is that I'm with Team Coffee."

The fact that they can joke around like this means that Rhine Control must be feeling pretty relaxed; that's a good sign.

Admiring this improvement in the situation makes Tanya sigh with a slight smile. *Usually they would be controlling interceptions, giving instructions until their voices turn hoarse as they handle all kinds of issues; the state of the war must be truly favorable if they have the mental freedom to conduct such a sociable, human conversation.*

"Oh, that's no good. The officer planning your welcome back function is with Team Tea. I'll try talking to him later."

"Fairy 01, roger. Thanks. So? What's our mission?"

"The short version is it's search and intercept, but only to the extent that you're authorized to attack if you happen to see anybody on your way back. Everyone is waiting for you heroes to return. Get here safe!"

Truthfully, Tanya nearly bursts out laughing at how considerate the controller is being. *To think the day would come when these guys who are always asking us to do the impossible would be this nice! What kind of miracle is this? I guess favorable prospects really boost people's humanity.*

"Understood. But the troops on the ground are working hard. We can't be the only ones taking it easy. I think we'll go ahead and take some of the load off for them."

"That's great. Conditions in the airspace consist of clear skies and little to no wind. Good visibility. Watch out for fire from the surface."

As a human, I find the wherewithal to help one another truly beautiful. As Tanya, too, with her altruistic mentality, a natural desire to do something charitable wells up within me.

"Fairy 01, roger. Any data on enemy mage units?"

"The details are as previously stated. We do, however, also have an unconfirmed report of fighting with a Commonwealth unit. It may be erroneous, but if it's true, their doctrine may differ from the Republic's, so be careful." The controller adds a warning. For that moment only, his voice was serious.

So Tanya asks right back, "The John Bulls are intervening?"

"Hotel 09 to Fairy 01. Sorry, but as a mere controller, I couldn't quite say."

Well, yeah, that makes sense, she mentally grumbles, simultaneously turning her attention to confirming the rules of engagement, which is higher priority. "Fairy 01, roger. Are we authorized to attack them?" Are we supposed to intercept or withdraw? You can't wage modern war very easily without knowing that much.

"There is currently no third country with legal authorization to enter the battle's airspace. You can eliminate any nonfriendly mages as enemies."

"Fairy 01, roger. Good to hear."

All her worries were for nothing. If it's the enemy, shoot them down. If it's not the enemy, support them. To an aerial mage that rule is very simple and therefore easy to follow.

And so, Tanya leads the select company from the 203rd Aerial Mage Battalion into the designated airspace over the Low Lands.

Unfolding below them is a massive encirclement battle the likes of which strategists have been dreaming of ever since Cannae.[6] It's a double encirclement on an unprecedented scale unlikely to ever be seen again, swallowing up not just a corps of the Republican Army but all its main forces.

When the Imperial Army has trapped this many troops, brilliantly surrounding them, it made an indelible mark on history.

After she thinks this, she recalls her life so far in the military with a start, and tears come to her eyes.

Come to think of it, we soldiers, steeped in war, have a tendency to

---

[6] **Cannae** The greatest instance of an encirclement and annihilation carried out by the famous Carthaginian general Hannibal. A landmark in military history. Hannibal is so Hannibal. He probably would have won if he hadn't been up against Rome.

lose sight of common sense. Yes, I want to cherish the reason and wisdom of a citizen versed in the norms of the modern age. If peace would just return, then all this will be replaced.

Imperial soldiers like me who had no choice but to volunteer are all combatants, but I should have remembered that we're citizens, first and foremost. Especially in this modern era, we must cultivate civil norms. So it's just a little longer. Just a little more patience.

In just one more attack, we'll turn the Republican Army into fertilizer that was once human and be able to end this war.

I will not let any Dunkirking happen. It's my duty, for peace and my own future.

"This is a general message for the entire army. Execute Attack Plan 177. I say again, execute Attack Plan 177. All units, follow the prescribed procedures and initiate combat."

"Fairy 01, the signal's good. Roger executing 177. We'll begin as of this moment! May the Empire be victorious!"

Having received the order waiting in the airspace from HQ to launch the operation, Tanya assents in a voice hoarse with determination. This is the usual Rhine front. The battle is being fought as usual. And crisscrossing around us are the various "fires" born of humanity's wisdom.

But today is just a little different. If you listen closely, you can hear the signs.

"Gale 01, the signal's good. We're prepped for phase two and standing by to sortie."

"Schwarz 01, normal signal here. Expect magic jamming. Roger executing 177. We're taking our prescribed actions now."

The wireless is perfectly clear. Although the typical noise of any battlefield interferes, each unit's reports come in as clear as during an exercise, proof that the enemy is lacking either the headquarters facilities or electricity to attempt jamming. Most importantly, the organized intercepting party that should be in the air to meet them is basically coming after the fact.

And to top it off, the Imperial Army has an enormous advantage in firepower, able to freely fire all types of shells, not the least of which is the 255 mm. The Republican Army doesn't even have enough 78 mm shells for infantry use. So much iron was invested in the firefight that the maps will need to be redrawn, and now it has turned into a one-sided massacre carried out by the Imperial Army.

And the Republican Army's response is...lacking in cohesion, you could say. The troops are in utter confusion, and with no unity, it's hard to even call what they're doing a military action. One unit is striking out with their small force to try to break the encirclement. Elsewhere, another unit has started digging a trench to prepare a defense, and yet another unit is looking to the sea for an escape route and advancing on the port facilities. They've thought of every possible solution, and since the structure of their army has disintegrated, they're trying them all at once.

The chaos of the decapitated Republican Army is hard to watch—it's just so pitiful. Meanwhile, the actions of the structurally sound Imperial Army can be praised as a triumph of organization.

First, the imperial troops have already cut off the Republican Army's supply lines to the main forces and have them under control, for the most part. No matter how much they brought with them, these units have been on the Rhine lines for some time now, so they surely need more.

Estimating from what a foot soldier can carry, it has to be three days' worth max. And shells for the heavy artillery must all come from the rear. Not only are these guys currently lacking hot food, but they're running out of shells as well.

Second, in order to prevent the localized inferiority unique to complete encirclement scenarios, they have a screen of aerial mages on a search and intercept mission.

"...Well, things are going pretty smoothly."

My initial order was to prepare mages for resistance as we cut through their supply lines. There was also a nonzero chance that the Republican Army forces would come together and try to break through the encirclement.

But the General Staff's worries were misplaced. Just as the Imperial Army was ready for a counterattack, the Republican Army units were all following their individual commanders, doing different things.

And that's how they lost the slim chance they had.

Now is the time for Tanya to knock the weakened Republicans sense-less and snag a promotion.

Her troops may have been partying on the submarine the night before, but they're vets who performed to their full ability even over forty-eight straight hours of recon in enemy territory. It doesn't seem necessary to micromanage them.

"Fairy to CP. There's no interception. I say again, there's no intercep-tion. We're headed for the designated sector."

The enemy is practically done for if this is all the resistance they can muster. Normally, there'd be a hail of anti–air fire flying at us, but now they're only shooting a handful of shells. Even though visibility is good, the rate of fire is so sad it can't even be called "sporadic." Appar-ently, they're really that low on ammunition.

It was so simple. I can't believe how easy it was to enter this airspace.

It's an awfully meager welcome. I almost want to ask if this is the same Republican Army we were fighting not so long ago.

There should be mages or fighter planes to intercept us, but there's nothing. Thanks to that, our anti-surface strikes are as successful as they are during exercises. It's a simple attack mission, just pummeling station-ary targets with interference formulas from the sky.

It's an easier mission than attending evening work functions.

…Well, back then I was a rank-and-file member, not a commander, so I guess in that sense it was less pressure.

Anyhow, I'm not interested in lowering my effectiveness by clinging to the past, but since we do need to learn from it, looking back can be meaningful.

"Viper 01 to CP. There's just a little bit of anti–air fire. Damage is neg-ligible. No obstacle to movement."

"CP to all units. Multiple mana signals detected in Sector Forty-Two. Watch out for long-range observation sniping formulas."

As you might expect, war is easier if you use your head. Sometimes it's not only my unit that is blessed with luck but the entire Imperial Army is in a superior position.

Communication lines to the Viper Battalion in the airspace next door are clear. Astoundingly, CP actually has a grasp of the broader district and is doing a brilliant job of finding enemies and analyzing data like they're supposed to. Thanks to that, if we're in trouble we can actually get help from our neighbors, and the artillery is providing appropriate supporting fire.

These are such basic things. But when the basics actually get done, it makes war so much easier. Or maybe it's the reverse? Maybe whether or not you can get the basics done determines whether you win or lose.

"Fairy 01 to the artillery—it's urgent. Target: Sector Forty-Two. Requesting anti-mage suppressive fire."

A ton of work must go into making these basic things happen, which is why the willing response to Tanya's request makes her smile.

Usually, supporting fire is provided only reluctantly, or denied completely with a bunch of excuses, but today the artillery is already installed since we lured the enemy over here. Plus, because of the way the sectors are divided, we're operating under ideal circumstances where you can get support the moment you request it. How reassuring it is to have the big guns.

"Artillery, roger. Firing now, please observe impacts."

"Frontline Control to all batteries, impact confirmed. Looks to be effective. No calibration necessary. I say again, no calibration necessary."

Seriously, I'm in love with this level of mastery.

"Fire for effect. I say again, fire for effect."

The observed area is doused in saturation fire at a large caliber that mages have a hard time defending against.

If the positions were heavily defended or they had a fortress, they might have been able to withstand it, but the burden was too big for the individually constructed defenses to bear.

A saturation bombardment of shells from 120 to 255 mm. And it's disciplined fire by artillery with observers.

"Sector Forty-Two confirmed silent!"

If you hit them when they can't move, even mages will succumb to shells. And that's why even though I don't want to, I fight up in the sky. Compared to the surface, there's much less chance of getting shot.

But today, I don't even have to lament such a passive choice because every last thing is going smoothly, and we can advance in safety.

Thus, Tanya's cheeks relax ever further into her smile. *Man, efficiency is wonderful.* If we can unilaterally problem solve like this, war starts to feel like a passable extension of diplomacy.

Granted, I fully agree that war is a waste of resources, so it goes without saying that we should get it over with quickly.

Sheesh, if the Republic would just surrender already, they could get out of this without squandering the nation's human resources. What point is there in slowly depleting your workforce?

It would be a real waste if they wiped themselves out without even considering economic rationality. Should I assume that our opponent can calculate their economic gains and losses and counsel them to surrender? Resisting an enemy you can't possibly beat—to the point of annihilation—is above and beyond a soldier's duty.

The state is basically telling these cornered troops to die. Shouldn't there be some limit to the suppression of human rights? I'm sure states have their logic, but there's no reason individuals should have to sacrifice themselves to it.

At this point, the state is expecting way more of individuals with rights than it should be able to. A soldier's duty is to fight. I have no objections to serving for national defense. But it shouldn't be anyone's duty to get obliterated.

"All first echelons, begin your operations!"

But this isn't the sort of situation where you can calmly think things through.

The friendly wireless signal in my ear tells me the operation has entered its next phase.

Apparently, we don't have much time to just fly around up here.

We don't panic, but we do up the pace on our anti-surface attacks. All we're doing is busting up defensive firing positions with explosion formulas, but that will probably be more than enough to frustrate the last holdout of organized resistance.

Looking down, I see the muddled Republican Army and the advancing Imperial Army maintaining discipline. It's already such a trampling that imperial rangers are getting into strike formations.

Usually, charges into defensive positions come with heavy casualties.

But when your side is superior, it's a different story. The sole cause for concern would be machine guns, but we mages already smashed them; it's truly a one-sided game now.

Maybe the reason the Republican Army isn't surrendering is that the Republicans want to fight about terms, but do they understand the situation they're in? It doesn't seem very rational to trade a bit damage to the Empire for annihilation.

So then are they that fanatically anti-Empire? Or are they simply war crazy beyond all hope for recovery?

Or maybe they're poor little lambs who have no idea what's going on?

If the latter, they can still be reasoned with, but if the former, that's the worst. I'm sure we have no interest in getting anywhere near maniacs like that.

"Airspace warning! Confirmed sighting of multiple fighters scrambling!"

"Not detecting any mana signals. All units, be alert for ambushes!"

...So apparently, they aren't going to completely fail to respond.

Well, they can send fighters up now, but it's still too late. But odds are good that I'm safer in counter–air battle than fighting those potentially dangerous lunatics.

I have the battalion cease anti-surface attacks. We get into combat box formation and contact control while ascending to combat altitude. Sounds like there are twenty fighter planes coming our way.

The imperial aerial flotilla will be up momentarily to intercept, but we're supposed to keep the enemy busy in the meantime. That's fine. I'm sure it'll be nothing more than a play fight. After all, mages and fighter planes generally don't handle each other very well.

Although mages are more flexible, they have a hard time when it comes to speed and altitude. Meanwhile, the planes excel at hit-and-run tactics but can't do as much damage. Apparently, they're a better deal cost-wise, though.

Still, since they get shot down more often than we do, the cost-effectiveness evens out.

"Enemy artillery is firing!"

"Hit confirmed. All trenches, report your damage."

"Theater report. Light damage."

"Counterbattery fire! Crush 'em in one go!"

On the ground, a so-called "battle"—an unopposed attack, really—is unfolding. Man, if we're in good enough shape to obliterate an enemy position in retaliation for a single shot fired, maybe I should have stayed helping with the anti-surface attacks.

That said, avoiding risk is logical and therefore a must. Now I need to focus on getting air superiority or air supremacy, as the case may be.

...Still, at this rate, we might be able to win this war.

It was a faint hope.

But the moment the leisurely thought enters her head, it's dispelled by a strange feeling, just a ripple but nonetheless strange, from the direction of the ocean.

"This is Rhine Control with a general notice. To the mage unit in the airspace that is not broadcasting identification! Make your affiliation clear now!"

A bit of commotion and a challenge.

"This is Rhine Control. I say again, to the mage unit in the airspace that is not broadcasting identification! To the unit passing through the maritime identification zone! Make radio contact or send identification immediately!"

Friendly warning signals echo across the theater like screams. Even over the radio I can tell from the desperate repeated challenges to the silent unknown that the controller has fallen into a kind of panic.

Bad feelings are always right.

An enemy from the sca...? That means...yeah, it must be the unpleasant relatives of the pleasant John Bulls.

"Fairy 01 to Rhine Control. I presume the unknown is an enemy. Requesting permission to turn around and intercept."

Tanya waves Lieutenant Weiss over as she contacts HQ via long-range wireless. It's much better to turn and attack than to be chased from behind.

"Rhine Control, roger. But an early warning unit is currently attempting to make contact. Limit your fire."

But although she gets permission to go back, she's handed limitations based on the rules of engagement. The whole principle of air combat is to be the first to find the enemy and the first to attack. On top of that, just a little while ago, control said it was okay to shoot. Getting slapped with limitations that flatly contradict that makes it pretty hard to fight a war.

The brass is always expecting the impossible from the troops in the field. In the end, a mage company is just one unit. Still, I'm not interested in dancing to their tune and then falling like autumn leaves.

So Tanya is about to press her case but suddenly realizes she's kind of losing her cool.

She pauses to divert her inner irritation with a deep breath. Then she puts serious effort into making sure her discontent doesn't come through and states her objection in an even tone.

"Fairy 01 to Rhine Control. I can't accept that. If we can't strike preemptively…"

But her efforts are all in vain.

"Warning! Unknown mages—a battalion—approaching fast!" A friendly warning comes over the wireless.

"No response to a friend or foe request!"

The radio waves are getting tense, and the exchange, muddled. When friendly troops who seem to have visual confirmation of the unit give a warning, Tanya makes up her mind—and she does it quickly.

Ever since Operation Lock Pick began, only one unit has flown from the sea toward the Low Lands, and that is the 203rd Aerial Mage Battalion's select company.

So she uses a megaphone to shout instructions to Lieutenant Weiss, who is now next to her.

"Lieutenant Weiss, we're going back. Let everyone know!"

"We're going back?!"

Suppressing the urge to chew him out for being so dense, she shouts, "Yes! I've concluded the unknown is an enemy! I want radio silence, and smother your mana signals! Let's get the jump on them!"

"It's too dangerous to judge them an enemy! We can't rule out the possibility that they're friendly marine mages from the High Seas Fleet!"

"If they were from the High Seas Fleet, they would at least give us the password! They're the enemy! Consider them the enemy and handle them!"

He finally seems to get it and nods his assent. Before he flies off to alert the rest of the company, she adds, "Before you go silent, give a theater warning about a bogey! A new one, from the sea!"

At the same time, the commanders of the opposing units became aware of their enemy's abilities and loudly clicked their tongues in frustration.

Lieutenant Colonel Drake, a Commonwealth commander being intercepted, was particularly vexed.

"...An enemy who doesn't hesitate is the worst, 'ey, Jeffrey?"

As he watched the imperial mages briskly prepare to intercept, the high level of discipline suggested by their movements made him feel completely out of his depth.

Changing the bigwigs' diapers was not his hobby. And anyone would complain if they were hurriedly dispatched for such a mission because the politicians failed to read the Empire's moves.

"Truly. You can think about it any way you like, but this situation is clear."

These men were told something unusual was happening on the lines between the Empire and the Republic and were sent posthaste to ascertain what.

But unable to establish contact with a Republican controller, and seeing that the only ones patrolling the skies were imperial air force units and mages, no one could misjudge the situation. As First Lieutenant Jeffrey, Drake's vice commander, grumbled, it was proof that the Imperial Army was overwhelming the Republicans.

"Commander Drake, should we pull out? We were instructed to avoid combat if possible..."

"We can't."

Hence, Drake's instinctually rejected his vice commander's suggestion of withdrawing. When the subordinate man asked why, he flashed an invincible smile and said, "If we let this chance go by, this encirclement will grow to become a thick wall... Right now, there's still a nonzero chance of breaking through. It's got to be worth doing some recon-in-force."

Drake's reading was that escape was still a possibility if they acted fast.

Of course, the supremely brisk movements of the imperial mage unit before his eyes astounded him, and they were forming up without even emitting any detectable signals, so he wasn't sure if recon was possible.

"Are you seeing these guys? They seem like an awful lot of trouble."

"I don't deny that. But can we really just leave the situation as it is?"

Drake could understand how Jeffrey felt—if it were an option, he would have wanted to pull out, too. But failing to understand how long the Republican main forces could hold out under these circumstances would prove disastrous for the Commonwealth, as well.

So Drake was determined to fight, even if it meant sacrificing his men. *If we can break through, then let's break through. If not, then let's at least tell the others what fearsome adversaries these guys are.*

"Besides, Lieutenant Jeffrey, have you forgotten what kind of person you are?"

"Ahh, right, you'll have to excuse me, Colonel... Now that you mention it, we're citizens."

"Correct, Lieutenant, we're citizens, not subjects. At least remember what kind of state you belong to. Too many long nights at the pub?"

So as Drake chatted with his troops, they prepared to resist the approaching imperial mage unit and awaited the beginning of the battle.

"Apparently, in the Republic, they call pubs 'bars.'"

"Hmm, sounds like a pronunciation problem."

"You think?"

And though he was joking around to keep his unit relaxed, Drake hadn't dropped his guard.

"Warning! Bogey up above! You're being targeted!"

Which is why he was able to respond immediately when the lookout's warning rang out.

Trained to break as a conditional reflex, the troops just barely managed to act. They dodged the rain of formulas so narrowly that they couldn't help but be shocked.

"Ngh, eight thousand? Is this that unit from those reports?"

There had been reports of an imperial unit who could operate at an altitude of eight thousand—higher than the commonsense limit, but until actually facing it, Drake had believed it to be a battlefield legend.

After all, he knew from personal experience how harsh the environment over six thousand was. A unit flying at the absurd altitude of eight thousand was mind-blowing.

"Intercept! They aren't that many! Shoot them all down!" Still, seeing that they were only a company, Drake put his troops' numerical advantage to work and roared orders to stop them. "Keep your fire disciplined! Suppressive fire! Close the altitude gap as much as you can!"

He chose to meet the enemy with disciplined fire because he was confident in his unit's numbers, their level of training, and their sharp shooting.

"Wh—? They dodged?!"

Hence his initial disbelief. This might have happened against a solo enemy, but how could an entire battalion's worth of disciplined fire miss every single target?

Drake returned to himself amid the shocked moans of his men—*Of all the*—and thundered out orders to prepare for a counterattack...but he was just a smidge late.

"Lieutenant Hawkins is hit! Shit, someone cover him!"

He hated hearing the reports of who was shot and the agonized groans coming over the radio. The only thing he could be happy about in this situation was that no one was down.

"They're even tougher than the rumors say! Don't take them lightly—they aren't some kind of tall tale! Ahh, geez, I can't believe that crazy story was true—goddamnit!"

It wasn't just some phantom the Entente Alliance and Republic cowards conjured up!

All those stories about the Devil of the Rhine, about an imperial unit running amok at eight thousand—what about that was just a legend? It's not nonsense at all; they're actually an elite, terrible enemy unit that we've been underestimating!

What were the intelligence analysts doing, those freeloaders?!

"Ngh! We're getting out of here! Slowing them down and collecting intel isn't worth any further risk!"

"…Ngh. I don't know this ceiling…"

Forcing his muddled consciousness to function, Captain Cagire Caine from the Republican Rhine Army Group headquarters took stock of his situation.

Okay, here he is, thought John as he casually pushed the nurse call button. He was being considerate because Caine had to be totally fatigued.

He must be on a potent drug, some kind of long-acting sedative.

Well, that's probably the kindest thing to do for a man who was half-dead from horrible burns and carbon monoxide poisoning, rather than letting him thrash around.

Anyhow, as long as I can talk to him, that's fine. I should just ask what I need to ask. That's what he decided to do, but…if he was being honest, he felt that someone returned from the brink of death had the right to a little peace.

His vision must be okay. If he can make out the ceiling, he can see colors. That said, since he can't move his body at all, his field of vision is limited. But his ears and mouth are working normally. It'd be nice if he'd realize I'm here.

Anyhow, he's alive. Given that, an Intelligence agent would be trained to wonder where he is.

Then John thought he should respond to Cagire's confusion. *If this pain-in-the-ass Intelligence guy mistakes me for an enemy, it'll be more trouble than it's worth.*

"So you're awake?" John addressed him calmly in a voice the captain should have been able to recognize.

"…Who are you? I beg your pardon, but please give me your name and rank."

John didn't expect to be asked that, but he couldn't fault the fellow for following procedure.

Although he would remember if he weren't utterly incapacitated.

"Sure. You're Captain Cagire Caine, and you can call me Mr. John. I'm from the Commonwealth. Haven't seen you in a while."

"Oh, Mr. John."

He pretended to understand. *Well, even I have to admit it sounds pretty fishy, but a soldier doesn't ask questions when they've been told not to go poking their nose around.* Anyhow, they knew each other's faces.

As far as the previous intel went, at least, they weren't enemies. They were on friendly enough terms to cooperate and exchange intel. Hence, "Mr. John" was enough to be understood.

"So, Mr. John, why am I tied down?"

No wonder he was so confused, questioning why he was bound to the bed.

"Ahh, you're not really tied down. Your meds are mostly pain-killers."

"Huh? So I lost almost all feeling in my body from pain-killers?"

From the file the nurses brought when he pushed the button, it didn't seem like he should be fully numb, though. *Maybe some of his nerves are shot.*

...And so young, poor chap. May the Lord have mercy...amen.

"If writhing in pain is a masochistic quirk of Republicans, then I suppose we've committed a cultural faux pas."

Geez, at this rate, it doesn't seem like I'm going to find out where the imperial mole is hiding.

And apparently, his pessimism wasn't misplaced.

Caine suffered from memory loss due to carbon monoxide poisoning. Frustratingly, he wasn't in any position to provide useful information.

"Get well soon."

With that, John left the room and heaved a sigh. Then he picked up the hospital telephone.

He had to notify the Republican Army that he'd just barely managed to save one of their officers' lives. But he had to say what he couldn't say earlier—that the way the man was, he was closer to a corpse.

The only thing he learned was that Caine didn't know what had happened immediately before he was injured. Sadly, his condition rapidly deteriorated after their conversation.

The top drily responded that he should be promptly turned over rather than probed for no good reason, so there was John giving the notice.

...*Given the Republic's changing circumstances, this is my only choice.* A calculating thought came to mind. It was true that if the fellow didn't last long, they would no longer need to have a "charity organization" based in a "hazardous region."

Also, John mentally added, *considering how furious General Habergram is going to be, the Republic should bear some of the blame.*

And it's regrettable that my flight back was set up so efficiently. Just the thought of how grouchy Habergram must have gotten made him want a smoke. *This is one of those times I just want to unwind with a few cigars and not think about anything.*

True to his desire, he took out a cigar, put it in his mouth, cut it, lit up, and puffed.

Thus exhaling smoke in lieu of sighing, John, with his somewhat aloof John Bull spirit,[7] cursed the heavens. Of course, he was proud of his ability to keep calm and collected in any situation, but even for him this one was a challenge.

I can handle the homeland's "cuisine," but spare me Habergram's angry screams. More than a few from Intelligence grumbled in that vein.

Reluctantly—well and truly reluctantly—John disembarked in the Commonwealth.

Besides tea, there was nothing that could soothe his heart.

Ahh, he lamented, but he would do his best. He just had to think of the cancellation of his vacation and sudden business trip to the Republic as earning money for his family.

Good grief. With that mental murmur, he plunged into the storm of making his report.

He got a sense of the situation from the looks on the faces of the people

---

[7] **John Bull spirit** An indomitable sarcastic spirit of taking both sports and war very seriously. Just their food is no good.

passing by, but he still had to go. Granted, he wasn't sure if his meager salary covered observing a man who was like a dragon when he flew into a rage.

Grumbling internally, he didn't let it show on his face as he entered the room.

He gave the waiting major general an oral report that covered the main points.

Maybe you could say "luckily," or maybe you would just say he was used to it, but he had enough time to plug his ears as he finished speaking.

Naturally, he made use of it immediately.

"...............DON'T FUCK WITH ME!"

Forged by salty tides, the natural voice of a seaman who had been with the navy since the days of sailing ships was loud enough to thunder over even a stormy ocean. And this angry general's screams were even louder.

Major General Habergram of the Foreign Strategy Division.

The fist he pounded down was bloodied, but it broke the desk nonetheless—the desk made of oak, known for its durability. *What magnificent power.* John watched with a somewhat faraway gaze and endeavored to understand his boss's eccentric behavior in an objective way.

He could probably even make a living as a baritsu instructor.

"Ah. That said, you know, the sole survivor was apparently burned before he knew it."

"Mr. John" feigned a sigh, all but saying he had plugged his ears because he knew he would be screamed at.

John had known Habergram for a long time. As a result, he also knew what might calm the man down a little.

"The survivor is in an extremely precarious condition. Unfortunately, I don't think he'll be able to hold out much longer. He only finally spoke just a little while ago." John explained why they couldn't question the survivor before being asked. "We have no choice, so I think we should send him to a facility in the Republic for urgent care to save his life and consider what we have, all the new information we were able to get. I don't think we can expect a follow-up report."

Chapter **II**

He knew, however, that these words would have very little tranquilizing effect on Habergram, who was practically exploding with rage.

"Thanks to the fires, there are no documents left. Everything's vanished."

To put it plainly, the results of their investigation were not good. All the classified documents they had collected had burned up. The loss of veteran agents who might have discovered something was also huge. The only thing they had managed to learn from the Republican survivor was that they had been burned up before they even realized what was going on.

Anyhow, in exchange for that meager piece of intelligence, they were now stuck writing letters explaining that all the personnel they had dispatched "died in an accident during training." And at this rate, they would have to blame someone for this huge accident and somehow fake it in a believable way.

The human loss was too major to brush off. On top of that, the questioning of the survivors was not going well.

"…How? How is it that a station so secret you can't even tell me about it gets targeted and attacked by imperial mages?!"

Agh, if there was ever a headache worth griping to the heavens for, this is it.

Now even John was being suspected. He had to sigh.

Is that any way to talk to an old man who's ground his bones down with hard work? Has the boss finally succumbed to paranoid delusions? John had to wonder for a moment as he retaliated with a hard stare.

But faced with Habergram's impatient return stare that confidently asked, *Got a problem with that?* John was the first to back down. *Well, with such serious suspicion that we have a mole, everyone will be under scrutiny.*

Not many people knew, but the Commonwealth's intelligence agency had been suffering a streak of failure. There were just too many "unfortunate coincidences."

It may have been an unfortunate tragedy that the section dispatched to the Entente Alliance got shelled into oblivion along with their observation post. When the imperial mages unexpectedly encountered the

Entente Alliance fleet, it was possible that their stray shots just happened to concentrate on one spot—even if, in a turn of bad luck, someone the Commonwealth was doing its utmost to protect happened to be in that location. Probability theory showed that it wasn't impossible.

And the subsequent discovery of their submarine was also theoretically possible. Given the nature of boats, the chances were nonzero.

In other words, even if they could declare the chances were too low for mages to have possibly encountered ships at sea, it was not unheard of. Thus, the current silencing of any discussion regarding the cargo due to confidentiality concerns might have been the result of the product of an unfortunate coincidence.

So yes, one could argue those cases were bad luck, despite the astronomical odds. Then this happened.

When people voiced suspicions that perhaps it wasn't a coincidence, that it could have been a leak, an investigation was only a matter of course. Naturally, in order to conduct such an investigation, it was necessary to keep secrets. So the Commonwealth's intelligence cooperated in utmost secret with the Republic's intelligence agency. The secret facility where they worked together was extremely well protected.

Of all the things that could happen in the great big world, perhaps imperial mages just happening to also attack that facility during an assault on headquarters was just one more possibility.

Well, coincidences are just horrible—horrible enough that it wouldn't be strange to discover a mole in the Commonwealth... There John stopped thinking.

Frankly, what they needed was a realistic plan of action, not idle speculation.

It may have been an unbelievable story, but if it was a coincidence, he had to prove it as such or the specter of suspicion would torment him forever. If it wasn't a coincidence, there had to be an awfully big mole scrabbling around. If that was the truth, he had to shine a light on it and drag it out.

"Well, all we can do is make an inquiry."

"...But we've done that several times."

Hmm. Maybe moles can burrow unexpectedly deep. Should we look even if we have to dig? John adjusted his appraisal of the spy. "I'll see what I can find."

It's a bother, but maybe I should shake down the Home Office, too.

He revised his plans in his head. If he was looking for a mole, he had to consider the possibility of leaks from other departments, too. Sadly, he didn't have much time.

The collapse of the Rhine front was coming. All military specialists agreed. Incidentally, "Mr. John" didn't have any issue with that judgment, either. It was more about whether he had time for a leisurely mole hunt or not.

John was the type who knew his limits. In other words, when something was impossible, he thought, *Mm, yeah, this is probably impossible.*

>>> JUNE 18, UNIFIED YEAR 1925, OVER THE OUTSKIRTS OF PARISII <<<

If I must confess my emotions at this moment, honestly, I'm feeling absolutely refreshed.

Good morning. Or perhaps "hello"? "Good night"? I'm not sure which greeting is appropriate, but I'm not averse to wishing everyone good day with a smile.

On the contrary, I'll smile and send a greeting to not only the people of our beloved Empire but everyone in the whole world—straight from the imperial Rhine lines where we continue mopping up enemy.

Yes, thinks Tanya, relaxing her lips into a gracious smile and recalling the moment they crossed the wasteland below. *That is what used to be the Rhine front. The abundant greenery, the brooks that used to be resting places, all shelled into nothing. Nothing but the desolate remnants of trenches remain.*

I was here with my fellow soldiers, and some of them are here still, their bleached skeletons buried beneath the earth. After crossing that bony soil, luring in the main forces of the Republican Army, and then encircling and annihilating them, there is nothing to stop us on the road to Parisii.

Yes, we're advancing on the escargots' Parisii. Now that ending the war with our own hands is more than just a dream, the scenery is so wonderful it makes me want to praise the Reich, crown of the world.

Was this as expected? Or was it strange that there was no resistance? The mage vanguard only makes contact with Republican forces on the outskirts of the city. But what luck—they manage to acquire the railroads intact, so they even have heavy artillery.

That makes the advance a bit sluggish, but all the officers of the Imperial Army, including Tanya, believe that the attack will continue unhindered and that the capture of the city is only a matter of time.

That scene, in a way, is something not just Imperial Army officers but officers from any army have dreamed of. The attack is so glorious that a competition even begins to see who can be the first to storm into the enemy nation's capital.

And then the 203rd Aerial Mage Battalion, part of that vanguard who reached the outskirts of Parisii, finally finds some Republican soldiers prepared to defend their capital to the death.

From above, it looks like it must be mainly units that were garrisoned in Parisii. What she can see seems like about two divisions—infantry divisions bearing no similarity to the armored or mechanized varieties. From the dearth of young people, she infers that these units must be mainly an emergency mobilization of reserves.

Though the army is currently building trenches in the suburbs, behind them, the city streets and their pristine rows of buildings seem to remain entirely untouched by field engineers—at least, as far as she can tell from the positions being constructed below her.

…They should have at least dismantled some structures, to give themselves a clear line for their defensive fire, and blown up bridge pillars, but they didn't.

Too bad for the guys who were emergency mobilized, but apparently they were being made to defend the city from the outskirts because the government was hesitant to wage urban warfare in the capital.

"…Those poor guys. They really lost the boss lottery. I—or rather, the Imperial Army in general—we're extremely blessed in comparison."

…Or maybe if they had been trained appropriately and holed up in sturdy, entrenched defensive positions with heavy artillery backup they would have managed to be a threat.

As it is... Tanya chuckles to herself.

A mere two divisions won't be enough to stop the tide of an Imperial Army fresh off its victory on the Rhine lines. The Republicans actually *are* pitiful for having a superior officer who would order something so ridiculous. On that point, Tanya is glad to be blessed with mostly good human relations, beginning with General von Zettour, but really from the bottom on all the way up.

"Fairy 01 to CP. It's just as we heard. Infantry two divisions strong are constructing defensive positions."

"Roger. Support the armored division until they arrive."

Lately, we're getting lots of easy jobs—it's great.

Just as she was thinking that, Intelligence had hit them with some enemy intel that could actually prove to be a threat: The Republican Army was building defensive lines around the periphery of Parisii. On top of that, multiple other divisions seemed to be gathering to defend the city. That has been the big news for a little while now.

Thanks to that, our plans to stand by got changed to a mission of recon and anti-surface attacks. It was news that suddenly made me wonder if I should I be happy about the additional pay or bemoan the reduction in vacation.

But, Tanya mentally murmured, *looking at my current situation, I should celebrate receiving such an easy task with odds in my favor. I might even earn a bonus.*

"Fairy 03 to 01. Data input complete. I've sent the observations to the artillery."

"Fairy 01, roger. Now focus on observing."

Normally, observers face the most enemy interference, but with none of that, the sky is calm. Considering that over Norden the Entente Alliance mages managed to give us hell, it's *surprisingly* calm.

That's how truly peaceful it is out here. Aside from the occasional explosion on the surface sending up smoke, the sky is blue—it's a fine sunny day.

And as such, it was pitiful how wimpy the normally terrifying anti–air fire was. Anti–air cannons generally stick out on the surface, but Tanya and the 203rd Aerial Mage Battalion didn't spot a single one.

Those Republican numbskulls probably thought installing cannons in their city would tarnish its beauty. Or maybe they didn't want to alarm the citizenry by intimating that the battlefield would come so close. In any case, as far as Tanya and her unit can tell, the enemy is extremely weak in anti–air fire.

Even flying through, all they spot are a few 40 mm machine guns. There are none of the terrible 127 mm cannons.

On top of that, there's no sign of what would usually be the mages' first targets, heavy artillery. Actually, the greatest firepower they see on the battlefield is an outdated field gun. The trickiest to deal with will be the mortars issued to the infantry. Long story short, the battlefield has relatively little enemy artillery.

In close-quarter combat, heavy artillery would have too high a chance of accidental friendly fire; given that the most firepower a foot soldier can use under those circumstances is the mortars, then that's what they need to be careful of... To put it another way, though, that means there's nothing else to worry about.

After all, to a mage, that's not enough firepower to constitute a threat. As long as they're in the air, it can't do much of anything to them.

"Fairy 03 to all units. Be aware of the artillery's firing lines."

Actually, grumbles Tanya in her mind, *the worst thing that can happen to us now is being mistaken as the enemy by our own guns.* As it stands, the only thing to do is roll our eyes and trample them.

I don't want to be blown away by friendly 180 mms. Tanya should be in the safe zone, but she decides to fly higher just in case.

Her altitude adjustment isn't enough to cause her to lose sight of movements on the ground. Luckily, visibility is great; there are hardly any clouds. I'll just enjoy my view of the imperial mages forged on the Rhine lines firing away at the Republicans and their 80 mm field guns.

The range of a 180 mm is very different from an 80 mm, so I'm sure things will develop in a one-sided way. We have them literally outranged. That should make this quite easy.

Since we're on an anti-surface strike mission, not a bombing mission, we're heavily armored, which weighs us down a bit, but this is just one of those times you have to bear it.

To be safe, we assumed the dregs of the Republican Army's mages would intercept, so if spotting artillery fire was too dangerous, the plan was to throw a ton of grenades on the ground troops' heads and move in for a hand-to-hand fight.

So we loaded up on potato mashers, but now the artillery is going to handle the ground forces, so we have no use for them. That said, I can't cast off ammunitions bought with the nation's money just because they're heavy—although maybe I could make the excuse that I needed to be lighter in case of hand-to-hand combat with enemy mages.

Ultimately, since no enemy mages appear, there's nothing to do but observe for the artillery carrying all this heavy stuff.

...So did General von Rudersdorf misread the situation?

"Fairy 01 to HQ. We've acquired the designated airspace. No resistance. No enemy mages in sight."

Yes, the Imperial Army has been advancing smoothly, but if we can really march right into Parisii with no resistance, something is off.

Well, but there is *some* resistance. But it's difficult to understand why they aren't gathering all their remaining troops for a mass effort.

Like, we're circling above the enemy capital with good visibility! This isn't just unexpected; it's unbelievable. It's so empty here it would feel more realistic to suspect we're getting lured into some kind of trap.

Nothing about this is what you would expect.

Usually, this airspace would be tightly secured. It's easy for mages to conceal themselves for an ambush. That's why we performed recon-in-force on the Rhine lines, to drag them out of their lair.

Our goal this time in Parisii was to draw the defensive units out by running attack missions on them, but...strangely, there's no sign of them anywhere. Even if there aren't any conspicuous measures like anti–air cannons, there have to at least be some mages. That's what we're all thinking, and I can hear people warning about the possibility of an ambush.

If the Republican Army tried to fly over the imperial capital, there would be a hell of an interception.

We were sure this whole area would be ready to saturate the sky with anti-mage fire that could penetrate defensive shells and protective films. The troops accepted that forecast with next to no objections. They'd learned on the Rhine lines how stubborn the Republican troops are, so it was only natural. But here we are with not a single shell coming at us. Unless a majority of the enemy are believers in passive resistance, they must just not be here.

In that case, it starts to feel like we really took out the Republic, but at the same time, a total lack of anti–air fire is kind of eerie. Are there a bunch of characters loyal to their duty holed up somewhere, waiting to blow themselves up to take us with them?

No, this is their capital. They aren't so politically blasé that they would blow it up themselves.

"HQ, roger. Keep observing impacts and stay on your toes."

But though that may be bothering me, I have to focus on other things right now. The army wants to avoid urban warfare; they'd rather obliterate the city before the enemy can hole up in it. I have no objections to that. You could say they have the right intentions.

Rather than fighting a tricky urban battle and sweeping through each area in turn to wipe out the enemy, it's much easier to surround and annihilate them. Above all, it's effective.

But if we take the time to blast the city with our artillery, we risk letting them escape. Or it's possible that units will drop out of the fight and begin withdrawing. In that case, someone will have to cut off their retreat in the rear.

Naturally, if there are no other airborne units, the mages will be put in that role. If we're unlucky, my unit might be sent on a mission to drop in and attack them.

Of course, this is much better than being in the trenches.

That said, getting jumped in a city in the middle of enemy territory doesn't sound like much fun. It's obvious that the best would be to not have to do it.

All we can do is pray the artillery gets the enemy movements and terrain down and does their thing. Well, and I guess we should consider if anti-surface supporting fire would discourage a retreat.

Chapter **II**

"Fairy, roger. We'll be on guard."

We made it this far without getting Dunkirked. Once we win the war, I should be able to enjoy the rest of my life. Tanya is extra vigilant precisely because they are fighting a winning battle.

If you don't survive until the end, you don't get to partake in the victory. I don't want to get injured during my final missions.

〉〉〉   JUNE 19, UNIFIED YEAR 1925, THE REPUBLIC, DEPARTMENT OF   〈〈〈
FINISTÈRE, BREST NAVAL BASE

The Imperial Army had breached the defensive lines outside the capital and entered the urban area, and the report stating as such reached the naval base at Brest promptly. Vice Minister of both Defense and the Armed Forces, Major General de Lugo had complicated feelings about the awful news.

Though he had been expecting the notice, to actually get it was incredibly irritating.

He was the one who had drafted the plan for just this sort of scenario, but he had only done so shamefully, weeping inside.

A plan to withdraw from the continent…

No other job in his life was so humiliating as drawing up this plan. Major General de Lugo had walked the path of light during his time as a proud Republican soldier, and now he felt utterly disgraced. Even more than that, however, he was filled with anger.

So many soldiers, his brothers, had died believing in the glory of the Republic. It was because of their voluntary efforts that they had been able to draw the Imperial Army's attention to the capital.

He knew that the time they were giving their all to buy would do more than anything else to keep the pulse of the Republic beating, so he couldn't waste a moment of it.

But as a Republican soldier, he couldn't help but feel disheartened. *Shouldn't I be there lined up with my brothers-in-arms?* The conflict plagued him

As a commander, though, he knew he had to lock those feelings up deep inside. Everyone was carrying the same burden.

Which was precisely why he couldn't undermine the importance of fighting through. He had managed to gather all the ships he could at the Brest naval base in the department of Finistère without the Empire noticing.

To make the most of the opportunity, they were departing packed full of heavy armaments and resources, from the common to the scarce, in addition to many soldiers. The land and people they were meant to protect they left behind.

The collapse of the Republican Rhine Army Group was more than the fall of a mere army group. It meant the Republic's home army had been virtually annihilated. That is to say, the Rhine Army Group included the majority of the home army units, and most of them had been lost. All that was left in the Republic's home country was a vast, empty military organization and the stunned bureaucrats at the top. Most of the combat units critical for the fatherland's protection had been lost in no time. That meant there was no longer an army standing in the Empire's way.

When the issue of how to reorganize the lines in the battle with the Empire to patch the gigantic hole came up, it seemed like collapse would be impossible to avoid. The Republican government and military leaders were prepared to mobilize every last unit along with Commonwealth assistance, though, frankly, some knew that it was only delaying the inevitable.

One of them was Vice Minister of Defense, Major General de Lugo, and though he was executing the plan to abandon their home territory, he certainly had more than the standard reservations about it.

Logically, if they had built trenches and put artillery and soldiers in them, the lines could have been protected.

He knew that was a reasonable thing to order.

But the hole ripped in the front was so gigantic that units that could have held the line had been erased from their formation forever, not to mention the loss of munitions and the heavy artillery. Having lost the majority of their war production and other heavy industry capabilities, they wouldn't be able to sustain the same level of consumption as before.

But still.

If we could have gotten a hand from our allies. If the Commonwealth had only hurried up and intervened two weeks ago. Or even ten days ago. If only their forces could have made land by the time the Republican Army's central forces were getting surrounded and annihilated...

If the expeditionary force had arrived and fought a delaying battle, maybe there would have been enough time to prop up a new front line. Even if they couldn't save the entire army, maybe they could have gotten some units out of the encirclement.

Having thought that far, de Lugo had no choice but to recognize that nothing good would come of going any further.

It was too late now. Anything else would be of as little use as crying over spilled milk.

The glorious main forces of the Republic were forever lost to the possibility of reorganization. Their home territory would be trampled beneath the loathsome Imperial Army's boots. That damnable prediction was now an inescapable future.

"...How's progress?"

He switched gears to dismiss the thoughts of missed chances.

The Imperial Army had wiped out their trained and outfitted elites. Forged in the endless combat on the foremost Rhine line, they were literally the best the Republican Army had. It was an utter shame to lose them. Sadly, the Republic would probably never, not during this war or any other, be able to muster a group of such elite soldiers ever again.

But the Republic still had a fair amount of men left, if it brought them all together. In their vast colonial holdings, they had troops and a wealth of natural resources. Of course, scattered as they were, they were only targets for slaughter or surrender and disarmament.

However—however... This also meant that if the Republic could band them together, could harness those human and natural resources, it could safeguard a bright future for itself. And if they looked at it as a means to control the weakened influences in the colonies, if they could get the remaining troops out organizationally intact—if, in other words, they could preserve the cluster of troops they had, they could build an immensely powerful anti-Empire army.

If they bided their time, it wouldn't be impossible to deal the Empire a painful blow.

"Armored Division 3 has finished boarding. A provisional brigade from Strategic Mobile Army Seven is boarding now."

That's precisely why I have to protect these heavy troops no matter what, thought de Lugo with a pained expression as he watched over the loading process below, practically praying. Armored Division Three was a precious asset, a tank division. And Strategic Mobile Army Seven was equipped with the latest computation, hot off the presses, as well as the newest capital tank model.

The combination of these forces was the blessing in this tragedy. That these two units had been in the rear training with their new equipment was surely unlucky for the front lines.

If they had been there, perhaps they could have saved the day. *But if they're here now, the Republic can still fight*. The Republic had managed to preserve units that could combat even the remarkably improved imperial mages, troops who could fight on a level battlefield with the enemy in this new mobile style of warfare.

Most of the mages were already gathered, thanks to their mobility. Meanwhile, given how doubtful it was that Strategic Mobile Army Seven would even be able to meet up with them, the way they rushed over showed their fighting spirit and indomitable will—both rock-solid.

You didn't even have to be de Lugo to be sure—the Republic could still fight. Yes, the Republic, as a nation, had not—by any means—lost yet.

It still had cards in its hand.

True, many of the Republican Army troops had been stationed on the Rhine front, and the shock of losing them all was enormous, but it wasn't as if the Republic had lost everything.

In a way, maybe he was putting up a brave front. But Major General de Lugo still had fight and drive left, so he scolded his discouraged heart.

What kind of soldier leaves the fate of his country dependent on the goodwill of another nation?

A soldier who can't save his own country is better off dead. They must stay on the lines of battle, fighting for the fatherland, their country, until the very end.

He wanted to scream that even if their opponent won the first round, the Republic would be the one left standing in the end.

So de Lugo wanted to gather all remaining forces in anticipation of a counteroffensive. He wanted every soldier he could get his hands on. But due to the nature of the operation, he was up against every commander's eternal scourge: time.

On the one hand, the longer it took, the greater the possibility the plan would leak. If that happened, the would-be core of his resistance army could get attacked.

On the other, considering the psychological effects of abandoning allies who were racing to be with them, he couldn't leave so easily.

Naturally, the decision was pressing.

"…What about the special-ops team? When will they be here?"

It was under those tight circumstances that de Lugo was expecting the elite special ops team.

They were a group of mages created to carry out special missions. General de Lugo expected the strength and experience of Lieutenant Colonel Vianto and the others who survived Arene to be a huge help.

The General Staff knew, too, that if those mages managed to join up with the others, the number of options they had would increase dramatically. But it was true that waiting posed a risk.

"Their estimated arrival is in about ten hours. Since they're coming from Parisii, however, it's possible they're being pursued…"

…If they're being followed, worst-case, imperial troops realize we're here. If they do, all our work so far will be for nothing.

That was a fearsome possibility. Under their current circumstances, that would be unacceptable. *Should we abandon them?* Some of the staff, especially officers of the fleet, were of that opinion.

"…We'll leave in ten hours. Mages should be able to catch up to us over the water, right? For now, load as much as we can in that time."

"Understood."

But de Lugo decided to wait right up to the last second.

He was making a gamble, pushing both cargo space and time to their limits. Yes, it was high-risk. But those mages were a valuable asset. If they could manage to accommodate them, it would absolutely boost the resistance's firepower later on.

"More importantly, what about the route?"

"The latest check-in from Escort Fleet Two says it's all green."

And most crucial of all...

Luckily, the sea was still free of imperial influence. The Imperial Navy was confident they had suppressed the Republican Navy, but that was just barely true, under a limited set of circumstances.

They still had enough muscle left to show the Empire that attacking head-on wasn't the only way a navy could do battle.

Furthermore, the Imperial Navy, with their objective of putting a check on the Commonwealth and Republican navies, tended to fall into the "fleet in being" pattern of thinking. It was hard to imagine them coming out for a decisive battle.

After all, with the Commonwealth's Navy on his side, it was de Lugo and allies who would prevail. The imperial military didn't seem to have much strategic flexibility.

"Telegram from Independent Submarine Squad Fourteen. No contact. The route is clear."

They were lucky that the Imperial Army hadn't caught on. There was no way ships full of supplies would be allowed to escape if they were detected. For now, at least, there was no sign of interference.

Given the way the imperial troops did things, it could very well be a while before they realized. Of course, once the escape operation was under way, they would figure it out. He was sure their pursuit would be fierce.

So they only had one chance. He was betting the future of the fatherland on this one venture.

The moment the cease-fire was called—that was their chance. The success of the operation depended on whether or not the Empire found the movements suspicious. Or whether they could distract the Empire somehow.

"Report from the embassy in the Commonwealth. The main enemy forces are busy monitoring the Commonwealth Navy's 'exercises.'"

Chapter **II**

Were they idiots? Or was it just business as usual? The Commonwealth's home fleet was performing emergency exercises as "surprise training" right on the edge of their territorial waters, completely distracting the imperial forces. Their fleet, air force, and mages were all paying attention to the exercises, which gave de Lugo a free hand.

Given that there were apparently no complications that would damage the gathered ships, the Empire must not have realized what was going on. Neither were there any reports of imperial scouts or suspicious characters in the vicinity of the naval base.

He didn't want to jinx it, but the situation didn't seem so desperate.

"…Good of them to assist."

"Let's get through this and retaliate."

"Even if I have to eat that stinking Commonwealth food, I'll fight through. Can't wait for the counteroffensive from the south."

His subordinates' spirits were unflagging. The troops could still fight, at least. Even if they had to give up the fatherland to the Empire temporarily, in the end they would take back the land that raised them.

"Well, it all starts here."

His resolve was firm.

Though he was suppressing his emotions, his voice brimmed with the spirit to fight the Empire to the last.

Major General de Lugo was a patriot.

He loved his country. He loved his fatherland. He was a firm believer in his country's glory.

If the Republic was no longer great, it was no longer the Republic.

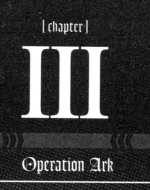

If even one of us remains, the Republic can keep fighting.
It may seem like a platitude, but all we need to do is be
standing in the end. That's how war works.

———— Vice Minister of Defense de Lugo during the escape operation ————

As usual, Major Generals von Zettour and von Rudersdorf were washing down lumps of off-tasting glop that most would hesitate to describe as food with awful ersatz coffee in the dining room of the General Staff Office.

The cuisine did absolutely nothing to whet their appetites, but even more upsetting was plating such awful fare on beautiful dishes.

The expensive tableware was on par with what you might find at a court dinner, but as the pair carved into the lumps of what could maybe be called food (but maybe not), they were long past the point of frowning at it. The key was to pay no attention to what you were eating.

As they did their best to look at each other instead of their plates, the theme of today's discussion was uncommonly abstract.

After the good news of the suppression of the Republic, the next debate was laying the groundwork for negotiating with the Kingdom of Ildoa.

"So? Do you think it would be best to arrange the surrender terms via the Kingdom of Ildoa?"

"Strictly speaking, General von Rudersdorf, the army's duty is to protect the Empire. Diplomatic strategy is out of our jurisdiction."

"Oh, well, that's true."

Rudersdorf felt they should perhaps put together peace terms, and Zettour advised him that doing so would be overstepping their authority.

Still endeavoring to keep their eyes off their respective meals, the pair were discussing policy not as the ones in charge but as a third party—a rare occurrence.

"That's the job of the Foreign Office, so we should respect their work. And we should probably focus on our own responsibilities."

"In other words, the administrative tasks surrounding the cease-fire, right?"

Which was why when Zettour reminded him of their job, Rudersdorf was quick to respond. Though it was only an administrative matter, managing the cease-fire would be a bit of a challenge. It was true that the one grumbling to that effect would have a pile of work to do as the one in charge of Operations.

Rudersdorf sighed. He still had to keep a tight hold on the reins and limit confusion to the extent possible.

"Out where they're actually shooting at each other, the mentality could spell trouble, you know. With emotions running high, we run the risk of a mix-up. Why don't we at least get an idea of what tack we're taking?"

"For now, let's draw up a cease-fire plan for the front lines. The standardized procedure for a local cease-fire should be applicable, but let's check just to be sure. Then we just have to show it to Legal."

Cadets learned the basics of forcing enemies to surrender and enacting cease-fires in the academy, but that was only a cursory look at elementary principles. When it came to officers in the Imperial Army who had experience dealing with the fallout of a major military clash between nations, there were only a few legal specialists, if that.

"Yes, if you want a status report, Lieutenant Colonel von Lergen just returned from observing in the field. Let's have him fill us in."

It was obvious that the knowledge the staff officer brought back from the front would come with extremely valuable suggestions, especially when the officer in question was a capable man whose reports could be trusted.

"That would be great… We have to finish this right. That was quite a show of confidence we put on for Supreme High Command. I have no intention of failing and ending up a laughingstock."

"Go ahead. Everyone's buzzing about how skillfully you're handling things. You really saved me by getting supply lines into the capital. I'm grateful."

The main thread of the pair's conversation had shifted from diplomatic matters outside their jurisdiction to the practical matters they needed to handle. As capable businessmen, Zettour and Rudersdorf knew there were a mountain of pending issues regarding logistics and the front lines.

"That's what friends are for. Well, you can thank me with coffee beans."

"...As soon as this is over, I'll get you all the imported coffee you can drink, you greedy rascal."

Thus, even while joking, the only thing on their minds was smoothly accomplishing everything necessary to ending the war.

"You're just as greedy. I'll have you recall that the Imperial Army was set up to function along interior lines. Please understand how much strife you caused us by doing whatever you saw fit."

"I do. Anyhow, shall we mop this up?"

"Indeed. Call Colonel von Lergen."

They were brave, loyal soldiers. Not only that, but it was fair to call them outstanding. They, however, defined themselves as staff officers who had to be constantly engaged in military business. Soldiers were the ones whose duty was to focus on the fighting.

>>>> THE SAME DAY, IMPERIAL ARMY SUPREME HIGH COMMAND'S <<<<
FOREIGN INTELLIGENCE ADVISORY BOARD

The conference room was full of frowning men, each one's suit as drab as the next. Normally, the atmosphere was tense, so solemn that the room's occupants would refrain from smoking, but now it was abuzz with the first good news in a while.

The major counterattack operation had been a success. The army had notified them that the troops had marched into the Republican capital and that a cease-fire was near. Both of those things meant victory for the Empire.

Their dream of the war's end and the return of peace was right before their eyes.

"How is the foreign minister thinking of handling the end of the war?"

So even the no-nonsense bureaucrats were bubbling with enthusiasm, already thinking about postwar tasks.

The end of the conflict entailed a lot of work after the fact. Just a little while ago, they were fretting over the enormous expenses, terrified at the crisis surrounding the loss of the Low Lands industrial region, but now they exchanged insuppressible grins and discussed the end of the war.

"Mainly, we plan to demand that each of the warring countries establish peaceful borders and pay reparations. We also plan to demand that the Republic surrender some of their colonial holdings and abandon some others."

"Oh? Taking the tough line, 'ey? Er, pardon me…"

The unexpectedly moderate answer given by the foreign minister sparked a somewhat surprised murmur in the room. To those who had suspected aggressive demands from a hard-liner stance, the conditions seemed very realistic.

"Hmm? From the way the young bureaucrats were talking, I thought they would come up with harsher demands," someone whispered.

And it was plenty loud enough to reach the foreign minister's ears.

"No, I understand how you feel. But we know what would happen if we wrote the peace treaty after drinking a swimming pool's worth of sweet victory."

"Which is to say…?"

"I'm embarrassed to admit the younger officials did just that. So we waited till their hangovers subsided and made them rewrite it."

Wincing a bit awkwardly, he presented the private meeting with an honest account of the behind-the-scenes workings and added that he realized other ministries were laughing at their somewhat extreme antics.

"In the current plan, with the vast concessions and large reparation bill, we're essentially treating them as a client state. It's not realistic in any sense of the word. Of course, I threw it back at them to have it redone!" He chuckled wryly as he related the inside story. "Ah, excuse me. That was a tangent. Please strike it from the record."

"That's fine. Secretary, as he says." The clerks dutifully gave their verdict with the benevolence of those free of the anxieties of youthful error.

"A question. Umm, how will surrender be handled?"

"Well, the army will take care of that. At least, it wouldn't be good to put restrictions on the military leadership before the war is over. What's important is for us to do a proper job on our respective tasks, don't you think?"

The conclusion they reached was to do what they could to respond to the military's requests. Then they diligently moved on to the next topic of discussion.

"Now then, our next order of business is the trade agreement with the Federation..."

 THE SAME DAY, THE 203RD AERIAL MAGE COMPANY'S GARRISON

"What? The Republican Navy is withdrawing?"

Major Tanya von Degurechaff's first response to the news was delivered in an even voice.

So Visha didn't notice her superior was working incredibly hard to maintain that monotone. After all, it was the afternoon after they had invaded the Republican defensive lines and finished their anti-surface support mission, and as far as Visha could tell, the message from high command seemed like good news.

"Yes, Major. It's a general message to all troops from home. Vice Minister Major General de Lugo has ordered the Republican Navy to stop fighting and move. Now the end of the war is only a matter of time."

Notice of a cease-fire and word that the Republican Army was abandoning their position and retreating—surely that had to mean the Empire's dream of victory was coming true.

"Lieutenant Serebryakov, did they actually say 'the end of the war'? Not 'cease-fire' or 'surrender'?"

"Major?"

So for a moment, Visha wasn't sure what her superior was finding issue with.

"Are those the exact words they used? 'The end of the war'?"

"My apologies. I didn't see those words written there."

Come to think of it, the major is such a stickler for accuracy. I really messed up. Adding my own optimistic view to a report for her is a no-no. As Visha was regretting her goof, Major von Degurechaff calmly asked another question.

"One thing. You said this is under Major General de Lugo's orders? Where are they withdrawing to?"

"Ah! Please excuse the omission. Apparently, they're gathering at the Brest Naval Base."

The message definitely included the detail that they were withdrawing to Brest on Major General de Lugo's orders. *Oh, brother, I can't be so irresponsible just because we're about to win,* reflected Visha solemnly, impressed by her superior's attention to detail. *You'd think I'd know how she likes her reports after being with her ever since the Rhine Battle. The whole base is in a celebratory mood, so I guess I've gotten a bit lax, too.* She finished her introspection with a vow to take after her superior's prudence.

"Brest Naval Base? De Lugo...? Sorry, can you get me a map?"

Thinking how amazingly attentive the major was—always ready to add more to her stores of knowledge—Visha pulled out a map and spread it across the table in a way that the major could see it well.

Her face as she stared silently at the map was so earnest that carelessness seemed like a foreign concept to her.

So just as Visha was about to ask if she should be bringing coffee if it would take a little while, Major von Degurechaff pounded her fist on the table and stood up, trembling all over.

"...Shit! These gigantic numbskulls! Why didn't they realize?!"

"M-Major?"

"Lieutenant! Prepare to sortie—on the double! We're taking all the V-1s! Get them on the runway—now! And get me Lieutenant Weiss!"

The fierceness on her face and the shrillness of her voice left no room to question the order. Visha knew better than probably anyone else how foolish it would be to oppose Major von Degurechaff when she was like this.

So she barely saluted and confirmed the order before running off. Just as she was told, she alerted Lieutenant Weiss that he was being urgently summoned, and then she went straight to the V-1 hangars to get them ready to deploy.

"Excuse me."

"Good, thanks for coming, Vice Commander. We don't have much time. I'll get straight down to business." Tanya speaks the moment Lieutenant Weiss salutes and enters the room where she is poring over a navigation chart in agony and distress. "The enemy fleet is concentrating in Brest. The brass thinks this is the Republic withdrawing as part of the cease-fire, but I say that though they may be withdrawing, what they're doing is escaping in secret."

To be blunt, what they are pulling is unmistakably a Dunkirk.

"They mean to extract what military organizations they still have and continue fighting. If we don't beat them here, the war won't end."

"Major, with all due respect, the cease-fire will be declared tonight. Attacking now would be…"

"Lieutenant, a cease-fire is not the same as the end of the war. It's something else entirely. And as of this moment, we're still at war."

He must not understand. Weiss's leisurely reticence to take her attack order is unbelievably frustrating.

We can't get Dunkirked. We can't let them escape. We can't waste this victory. If we don't eliminate him—de Lugo—now, the war won't end. No—we won't be able to end it.

And if that happens, the path forward leads to a morass, and the only way out of that is ruin.

She can't let that future come to pass. Not after being worked like a horse in a total war. She can't let her organization, the Imperial Army, go out like that in this nightmare scenario. My employer going bankrupt is the worst possible outcome, so it must be avoided at all costs. *Therefore,* Tanya is determined.

"But…"

"Lieutenant, the record will show that you raised an objection. Now you must act. There is only action."

They may scream, but we will act. I'll ruin my military career if it will prevent us from getting Dunkirked.

Chapter **III**

If we act now, that fate is still preventable. Tanya is sure she can get authorization for recon-in-force. The general notice of the coming cease-fire is a sizable obstacle, but since her unit reports directly to the General Staff, they should have the power.

In the worst case, a single mage platoon would be enough to get the job done. She could drag them out under the pretext of officer reconnaissance. Once they were off the ground, no one would be able to bother them. The radio silence inside the V-1s flying at top speed would be the perfect excuse. We should at least kill de Lugo along with his capital ship rather than kicking ourselves for letting them get away.

"Excuse me, Major!"

"Is the unit ready?"

"Yes, but base command is calling you."

Even with it happening before their eyes, any sensible imperial soldier would find it hard to believe.

Or hard to watch, perhaps.

"Please let us go! I'll do anything! Just let me— Let my unit go!"

The agonized scream was almost like a curse.

"Authorize us, even just my unit, to sortie! Please!"

The hands clutching his lapels were at once powerful and tiny.

The warped expression and pleading tone of voice were a petition to avert destruction. No, her voice was more like the wail of one desperate for salvation.

And the one acting that way, with no regard for appearances, was the capable Imperial Army officer said to have maintained unparalleled composure during the Rhine Battle.

"The events of this hour—this one brief moment—will determine whether the Empire gains the world or loses everything!"

"Please," she said. "Please let us go."

Major Tanya von Degurechaff had abandoned rules, norms, and regulations, and that was her plea.

Yes, the one declared a model soldier by everyone, the officer von Lergen admitted to fearing on an instinctual level. She had unhesitatingly cast all that away under the gaze of everyone nearby and grabbed the lapels of a superior officer. She was practically threatening him with her shouts.

Which was why everyone present was so confused that they simply stood there, unsure what to do.

Even her subordinates, though they stood perfectly still in utterly silent rows, were wearing expressions that said they were shaken and perplexed by their superior's incomprehensible clamoring.

She was a veteran field commander, a proficient officer who got through any impossible challenge unfazed, a fearless mage who could penetrate a fleet's air defenses, a night fight professional who crawled around under the veil of darkness as if she owned the battlefield.

Of all the people in the world, she was probably the one most unfamiliar with the emotion of fear, and yet here she was shouting with a face that was unmistakably pale.

Her subordinates had no choice but to stand there at a loss.

"Just—just five hundred kilometers! That's all we have to advance! The key to the war, to the future of this world, is so close!"

Her right hand gestured to the map hung on the board. She was pointing at a strategic Republican Army position where a group of suspicious transport ships had assembled according to a report they had just received: Brest Naval Base.

Brest Naval Base, one of the Republican Navy's principal bases, was one of the places the Republic was expected to concentrate their fleet prior to the cease-fire.

Which was why everyone in the Imperial Army interpreted the Republican fleet gathering there as preparation for a cease-fire to end the war. Of course, legally, the war wasn't over yet.

Still, everyone was compelled to say, *surely it's impossible for the Republic to continue fighting now that they've lost their capital. The end of the war is only a matter of time.*

Then came this request—no, more like an entreaty—for authorization to attack the Republican fleet.

That base was tightly defended under normal circumstances, but with the additional fleet's cannons, it had to be a veritable porcupine. Anyone

Chapter **III**

who wanted to go charging in there had to have something wrong with their head. Any reasonable commander would hesitate.

And yet. And yet here she was practically beside herself, insisting on an attack plan that could spoil the negotiations to end the war.

"Now! We must act now! Please, please! Give me the forces to suppress the Republican Army at Brest. Please let me, let my unit go!"

"Major! Major von Degurechaff! Please calm down, Major!"

"Colonel, please! Please send some troops! If we let them get away, they'll become the root of all the Empire's problems!"

It was hard to imagine how all that fury came from such a tiny body as she pulled the base commander down to her level by his lapels.

"Major, I beg your pardon!"

The military police officers who couldn't bear to watch any longer tried to come between the two, but furious, Degurechaff continued to shout, keeping all attempts to quell her at bay.

"Colonel! Please, please let me talk to the General Staff Office!"

A wounded lion would probably be less of a handful.

The MPs had training and boasted a fair amount of strength, but with the caveat—surely, they would agree—that their opponents were normal humans.

If any mission would give someone second thoughts, it was fighting a mage. Every soldier had a visceral sense of how troublesome confronting a mage could be. The only ones who could pick a fight with a mage wearing a computation orb was another mage similarly equipped.

And their opponent in this case was…a recipient of the Silver Wings Assault Badge with Oak Leaves—a *living* recipient, at that.

Her medals, enough to warrant calling her a human weapon, were not merely decorations. Even in the rear, they called her by the alias "White Silver" in recognition of her achievements, while other voices called her "Rusted Silver" out of fear.

If she were an enemy, they wouldn't want to get anywhere near her. Even as allies, they didn't want to get in her way.

But the imperial soldiers recalled their duty and obstructed her.

Though slick with cold sweat and trembling in fear, they were faithful to their duty through and through.

"Major von Degurechaff! Please, Major!"

She may have been a little girl, but she was still a mage. Having steeled their resolve, they all leaped at her at once. And it was when her protective film repulsed them that they finally realized how uncommonly earnest she was as she shouted.

"Colonel, I beg you. Please, please reconsider this. For the future of the Empire, we must act now!"

"...Ngh. Major von Degurechaff, you need to calm down!"

But even the commander of the base was an imperial soldier. If he could be coerced by a commander stationed under him, he wasn't fit to be in charge.

"The fall of Brest is only a matter of time. We don't need to pointlessly wear down our forces! Major! I can't let you ruin the cease-fire!"

"The cease-fire hasn't been declared yet! We can still save our army if we act now!"

"Major von Degurechaff! That fleet has already been defeated. It no longer constitutes a threat to our army!"

With a glance at the hesitating MPs, the staffers raised their voices to forestall her. They didn't think they could convince her with muscle, but they figured if she was a soldier, she could be persuaded with words.

So they tried it.

"Ahh, please, you have to understand. Time is the issue. There's no time! Colonel!"

But although Major von Degurechaff was said to be so sensible words weren't even necessary, today she stubbornly held her ground. Not only that, she insisted, openly impatient, that they should attack with all they had.

It was almost as if...

Yes, without a doubt, she was pleading as if she were afraid of something.

How absurd. Rusted Silver? Afraid?

That can't be, thought several of the bystanders.

They just didn't understand yet.

"They mean to escape in secret, to abandon their fatherland like rats!"

...And what about it?

The question popped into the staffers' heads instinctively, and they weren't wrong. True, armies did eat a lot even during peacetime. Since there would be a starving stomach for every man, the outcome was clear. A tragic fate awaited an army cut off from its supply lines.

Above all, the collapse of an army with no base was only a matter of time.

If one considered this, then the troops gathered at Brest Naval Base were surely units for rebuilding the defensive lines. Most of the soldiers followed that analysis and concluded that perhaps they should be on the lookout for a counter-landing operation instead. *Aha, it would be problematic if they did the same as us and threatened our supply lines by landing in the rear.*

"But won't they just self-destruct? Isn't that all that would happen?"

What is she afraid of? Slaughtering a single isolated army isn't so hard to do!

But it wasn't as if everyone was perfectly at ease.

After all, the young girl practically losing hold of her sanity before their eyes was universally acknowledged for her excellent brain.

People knew her as a genius from the war college or even the General Staff's darling or an underrated strategist.

"Self-destruct? No, they won't! They're— No, he's trying to facilitate an escape for some of his forces! We cannot let that happen!"

The shrill roar of her voice echoed surprisingly loudly over the base's runway. Yet, still no one could understand what made her keep screaming like that, though she was running out of breath. Anyone who saw her knew she was calling for something, but they couldn't figure out what it was.

Why is she being so insistent? How did she reach that conclusion?

"That theory has nothing to back it up! It makes the most sense to consider the units as replacement defenders or counterattackers."

"If we let them escape, the Empire's victory will be jeopardized! We'll eventually collapse!"

A few people tried to think. But cruel though it may have been, it was too late.

The Empire's victory will be jeopardized. The Empire will eventually collapse.

The response to those shouts was quite different from what the shouter expected.

"All right, hold her down! Major, that's enough!"

As if everyone's patience had run out, the order was given to get her under control. The MPs and her unit reluctantly set about tearing her off the commander, but Degurechaff's resistance was unusually fierce. Even though it was five men against a little girl, it took all their strength to pull her away.

"Colonel, please! Please!"

It was a scream that lingered in the ears.

"Can it, Major!"

"We must destroy them at Brest Naval Base! This enemy is a threat to the Empire! We have to annihilate it here and now! Please, you've got to understand—I have to do my duty as a soldier! This isn't what I want, but I know we must destroy Brest Naval Base!"

"Major, it's not happening!"

He still brushed off her prayerlike wail.

"…Would you please allow me to go?"

"Give it up!"

"Major!"

"Please don't try to stop me. Commander, I should already have the authority to do this."

The base commander's logic was crystal clear. Her action would endanger the cease-fire. But Major von Degurechaff's refutation was also clear: *I don't give a damn.*

"By the authority invested in me by the General Staff, I'm going ahead with a recon-in-force mission."

Then, unbelievably, she turned her back to the general shouting himself hoarse trying to get her under control and raced with determination back to her unit.

The MPs braced themselves, thinking they should stop her, but the look in her eyes froze them solid. In later days, they would talk among themselves about those eyes: "If we got in her way, she would have 'eliminated' us..."

With a glance at the officers gathered for an emergency meeting at command, Tanya thinks to herself.

Major General de Lugo... That's a sinister name. You could even call it an extremely sinister name. It's the kind of name you'd expect to conduct nuclear weapons tests or quit NATO.

I get the truly ominous feeling that he might start declaring the Free Republic or something. We really can't let a guy like him get away.

I'm utterly disappointed that command doesn't understand this. Sadly, I'll have to help myself if I want to end the war. So how should we attack on our own?

If I don't do anything, there won't be any trouble, but that's completely missing the point. Think of Rudel—I shouldn't be reproached for attacking an enemy country. In other words, if I'm not going to end up before a tribunal after the war, then...this is a permissible risk.

Let's assume we're attacking. Until just a little while ago, I argued the best I could, but I'm no longer in a position to receive official support.

Probably the only contact I have at this point is the submarine we worked with when we used the V-1s. They've probably established a patrol line.

But honestly, it'd be risky to attempt a pickup over the water without arranging things ahead of time. Considering the possibility that we don't find each other, it's probably safer not to count on it to begin with.

I don't want to attack alone, but it seems like the only way. For better or worse, if we use the V-1s we have, we can break through to Brest unimpeded.

Then, at the very least, I can have General de Lugo take his leave from the world.

In a way, this is like a hostile takeover of a remarkable new company on the rise. We need to nail down our patents and assets and eliminate any future threat to our company—it's only logical. We'll have a much easier time if we take him out now.

I can't stand the idea of history mocking us for our irrational hesitation when we should have intervened.

"Attention, Battalion!

"Thanks. All right, troops. We're going to attack Brest Naval Base."

So Tanya states their objective in her usual manner. This enemy is no different from any other they must shoot, and since that is the case, they'll just do the same as always. So she is shocked to see the officers' tense expressions and understanding the effect her announcement has on them.

Sensible First Lieutenant Weiss and the other officers all look dumbfounded. Tanya realizes that what she has said sounded strange.

But the first thing she feels is confusion. Knowing her war-loving troops, she thought they might be happy, but she never imagined they would be dumbfounded. It's a bit embarrassing.

I thought they were all about pursuing the enemy anywhere if it meant additional achievements.

As someone from human resources, I thought I understood their feelings, so it's a bit of a shock to discover I don't. I'm supposed to be managing these troops, so if I don't understand their hopes and dreams, it can only mean I'm inept.

…No, let's think about this calmly. Haste makes waste. I'll suspend judgment for now.

"Commander?! That's…"

"We're going to act on our own authority. Why else have us report directly to the General Staff? Why else allow us to act independently?"

Just like insurance, it's better not to use it, but it's precisely for times like this that we have this wild card.

The higher-ups resent her authority because the standard chain of command is often tangled, but to Tanya, if you think of her unit as a project team, it's easier to see how they should be used.

The reason no one but the officer they directly report to can interfere is because they're a team doing an important project on special orders from the CEO. A team like that needs to be given a degree of autonomy. And anyone given authority to act is expected to use it appropriately. There's nothing better than solving a problem with minimal effort.

Medicine shows us that prevention before you get sick makes life easier. And the best part is that you can save on medical costs. Avoidable waste must be eliminated.

If you can prevent multiple risks with a single inoculation, it behooves you to do so. Humans tend to overestimate immediate risks, but it's equally foolish to forget terrible long-term risks.

Considering how well it manages costs for society, preventative medicine is truly wonderful. Momentary pain and certain types of risk can't be completely ignored, but obsessing about those things is missing the point. This operation to have General de Lugo take his leave from the world is quite similar to preventative medicine. It's worth doing even if it entails some risk.

We must prevent this plague that would eat away at the Empire. If we don't prevent it, the cost to society—the very society that gave Major Tanya von Degurechaff the authority to act—will be irrecoverable.

That must be avoided at all costs.

"B-but I don't really think our battalion can attack Brest Naval Base on our own. And besides, the only ones who used the V-1 before were the members of the select company. It's not enough. Please reconsider this," urges Lieutenant Weiss, but to Tanya, this is nonsense stemming from an attachment to preconceived notions.

Certainly, it would be logical for the Brest base to be heavily defended. Yes, I see how even an elite battalion could suffer serious casualties if they are shot at head-on by a unit lying in wait for them.

Still, to Tanya, even taking all that into consideration, it must be done. And they have a way to do it. There's no reason not to.

"Lieutenant, we're only going to hit them and run. It's less of an attack than a recon-in-force mission. I'm confident our battalion can handle it and that it's a worthwhile objective."

So Tanya argues. *If anyone can do it, we can.* After all, their defenses are configured for sea and land, and in the first place, we're only going to zoom in there on the V-1s and then get out after delivering a single blow.

In addition to those basic assumptions, she imagines Brest Naval Base's defenses are outdated. They didn't take aerial technology or paratrooper mages into account.

"On top of that, their defenses are an anachronism. And with no pressing reason, they probably aren't rushing to update them. You can probably assume they're operating with old safeguards."

Brest Naval Base's location makes it a good natural harbor. It originally developed into a port to shelter in a storm, and the topography allows large ships to dock. Geographically, it also has the distinction of being difficult for a land army to reach. There's a reason the place has been used as a base since ancient times. Another important point is its distance, safe in the rear, from the Empire, a potential enemy.

But that "safe in the rear" assumption brings with it an interesting proposition. In an arms race where every moment counts, there aren't very many resources available to outfit areas besides the front lines. So would a place considered safe like Brest be given priority? It's a very interesting question.

But what if the enemy is counting on using the fleet's defenses and firepower? It doesn't seem strange to expect that Brest Naval Base's defenses aren't much to speak of.

After all, compared to the state of defensive fire at the end of World War II, these anti–air measures are like peashooters. We'll definitely be able to limit our amount of wear and tear as long as we don't drag out the attack. Besides, the Republican Army isn't very experienced.

The imperial and Republican fleets have been staring each other down on the "fleet in being" principle for ages. That is to say, both of them are holed up. Of course, individual ships have participated in battles here and there, but we can assume that on a fleet level, they don't have much experience with fighting against air or mage forces. Well, it's no wonder, given that most of the mage units from both sides were pitted against one another in the attrition battle on the Rhine front.

And even if the group included troops who lived through their baptism in the hell of the Rhine lines, most of them were reserves anyway. The inexperienced units won't be able to keep pace with the elites. The difference between having even a little frontline fighting experience and none is huge.

"And I'm in contact with a friendly submarine near the base."

I confirmed that a friendly sub was patrolling the area, even if the most we can expect from it is alerts rather than preventing the escape entirely.

Still, if we can succeed in catching a lift, we can attack more than once and make our getaway underwater. I'll be glad to have additional choices. And as long as submarine command doesn't interfere, it will be possible to attack simultaneously with torpedoes.

"Given all that, I've determined that the best course of action is to directly attack Brest Naval Base with V-1s and then board the submarine and attack once more. In other words, we'll assault them with the V-1s like we've done once already. I'm confident you guys can pull it off again."

It's a rehash of a past operation. Since we're acting on our own, we can't get support to draft a new one, so there's no helping it. To have the most surefire plan, Tanya references the easiest operation she's been involved in.

Of course, she doesn't want to use the V-1s, but Chief Engineer Schugel's invention played a critical role in their previous operation. Tanya figures that destroying a ship is more than doable with the destructive power of those warheads.

Plus, using those, we won't have any trouble with enemy interception or any allies trying to stop us. If the tanks full of fuel score a direct hit on the ship, we can expect results on par with anti-ship missiles. Even a battleship won't get through that unscathed.

And with a whole augmented battalion going on the strike, that equates to forty-eight missiles. That should be enough to do some serious damage. Of course, we don't have much experience operating them. Even if everything goes smoothly, we should be ready for a low rate of direct hits.

But the V-1s should be packing plenty of punch. Maybe we can estimate half would be direct hits. Twenty-four doesn't seem unreasonable considering the target is an anchored ship.

And twenty-four missiles is more than enough to get results. And if mages attack on top of that, I have no doubt we'll get our sworn enemy Major General de Lugo promoted to full general in no time. We'll even give him a battleship for a gravestone.

No, "no doubt" isn't the right way to put it. We'll *definitely* execute this plan. Yes, rather than let him become a marshal, we'll present him with a double promotion and a jumbo gravestone in the shape of a battleship.

"Major, I have a question."

In response, her subordinates seem skeptical. She knows this, but if she can't get them to understand completely, the plan could fail. She nods benevolently, both cautious but with no guilt on her conscience. "Go ahead. What is it?"

"Commander, where are we going to get the V-1s?"

I didn't expect a technical question. She misses a beat but figures it's fine and answers matter-of-factly, "The Technical Arsenal just happens to have some here. We'll use those."

"So we have permission?"

That's an annoying question, but I have an answer prepared. I can handle it. I've prepared the minimum argument necessary to avoid getting court-martialed.

It really is the bare minimum, though. But no, making sure we have enough time to attack is more important than establishing the just cause.

Working beyond my pay grade is gut-wrenching, but considering it's to stay alive, I have to do it.

"What are you talking about? Didn't Chief Engineer Schugel request a combat test? We're simply following through."

I never imagined a request from *him* would come in handy. Fate sure is ironic, but if we can use the V-1s, then problem solved—we'll be able to attack Brest Naval Base.

The General Staff received a request from the Technical Arsenal asking for more combat data and a reassessment of the fine-tuned V-1s. We're the only unit that has ever used them, so no one should mind if we're the ones to do the follow-up test.

"It could be seen as not just assertive but overstepping your authority…"

"If we don't make a move, historians in later generations will call us negligent. I don't want to let them laugh at me. Really, we don't even have time to be debating like this. If you have nothing left to say, then let's end it here. The operation is go—now!"

We can't let him get away. If the withdrawal from Dunkirk hadn't succeeded, would the British and the French have been able to hold Britain's defensive lines?

No, not only that, but if the British hadn't scraped together enough troops to defend their home country, would the inept Italian army have gotten such a beating?

Not only *that*, but to think for just a minute: What if? Perhaps I'm talking irresponsibly, but if Germany had been able to smash Britain, maybe they could have fought the Soviet Union without worrying about their rear. The same could go for the Empire.

…To put it in extremes, if we beat the Republican fleet here, not only will the Commonwealth have to worry about how to control the sea, but with the Republic dropped out, it will also be facing the nightmare scenario of having to confront the Empire.

If that happens, the Empire might even be able to create an environment that gives it the strategic advantage.

In other words, an endless draw. The Commonwealth definitely can't defeat the Empire's land arm on its own. And the Imperial Navy is strong enough to keep up its staring contest with the Commonwealth's. Then… Then! That face-off works in the Empire's favor. We can use the manufacturing bases in the regions we control, get our forces in order—heck, we could even make ships if we took the time.

If we could establish such a broad foundation—no, when we do, if the Commonwealth realizes that, we could even end the war.

Then we won't have to do these dangerous things anymore. Then a peaceful world will be right in front of us.

In order to end the war…

We have to decide things right now.

We will end the war.

I'll grab peace with my own two hands.

Therefore, Magic Major Tanya von Degurechaff gives her troops strict orders in a decisive tone to make her reluctant subordinates get moving. As she expects, the soldiers respond crisply.

Her battalion personnel are in ranks. The engineers and mechanics are here to work on the V-1s that were brought over. The V-1s, virtually hijacked from rear depots using the shield of the Technical Arsenal's request, are already lined up on the runway. The engineers move them to the launchers and begin final checks.

Seeing that preparations to sortie are going smoothly, Degurechaff is able to look over her troops in satisfaction. It's great that they were able to get V-1s outfitted for the larger fuel tanks envisioned for longer flights. And to up their destructive capabilities, I had to give up on the 80s, which are specialized for anti-ship attacks, but we managed to add warheads to the 25s.

Any ship that gets hit with these going faster than sound will probably be sunk in a single attack. I doubt even a battleship's armor could stand up to these. And above all, we're targeting an anchored vessel. We should be able to get a great rate of bull's-eyes.

Those prospects of a brighter future cheer Tanya up quite a bit.

Even if we don't know which boat General de Lugo is making his capital ship, if we target them all, we're bound to get him at least once. That forecast alone makes her want to burst out laughing, it makes her so happy.

We can expect a payout that will, in the worst case, still be plenty to have de Lugo take leave of this world. And even just whacking the residual units he's got with him would be a pretty good result.

"…Commander, all units are here."

"Very good. The V-1s are all prepped, right? I don't even want to say this, but I'd hate for one of them to blow up with one of my men inside."

"They were careful. The mechanics swear by their work and guarantee the machines are tuned up safely."

"All right, then… What is it, Lieutenant Weiss? You look like you have something to say, so hurry up and say it."

"Major, this seems… Isn't this too contrary to the wishes of the home country? I have no choice but to follow your orders, but I think this is an extremely dangerous move for you, too…"

In contrast to Tanya's expectations of high payout, the leading officers in the battalion seem to have reservations.

Oh, brother, she'd like to moan, but it's hard when their reservations aren't unfounded.

That said, all they need to do is get results.

Once her unenthusiastic vice commander sees the results of their attack, he'll surely come around. Well, Weiss is the type who finds these sorts of unilateral actions unnerving. I should just be happy he can't stop me as long as we're operating within my discretionary powers.

"Lieutenant, I gratefully accept your warning, but I have no intention of changing my orders. Anything else?"

He's a soldier, after all. He won't slack off just because he's reluctant. I can trust him completely on that point. It's wonderful when people have so much passion for their work.

Agh, how many times have I been annoyed by temps who passively resist instructions just because they don't feel like it, as if that's a good reason? And then to watch them giving the company a bad name, all the while paying their salary—it's a vexing situation, to be sure.

Soldiers are different. They're much more reliable. Well, it's because if they slack off just because they're not into their job, they'll die. Of course, that's because the work isn't easy enough to let you slack off, but anyhow...

"No, ma'am... But are you sure you want to do this? The base commander is outraged and said he was going to have a word with the General Staff..."

"With the General Staff? As long as I'm not overstepping, he can't do anything."

Proper procedure. I sound like a jerk saying it outright, but fulfilling the Technical Arsenal's request is guaranteed as a valid move given the chain of command. *Learn laws, learn the regulations. Then you'll be able to find a way to justify any course of action*, I was taught in the past—fond memories.

Rules are not meant to be broken—they're meant to be exploited and wriggled out of.

That the commander on the ground rejected my proposal is regrettable. But nothing about that limits what operations I can undertake.

Following the usual procedure...no matter how much authority we have to act on our own as a unit reporting directly to the General Staff, attacking Brest Naval Base probably wouldn't be allowed.

But now, when we're in the middle of suppressing them, it's possible to broaden the interpretation of what discretionary powers are granted a unit serving in the war. Even if the base commander protests to the General Staff, the General Staff won't publicly rebuke me.

Of course, getting a stern warning below the surface can't be taken lightly, but either way, at that point, what's done is done.

The fact that I can secure the freedom to act now, at this do-or-die moment, makes me happy.

If I succeed, I'm plenty capable of handling whatever comes next. In order to think about the future, I have to eradicate the pathogen in front of me.

"...Commander, from Group Command."

But unhappily, in comes orders from Group Command. Inadvertently scowling at the radio operator who had the misfortune to be the messenger was a mistake on my part.

With an apology, Tanya takes the message and skims it.

It's some simple advice about her conduct. That is, a gentle warning to *Simmer down*, from Group Command. Though her unit is nominally independent, that's their request.

From the position of someone who has to comply whenever possible, it feels like interference.

Normally, even Tanya would step down at this point. That's how forceful the stance is. But under the current circumstances, she simply can't.

"Tell them I *understand and respect* their request," she instructs, wording her brief response carefully. As long as they can't deny that she's understanding and respecting the request, it's hard to imagine they'll contact her again. *I'm not lying per se.* She scrutinizes her words again, making sure they're not problematic.

Yes, all I have to do is understand and respect the request and then act anyway.

Luckily, perhaps it should be said, by the time someone clever at Group Command realizes what we're up to, the V-1s will have struck Brest. There'll be nothing they can do to stop us, then.

But Tanya realizes her predictions were a bit optimistic. I'm not a fan of the fact that the efforts to hold her back are so serious. It means some department has its eye on her.

It will only take a little longer, but there's no telling what will happen during that short time.

"Seems like they're going to bother us. Let's push up the launch schedule."

So Major Tanya von Degurechaff makes an executive decision to hurry.

Considering the risks, she resolves to move up the launch schedule. It took no time for her to decide that it was more important to prioritize going faster than humanly possible over securing perfect conditions.

Normally, the itinerary would be decided upon checking the weather forecast and analyzing enemy movements, but all that has been omitted. They'll get a rough outline of the situation over the wireless, and that's it. She's decided on the shortest attack route. That will use the least fuel, which should give them the secondary effect of a bigger bang when the V-1s hit the enemy ships.

Either way, she's going with speed over polish.

Luckily, the engineers really are engineers. The way they briskly perform all necessary tasks provides a glimpse of the high caliber of technological support the Empire is so proud of.

I'm genuinely thankful to have these precision machines properly serviced.

It's only a little longer now.

No, we can go in just a few more minutes.

Should I order everyone to board?

Just as Tanya is thinking to act, she sees a soldier from the communications facility racing toward her. It's the same soldier who had come with the warning from Group Command earlier. Tanya wonders if it's some other notice, but her expression gradually stiffens.

It's the same radio operator from before, but he's changed color. He's running so earnestly, and that look in his eyes says he has something to tell her...

She realizes at that point that he's frantic to get some message to her.

"…Ahh, damn it."

So Tanya has no choice but to grumble to the heavens.

It's not as if she believes in intuition, but she gathers that this will be bad news. She immediately looks over the unit, but it will be a tiny bit longer before they can launch.

How fatal even an infinitesimal delay can prove in combat!

It's only a few minutes' difference, but it's enough for whatever that soldier is going to say to come out of his mouth.

It's too late to wish she could have gotten them moving a bit sooner; she regrets it from the bottom of her heart, but the giant mistake has already been made. She abruptly considers knocking the messenger unconscious, but there's no way she could do that with so many people watching, so she discards the idea immediately.

Panicking isn't going to improve the situation one bit. Is this what it feels like the moment before you get executed? In any case, this is the height of bad luck.

"Commander! Special orders from the General Staff!"

Ahh, I don't want to hear them. I don't want to hear *anything*. He doesn't even have to say a word for me to know it's lousy news.

Agh, can't you be a little more considerate?! You could have done your job just a little slower!

…I know quite well that my emotions are wailing irrationally. Just moments ago, I was admiring him for his loyalty as a soldier. It wouldn't really be fair to take that back right afterward.

Still.

Tanya can't help the urge to throttle him.

"The cease-fire has been declared! This is from the General Staff with the highest priority to all units!"

"The cease-fire? They declared the cease-fire?!"

Before she can stop him, Lieutenant Weiss asks the messenger again, thanks to which all the others hear the news. Now there's no way we can launch the attack claiming we didn't hear.

Not only would I not accomplish much on my own, I'd be shot for breaking the cease-fire.

"Commander, please halt the sortie at once!"

There's no misunderstanding that scream.

"It's a cease-fire! Please halt the sortie at once!"

He's raising his voice to tell me to stop.

Yeah, I hear you. Tanya waves in response. *As long as this is your job, I should respect you for doing it.* He's an ideal soldier; all noncoms should be so faithful to their duties.

But Tanya refuses to accept this news. She's come this far with her solo action plan, resigned to some kind of punishment—because she knows that this is the last chance for the Empire to avoid defeat.

Now. If we don't act now, we'll have no way to make it in time. Major Tanya von Degurechaff knows this horrifying truth. If we get Dunkirked, victory will slip away to a place beyond the Empire's reach.

So we have to do it now. If we don't, we probably can't save the Empire.

At the same time, she knows. If they sortie, she'll be the one responsible for violating the cease-fire.

If she could find some way out of that, things might have been different. But now that she has been clearly instructed to halt the sortie due to a cease-fire, she's left with no room for fuzzy arguments.

Which is why Tanya's expression is extremely conflicted. She can see that if they don't go now, catastrophe and ruin will eventually befall the Empire. It's inevitable.

But to go means her personal downfall. That is equally inevitable.

In other words, for an extremely simple reason, she is unable to sortie. But not sortieing could mean the slow death of a collapse awaits. It's painful; she can see the chance to completely obliterate that possibility right in front of her, but she has to let it go.

And so.

Erupting angrily, she crumples to the runway with no regard for who might be listening and bitterly spits in an almost despairing tone, "…Ngh. Shit, shit, shit! Abort! Abort the sortie!"

Glory to our Reich!

Unnamed imperial soldier

"Reporting in!" Second Lieutenant Grantz runs over and delivers the words the moment he arrives in a tone that is kept crisp out of a sense of duty despite the tension.

First Lieutenant Weiss gathers from his expression that preparations are complete and promptly straightens up and faces him, feeling quite tense himself.

"Lieutenant Weiss, all battalion members are present!"

"Thanks, Lieutenant Grantz. Any logistical delays?"

"None at all, sir! We're fully equipped with both provisions and gear!"

That meant everything was ready. It was such a significant report, but it went not to Major von Degurechaff but the second-in-command, of all people.

He made his judgment upon receiving it.

Considering how important the matter was, the commander herself should have made the call, but the senior officer at the moment was First Lieutenant Weiss.

The duty and the tension of being in command... Above all, the immeasurable anxiety of assuming the position instead of Major von Degurechaff... *She told me I might be promoted before the year is out. The world is a strange place.*

"...Sir?"

"Ah, it's nothing, Lieutenant."

But now was no time to hesitate. This moment called for his decisive judgment as commander. He knew as an officer that throwing cold water on this strained, expectant mood would be an unforgivable error. What his duty required of him now was to carry out his responsibility.

Chapter **IV**

"Company leaders, report your status!" he cried.

Though he was endeavoring to maintain the composure of a pro, he couldn't hold back his anticipation entirely.

"All units present. Type one battle stations manned!"

In response to the roared order, a report of readiness.

"What's your status?"

The voice indicated the start of a battle was near.

"Beer, check! Wine, check!"

The response was proud.

"Meat, fish, check, check!"

Their extra rations were so generous that it seemed like the food and drink was challenging them to finish it off. The battalion's full fighting power was unsparingly committed to cleaning out all the items they'd swiped and stashed.

"Ocean, check!"

And Weiss had unwavering confidence that he had chosen the right spot for it.

"Great, troops, this operation is go!"

Clear water, blue sky, and the refreshing sunshine of early summer... The grills and cooking tables were equipped with mountains of many varieties of meat. Naturally, cases of bottled beer had been delivered by the cooler. There was even wine and champagne from who knew where.

On this day, the elite mages of the 203rd Aerial Mage Battalion were resolved to devote their bodies and souls to enjoying the beach.

Everything had been for this day.

"To victory!"

"To my brothers-in-arms!"

"To the Reich!"

""""Cheers!"""""

Three toasts and a hearty shout.

With that, the men dropped all formalities for this day only. Beer-drinking contests ensued. Champagne corks flew. Then shoulder to shoulder, they all sang "We Are the Reich, Crown of the World."

Their voices thundered from the pit of their stomachs to fill the

Republican vacation spot. The beach was the best chance to sing unin-
terrupted odes to the sweet, ice-cold nectar of victory in their hands.

"To the Empire," they cried and downed their beers. They would take
full advantage of this opportunity to sing praises. Several soldiers took
their shovels to the sand and began to play, never mind that they were
grown men; soon, platoons were pitted against one another in digging
competitions. Others jumped straight into the water, while others still
made a beeline for the grills with a shout of "First, the meat!"

Everyone there was right and truly intoxicated—on victory, on the joy
of surviving, and on the sense of accomplishment they got from carrying
out their duty.

>>>>   AT THE SAME TIME, IMPERIAL ARMY BREST BASE   <<<<

Reading the message her adjutant handed her, she rubs her temples and
groans. Then, clinging to the overly optimistic hope that her conclusion
will change upon a second reading, Magic Major Tanya von Degurechaff of the Imperial Army, General Staff officer, looks at it again.

But it doesn't matter how far between the lines she reads. After all, it's
clearly an official notice from the General Staff.

"...Sorry, Lieutenant Serebryakov, I'm going out for a moment."

So with a word to her adjutant, Tanya puts her cap on in annoyance,
slowly rises, and heads for the residential building adjacent to battalion HQ.

Looking up, she sees fair skies, in contrast with her mood.

"It's almost summer, huh...?"

It isn't too hot yet, but summer is probably near. Tanya was the one
who cleared First Lieutenant Weiss and the others to take leave and go
on vacation. It was also she who approved expenses from the battalion's
coffers, as a recognition of her subordinates' services, for them to spend a
day having a barbecue at the beach.

That's...well, it's fine.

They're just officers serving in the field. It's only natural that they
should have the right to taste the sweet nectar of victory. And Tanya is

not at all averse to respecting the rights of others. She knows it's unforgivable for a superior to take advantage of their subordinates simply because they are subordinate and infringe on their rights.

So Tanya doesn't blame the troops for celebrating their victory. It's fine. They gave their all from the positions they were in.

The problem, laments Tanya, just barely holding back her hellish rage and looking to the heavens, *is that the same optimism has tainted the brass. It's hopeless.*

Her pent-up anger and distrust completely exploded with this congratulatory message from the General Staff. A personal congrats would be one thing, but this was an official statement from the General Staff, of all people, aimed at the entire army and naively praising our "great victory," of all things.

The moment she understood, she had a hard time reining in her emotions. With her scant remaining self-control, she avoided a total explosion on the spot, but she was literally seething with anger.

The moment she closes the door, she hurls her cap to the floor and screams her true feelings. "Shit! The sweet nectar of victory?! We missed our chance to end this war! You may know how to win, but you don't understand how to use it!"

With the coolheaded corner of her mind, Tanya understands that telling everyone to piss off is pointless. That's why she has enough sense to get it all out in her room where she doesn't have to worry about anyone overhearing.

But once she is in her room, she can't hold it back: *How stupid must the General Staff be to get so giddy over this "great victory" when the war isn't even over yet?! What are they thinking?* She curses them as the urge takes her.

"This can't be possible! Why isn't the General Staff putting this victory to good use?! Why?! Supreme High Command isn't even doing negotiations! Are they not interested in ending the war?!"

A war is broken into multiple stages. Yes, the officers and men carried out their duty fine as far as the front lines; they were able to contribute to this great victory. As such, they should be allowed to celebrate. They have that right.

But if the General Staff, meant to be directing the war, and the organization above it, Supreme High Command, are getting all excited about winning and breaking into the celebratory wine...

That's negligence.

That's a mistake.

No, more than that, it's evil. It's a criminal lack of action.

"Shit! Why is this happening? How did the General Staff suddenly get so...?"

How did they suddenly get so dim-witted?!

In any case, practically pulling her hair out over this mess, Tanya turns on the alcohol burner in her room to boil some water and reaches for her mill.

She carefully grinds the fine arabica coffee beans she acquired immediately after the capture of Parisii and readies a drip filter. Then, with the water at the right temperature, she lets the bloom form on top of the grounds before meticulously pouring and transferring the results into a mug. Finally, she takes a deep breath, seeking peace of mind in the fragrance, and relaxes.

"The General Staff doesn't understand the situation. But why is that?"

Her question is genuine. *Why did this happen?* The Imperial Army is bunch of sticklers for efficiency who make sure even lower-ranking officers are well versed in planning and drafting operations. At the war college, they hammered in how to not only cope with encounters under unknown circumstances and make snap decisions but also plan as far as possible to minimize the fog of war, among other things.

"...I just can't understand it. What happened?"

Which is why, having regained composure, albeit temporarily, Tanya cannot fathom why the General Staff is so high on victory.

The General Staff was supposedly of particularly rational officers, even considering the makeup of the Imperial Army at large. Probability theory doesn't seem to allow that every last one of them would lose their minds at the same time.

How is it, then, that they're all wasted on the wine of victory?

"Yeah, I really just don't get this change in the higher-ups. Agh, well, a picture is worth a thousand words. I guess I have no choice but to go over there in person."

So she makes up her mind as she finishes off her coffee. There is nothing for her to do but go ask them herself.

Luckily, the battalion is not currently on rapid response standby. It's not ideal for a commander to leave their unit, but no one should object to her visiting the General Staff for a few days.

In that case, thinks Tanya, *time is a finite resource, so I can't waste it.* Once she decides on a course of action, all that's left is to promptly act.

She picks up the internal communications device in the corner of her room and calls up battalion HQ.

"Duty Officer Second Lieutenant Serebryakov speaking."

"Lieutenant, it's me."

"Oh, Major. What can I do for you?"

With a slight sense of satisfaction that Serebryakov was quick enough to pick up in two rings, Tanya briefly states her business. "I'm going to pop in on the General Staff. While I get permission from HQ, please prepare our bags—yes, mine and yours. And get word to Lieutenant Weiss."

"Understood. I believe he's currently on leave, but I'll let him know. Shall I reserve long-distance railway tickets?"

"Oh, if he can't come here, you can just radio him. And we don't need tickets. I'm getting authorization to fly straight to the General Staff Office. Do, however, secure accommodations for us in the capital."

Time is short, so we don't have the leisure to take it easy in a train. Tanya has already decided on cutting across the former Rhine lines and flying in directly.

Luckily, perhaps it can be said, Type 97s will allow them to get to the capital with plenty of energy remaining. Regardless of how it would go if it were a combat flight, simply passing through friendly airspace should be plenty doable.

"Understood, Major! How many days will you spend in the capital?"

"Not many, but three for certain."

She knows she has to take General von Zettour's schedule into consideration, so she's already resigned to the fact that this will be a time-consuming endeavor and figures it's best to overestimate the length of her stay.

Of course, really, she doesn't want to be away from her post for long... but she's already decided that she'll wage a fierce battle of words in the capital if necessary.

"Understood. Right away, ma'am."

All right, then. Tanya gets her things together and packs her type I dress uniform. Then she turns in two flight plan approval forms, one for her and one for Serebryakov, as well as a plan assuming a direct flight, and receives authorization almost immediately.

Meanwhile, Visha had received the orders and was making her preparations for their trip to the capital just as briskly, not about to let Tanya outdo her.

She contacted the magic officers' club and reserved two rooms. Then, using her status as the adjutant of the commander of a battalion reporting directly to the General Staff, she secured the use of one official car from the General Staff's rear section.

Times like these it really hit her. *The 203rd really gets a lot of respect for being directly under the General Staff. Usually the higher-ups hate doing anything over the phone where they can't see your face, but even a young officer like me calls and the staff in the rear generously consents.*

"So instead of the beach I'm on leave in the capital...? Well, it's not so bad. Maybe I'll get to see some old faces."

Which is why, for just a moment, she thought maybe she should be able to enjoy her vacation as well. *If I can make time, maybe I'll be able to talk to friends in person instead of updating them in letters.*

Of course, she would only do that after quickly accomplishing the things she needed to do. So Visha proceeded to take care of those tasks in an orderly way. Lodgings were arranged; transportation was locked down. The report for the incoming duty officer she put with the battalion logbook and the report of her activities. Lieutenant Weiss would be able to glean all he needed to from a single read through.

Major von Degurechaff told her that she understood Lieutenant Weiss was on break, so all Visha had to do was contact him and her part was done.

"Excuse me, this is Second Lieutenant Serebryakov. May I speak with First Lieutenant Weiss?"

Okay. She called the vacation facility number she was given "just in case" via long-distance telephone and asked for Lieutenant Weiss.

"This is First Lieutenant Weiss."

"Lieutenant, this is Second Lieutenant Serebryakov. So sorry to call you while you're on leave."

And because he was on vacation, Visha had intended to say only the minimum: *Please contact the major.*

"Oh, Visha. Are you calling to cry to me that you wish you were at the beach, too? We're having a grand old time."

Yes, it was unexpected.

Usually, Lieutenant Weiss was more composed and thoughtful, but this time he was drunk and slipped up, and what he said made Visha just a little bit mad.

Up until that moment, her thoughts on the matter had been, *Well, of course I'd like to go with everyone, but if the second-in-command is out and my superior the major is staying behind, then as her adjutant I have to serve as duty officer.*

But things didn't play out that way.

"...No, I have a message for you. The major has some business at the General Staff Office, so we're leaving for three or four days."

So Visha was true to her miffed feelings. Taking advantage of his slip, she matter-of-factly stated the truth.

"So you're letting me know so I can take over?"

"Yes, I was to inform you."

That was everything Major von Degurechaff had told her. *We're going to the capital, so contact Lieutenant Weiss to let him know.* Since that was her assigned duty, she was telling the truth.

"...I guess now that you told me that, I should go back and talk to the major, huh?"

"As you like. I've delivered the necessary message, so I don't presume to have anything else to say on the matter."

Sadly, that was the unadorned truth. Sticking her tongue out in her mind, Visha took a bit of revenge.

The major had told her not to force him to come. Put another way, she didn't say clearly to have him come or not come, and guessing what she meant was not part of Visha's job. Of course, given their superior's utilitarian mind-set, Visha personally felt that over the phone was good enough.

But she had no obligation to say as much to him.

"Got it, Lieutenant. Yeah, I should talk to the major directly about this. Okay, Lieutenant Grantz! The rest is up to you! As for me, I've received an invitation from a beautiful lady!"

So when Lieutenant Weiss, seeming to have decided on his own what needed to be done, left everything else to Lieutenant Grantz in a voice more cheerful than he ever used, Visha couldn't help but laugh.

"Yes, sir, Lieutenant! Don't worry about a thing! Every last one of us will stand our ground against this formidable enemy and fight through!"

Then, imagining the scene on the other end of the line, something occurred to Visha. *Lieutenant Weiss is probably actually drunk and not thinking up to his usual speed...*

"Aww, shit! I'm so lucky to have a report like you!"

"Lieutenant! If you're going to meet a lady, I'd sober up first!"

"Hey! All you all better have hangovers tomorrow!"

Having left them with that, he grabbed a ride to the base and sobered up on the way. When he arrived, he changed out of his civilian clothing and promptly went to battalion HQ.

If his superior was going to the General Staff Office now, maybe something was happening. If anything, it could be related to her attempt to act independently that nearly violated the cease-fire. The possibility might have caused him to overthink it.

Hoping his breath didn't stink of booze, he entered the room and announced himself. "First Lieutenant Weiss reporting in." The first thing he saw was Major von Degurechaff and Lieutenant Serebryakov with their flying goggles on and their luggage ready.

"Oh, Lieutenant. Good timing. The situation is a bit of a mess. It seems like the staffers are so excited they're not even thinking about how to end the war. There's nothing else I can do but go over there personally. It'll only be a few days, but take care of things here while I'm gone."

"Understood."

He would be in charge while she was away.

That was exactly the same as what he had already heard on the phone. *So now she must have something important to tell me.* He braced himself and devoted his entire being to hearing the words she would say next.

"I did call you, but I knew you were on your vacation. I didn't think you'd come all the way here when a phone call would have sufficed. You were probably thinking of me, but I'm sorry I interrupted your party, Lieutenant."

For a moment, his superior's nonchalant tone had Weiss at a loss. He had been convinced there would be something important he would need to hear in person, but it turned out she was simply getting in touch about being away.

…And that was when he finally realized he'd been putting in way too much effort and running around for no reason.

"Oh, uh, no. It's no big deal."

He was confused until he carefully remembered the earlier conversation and realized just what *"As you like"* meant when he had asked if he should return or not.

"Hmm? What is it, Lieutenant Serebryakov?"

"Oh, I'm just impressed by Lieutenant Weiss's kindness and attention to detail."

After all, Major von Degurechaff wasn't the type of officer to give vague directions. Weiss should have understood the moment Serebryakov said, *"As you like."*

He regretted being under the influence while receiving a message. If his head had been clear, he probably would have been able to catch Serebryakov's drift, even over the phone.

Well, I was on vacation…but I guess I should be ready to be called up at any time, even on leave, he thought and then added, *I probably shouldn't have made that remark, either.*

Well, the unfortunate truth was that for Weiss and other imperial soldiers, "wartime leave" usually amounted to medical treatment in the rear or being off duty in the trenches, so he had been enjoying his first real vacation.

"Yes, he's a model communicator. Well, we'll be off. Take it easy while I'm gone. Drilling just enough to maintain discipline is fine."

"Understood. Have a safe trip, Major."

"Will do, thanks, and sorry again."

"…Hello, I'm Major von Degurechaff. Please get me General von Zettour; it's urgent."

"Oh, Major, I'm terribly sorry, but the general is currently out."

Hmm, that doesn't happen very often, thinks Tanya, but she figures if he's busy with military affairs, it can't be helped. She adjusts her expectations and tries again. "Then, sorry, may I see General von Rudersdorf?"

She says it simply, expecting to just see General von Zettour's friend first, but she gathers immediately from the troubled look on the staffer's face that this request is also impossible. She asks with her eyes what it could possibly mean.

"You'll have to excuse me, Major von Degurechaff, but, well, everyone from the General Staff Office is out…"

Tanya had braced herself for some reluctance to reply, but the duty officer revealed the issue with unexpected readiness.

"I see. And where might they be?"

But actually, the answer came so readily that all she feels is a sense that something is amiss. After all, she's certain that the General Staff officers are terribly busy at all times. And she knows from experience that she can drop in unannounced if something is critical and get them to look at it.

That adaptability, that flexibility, is the Imperial Army General Staff's strength, and it only works because of the close contact between the officers directing the operations.

Which is why Tanya can't believe it.

Even when she is informed that the office is practically empty, she doesn't quite get it.

So compelled by necessity, she comes up with a reason. For example, maybe their attendance was required at some big function at court. Or maybe they had to show up for some occasion, a party or whatnot. That is her naive expectation.

That straitlaced bunch would never leave the General Staff Office empty at such a critical juncture for no reason.

"…I think they're at the *beer hall*."

"The beer hall?"

Which is why all she can do at that moment is parrot the words back at the duty officer.

What did he just say to me?

Beer hall?

What's a beer hall?

Beer hall.

It's a place for drinking alcohol.

So what need can there possibly be for the entire General Staff to go there all at once?

"Yes, they were shouting about drinking to celebrate our victory. I wanted to go, too, but you know how it is."

"Yes, thanks for your service. If you'll excuse me, then."

Hearing this reply, she is forced to devote nearly her entire being to maintaining her blank expression and nodding.

"All right, Major. Good night."

After receiving an easygoing send-off from the duty officer, Tanya burrows grimly into bed.

The next day, the staff officers, having drunk like fish for the first time in quite a while, are also nursing their first hangovers. It's been so long it's almost nostalgic competing to see who can feign normalcy most skillfully, until into the General Staff Office marches the fierce Major Tanya von Degurechaff.

"General, excuse me, but…"

She has resolved to speak directly to General von Zettour, at the center of the General Staff, and find out the whole story.

Chapter IV

"Oh, Major. I heard about the fleet. And the base commander's gripes. But my conclusion is that both of you erred in the course of your duties."

But what the hell is this now?

"As long as you are both correct, it's only a matter of reprimanding the pair of you to exercise more self-control. That said, Major, it seems you went a bit far this time."

The answer she is given misses the mark so completely she finds herself glaring at him, despite realizing it's rude. *What the hell is wrong with all my superior officers?*

"What? Don't worry, Major."

But he continues to astound her.

"We beat the pants off them. No one's going to get upset at you now that the end of the war is near."

But she freezes at the sound of "the end of the war." Those words can cause so much damage. Apparently, Tanya is the only one who knows. *It won't happen.*

Then, having trouble holding her expression steady, she averts her eyes to the window and realizes she was wrong.

The staffers going to and fro in the office look so ecstatic. Catching them out of the corner of her eye, she's racked with grief. They're all so excited about the great victory.

They're all savoring the taste of their triumph on the Rhine front and the capture of Parisii. Swept up in a euphoria, they are living in a moment so happy they went to the beer hall to let themselves go for once.

Ahh. It dawns on Tanya.

Major General von Zettour is an outstanding officer on both the political and military fronts. On top of that, he's a pragmatist who sees things objectively and, when necessary, as numbers or statistics.

Even he is drunk on sweet victory.

…Probably he convinced himself of the victory *with* his logical prowess.

He probably thought that any further fighting would not only be useless to the Republic but harmful. And if waging war no longer benefited them, then the war would surely end.

…General von Zettour must not understand that the Republicans will continue to resist with no regard for odds, rationale, or profit and loss.

But in the next moment, Tanya wonders objectively if maybe she has only lost hope because she knows the outcome of being Dunkirked.

The remnants they let escape are seeds of resistance, so to speak. Some will fail. Some can be stamped out under the Imperial Army's boots, while others can be plucked out by air force attacks.

Many of them won't have the moisture of the people and will thus dry out completely, unable to produce a resistance bud. But if those seeds are sown in the soft soil of a colony, eventually they will bear fruit capable of launching a counteroffensive. That is a real threat.

But even with that in mind, objectively speaking, the current situation is one of great victory. Anyone would agree that the Empire won.

Despite the Commonwealth's intervention and ultimatum, the Empire performed this amazing feat in no time.

The Republic was slain in the blink of an eye, the Entente Alliance is being brought under imperial military government, and the governance of Dacia is proceeding apace. The world can only watch transfixed. The Empire's victory, its glory, is genuine in this moment.

That's why, thinks Tanya darkly, seeing the point of divergence between the truth that she knows and the conclusion reached by logic in reality.

The attitude she's getting from General von Zettour—that, thinking rationally, this is where we end the war—is correct. After all, the Empire succeeded in annihilating the Republican main forces. It's a triumph that will surely be remembered in military history. The Empire achieved an overwhelming victory in the field and has only a very few things to worry about.

Victory, oh, how spellbinding you are. The Empire has earned the right to be drunk on your sweet wine.

"I'm relieved to hear that, sir. I only hope there will be a chance to make up for the trouble I caused."

"That's fine. Then to victory."

"To victory."

Chapter IV

She suppresses her emotions with sheer self-restraint, exchanges salutes, and maintains proper manners as she exits the room.

But even Magic Major Tanya von Degurechaff is human. So when Lieutenant Colonel von Lergen passes by her on his way to get General von Zettour's approval on some documents, he notices that her expression is more warped than he has ever seen it before.

"Excuse me, sir... Did something happen? Major von Degurechaff had a strange look on her face just now."

He hesitates to say it looked like a tearful grimace befitting a girl of her age. After all, the dark expression belonged to Major von Degurechaff. That could be worth worrying about.

"Oh, Colonel von Lergen. What do you mean, 'strange'?"

"Well, it just seemed to me that for a moment she looked awfully grim..."

"Hmm? Oh no. Perhaps she had some advice for me."

So Zettour would never learn the truth—that she looked like she was about to cry from hopelessness.

Though he sensed that something had been left unsaid, even Zettour didn't intuit that she gave up in resignation.

"Shall I call her back?"

"No, I'll talk to her the next chance I get."

He decides to wait for her to come to him again and turns to the countless papers he needs to approve. After all, he is the deputy director of the Service Corps, so he has a mountain of important work to do.

At that time, everyone had faith. The war would end, and the Empire had won.

But it wasn't a future they were glad to welcome, which was why various countries, the Commonwealth at the forefront, roared that they would resist to the last in order to avoid that nightmare.

The remnants of the Republican Army that escaped from the mainland joined the remnants of the Entente Alliance Army, and together they based themselves in the Republic's overseas colonial holdings and declared that they would continue the war against the Empire. They called themselves the Free Republic, and their opposition was already posing a challenge to the military government the Imperial Army was establishing on the mainland.

And near Mary Sue, people were both hostile toward and frightened by the Empire.

She was being raised among people who had escaped the Entente Alliance to hope for peace from a safe place. To the majority of the refugees, the fact that even the Republic had dropped out of the fight was a huge disappointment.

They had anticipated the fall of the Empire. That was why they were so happy to see the Republic's offensive. So when they saw the deadlock, they tasted despair, and everyone was shocked to witness the collapse of the Republican Army.

Can no one seal away the evil of the Empire?

But they couldn't accept that. So the refugees immediately rejected their own weak-willed doubts.

That can't be. Believing that justice wouldn't overlook this wrong, they hoped and prayed. Many refugees joined their voices and protested further expansion of the horrible Empire.

"We'll fight, too."

Inspired, or perhaps intoxicated, by that cheer, people began to volunteer for the army. And touched by their passion, the countries began accepting them.

And it wasn't just the refugees. Young people of each nation raised their voices in a frenzy. *We must join the Commonwealth Army confronting the Empire and fight!*

At the same time, newspapers began to print editorials cautioning against the birth of an Empire too large, complete with expert comments, and even in the Unified States, some sounded warning bells that they were not so terribly removed from the situation on the continent.

Everyone, whether they wanted to or not, had to understand that a period of violent upheaval in the balance of power had arrived. The tone of the debate stemming from that anxiety eventually began to naturally turn to exhorting countries to prepare, for their own safety, against the Empire.

Hence, everyone's heartfelt cheers for the remaining troops of the

Republican Army, who reassuringly declared they would continue to resist the Empire as the Free Republican Army.

The Commonwealth had also declared that they would resist the Empire to the last, and everyone expected much from its new prime minister, the Duke of Marlborough, and his war leadership. Likewise, they felt they should fight under said leadership and began to join forces.

She had power.

That is, she had magic abilities she inherited from her father, Anson. And they were a gift that put her in a league of her own. If there hadn't been a war, her talent wouldn't have been much use to her, so perhaps it would have remained hidden.

In fact, Anson had always explained to his family that just because they had the aptitude, that didn't mean they had to become mages.

Mary could still remember the kind voice of her father telling her not to limit her options. He had encouraged her to walk her own path and always said he would support whatever future she chose. That was precisely why she was so determined.

Meanwhile, the Empire was reluctantly coming to terms with continuation of the war and readying itself to claim another great victory.

However, perhaps it should be said…

Unlike with the other countries the Empire had fought, the army couldn't avoid crossing a sea to do battle with the Commonwealth. Of course, this was the Empire that had cut off the Entente Alliance's supply lines by conducting a landing operation in the enemy's rear territory, so it wasn't as if the option of an amphibious operation wasn't on the table.

But as always, that entailed a caveat: "as long as it could secure command of the sea." And when asked about the prospects of securing command of the sea, Fleet Command only answered that it might be possible if they risked annihilation.

So the Empire was facing a serious dilemma.

If it engaged in a naval battle, maybe it could eliminate or check the

Commonwealth's resistance for just long enough to get troops onto the mainland.

But if the Empire's fleet got wiped out, it wouldn't have the where-withal to take on another naval battle. At that point, no matter how many units landed, it would mean nothing because their supplies would be cut off, and they would be annihilated just like the Republican main forces were.

That said, leaving the Commonwealth mainland alone would be tan-tamount to ignoring the enemy's powerful strategic base. Of course, the Commonwealth Army had a limited number of soldiers, so it wasn't a terribly worrisome direct threat, but… At the rate things were going, it would be an endless draw.

Perhaps this needs to be reconfirmed. We are soldiers. As such, if the government of the fatherland wishes something, we fulfill. One's personal will at such a time is unimportant.

—— Lieutenant General von Zettour, from General Staff meeting minutes ——

The being there trembled with joy.

"Hoo-hoo-hoo. Wonderful!"

He was so happy he nearly praised the glory of the Lord in spite of himself. No, he did. To solemnly praise the almighty Being, he raised a pious face to the heavens and shouted hallelujah.

Of course, no one in this place would reproach him for such an act. Rather, they would join in. After all, they were creatures of that Being as intelligent as the Spaghetti Monster.[8]

"Cherub, sir, did something happen?"

"Oh, Archangel, keep up the good work. I'm just so happy that faith has been growing by leaps and bounds lately." Having finished his exalting prayer, he responded to the address with a smile and praised the *Homo sapiens'* return to the life-and-death cycle.

What wonderful news, the cherub's manner all but proclaimed, expressing his relief that order had finally been restored. These beings were charged with leading the creatures known as *Homo sapiens,* guiding their souls, and this was the first positive report they had received in quite a while.

And it was only natural that the archangel, upon hearing it, would smile and express his approval. Naturally, he celebrated that things were as they should be. It was a hymn for the Great One, nearly overflowing from his heart and very being.

O God, Creator, you are great.

---

[8] **Spaghetti Monster**   A being possessing great intelligence. So noble that even atheist scholars believe. RAmen.

"That is very good, indeed. But that's strange—hold on."

Yet, doubt appeared on the archangel's fine features. Restored faith and a promised return to the cycle of life and death was wonderful. If their appeals to the people had been effective, then eventually they would be able to guide their souls.

But something suddenly confused the archangel. He had the feeling that only a short time ago, he had heard something different.

They were all equal before the One-in-All, and outside the hierarchy of their obligations, rather tolerant. Thus, it was permissible for him to second-guess the words of a superior being. Which is why, perhaps it should be said…

As long as the archangel was engaged in holy work, he had an obligation to ask the cherub anything he didn't understand.

"Hmm? Is something wrong?" And the cherub was obliged to answer.

For them, delays in holy duties were unforgivable, so any and all obstacles had to be overcome.

Naturally, the cherub politely responded with good intentions, his voice soft. To him, it was proper to work together in the fight for the glory of the Lord.

Both of them only meant well.

"I hear evil atheists have infested their world."

That was why they had to stand up and bravely confront evil.

It was their sacred duty.

"What?! Nothing like that is happening in my jurisdiction. Do you know whose it is?"

But the archangel had raised an issue the cherub hadn't heard of.

In his area, the people were definitely beginning to sense the presence of God.

Yes, they all clung piously to his voice, acted as was right for his creatures to act, and fervently wished for the almighty Father's grace.

To the cherub, protecting and guiding humble believers was a delight; nothing made him happier. No, it was his raison d'être. He was created for no other purpose but this.

Which was why he smiled happily.

These beings had transcended the loathsome habit of sectionalism, but paradoxically, the news that the horrible, well-meaning evil of atheism had filled the little lambs they were meant to protect and guide pained his heart to the point of bursting.

Just hearing that atheists were running rampant cast a shadow across his beautiful face. For such a thing to happen in one's jurisdiction was a great sorrow indeed.

Therefore.

Out of utter kindness and a sense of duty, he had to ask. If such terrible tragedy was occurring...

"I'd like to do anything I can to assist. Does anyone know whose jurisdiction it is?"

He felt he had to extend a helping hand.

"Alas, I'm ashamed to admit it is my own."

Naturally, rather than conceal this awkward problem, it was better to solve it together. After all, that was their job as guides. No, it was their holy duty as creations of the Lord.

If they couldn't lead the lost lambs properly, how could they claim to be guides? Ushering lost lambs down the path of righteousness with joy, to be as they were meant to be, was their raison d'être.

Anyone who neglected it could only be seen as a fallen, evil being beyond all saving.

So an offer of aid on the path of salvation was always welcome. That said, while these things sometimes happened, the unspoken expectation was that it was relatively inexperienced beings themselves, liable to stray, who would fail in their guidance.

Which was why all the beings present were shocked to hear that their supervisor wasn't sure how to proceed with his guidance.

"The ones under your guidance, Sir Seraph? How could such a thing have come to pass?"

The seraphim served the Father most closely of all.

Yet, this one's guidance wasn't reaching the people? The guidance of this truly faithful seraph who was trusted just as deeply by God the Father? If a seraph wasn't enough to save them, then it really was a puzzle.

"Yes, lamentably, the fools have not only abandoned their faith, they even, if you can believe it...blaspheme."

Chapter V

Blasphemy? How could it be?

Rather than understanding the sheep, the beings could be described as basically unconcerned. Only rarely did something occur to cause a change in their attitude.

But this was even rarer than that—it was that shocking. They were up against mass atheism. Not only that, but reports indicated that behavior judged blasphemous was happening on the same scale?

They were committing the sin of holy sacrilege!

But if that was true, *Why? Would it spread to them all?* Those were the questions on their uncomprehending minds.

"It shouldn't be possible. I heard there is even an outrageous movement to deify their rulers."

But the seraph spat the reply, as if saying it disgusted him, and removed all doubt from their minds.

For a moment, all were silent. A beat later, the meaning of what he had said sunk in, and astonishment followed.

"Have they really so little fear? What sort of person would you have to be to do such things?!"

"It's revolting to even say, but apparently they lump God in with opium."

He provided the explanation reluctantly. How could the origin of the world be equated to something so unclean? There were even some recalcitrants aiming to replace God the Father. Even the beings who fell in the past hadn't come up with something so awful. That was why it was so unsettling; they were simply stunned.

"What...?! Is there no limit to the horror?"

That was more or less how they all felt.

There was one thought that didn't get voiced.

How could this have happened?

"This just isn't going very well, is it?" the cherub lamented with a sigh, in spite of himself, but it was likewise the unmistakable sentiment of all present.

His overflowing joy of a moment ago had been replaced with sadness, as if it had never been.

"But half the world is still filled with pious little lambs seeking salvation."

They had finally managed to bring the voice of God to the believers. During the war, the humans had finally begun to seek salvation from a transcendental being.

"I can't believe the other half have fallen to the wickedness of atheism."

That half the world should have fallen into darkness where the Good News wouldn't reach!

"...With all due respect, I find that hard to believe. They've received the Good News! How could half the world have descended into the primitive darkness of atheism or what have you? Is that really possible?"

At the same time, the archangel and other angels sighed their doubts.

They questioned whether it could really be possible. They agonized over whether it could really become a majority. It was truly unthinkable. No, they were in denial of the impossible phenomenon.

For something like that should never happen to a group who had been given the Good News.

Perhaps it could happen to a single person. There were examples in *Homo sapiens* history of individuals being seized by such insanity. Their policy on those isolated examples was to deemphasize them. Though they were interested in humans as a group, they were nearly indifferent to them as individuals.

But a group who had received the Good News descending into such darkness was worrisome indeed. It was virtually unheard of. If they searched the past, they could find examples of new forms of faith or reduced faith, so they had experience dealing with such problems.

But this had never happened before, and neither had they anticipated it.

"It certainly is strange. Good grief, what came over them?"

That said, they couldn't simply weep and fail to act. They were tirelessly faithful to their duties, and as such, they scraped together all their wisdom.

"If we want to restore faith, what about sending in...you know, that one?"

Chapter V

"The glory of being God's servant is too great a responsibility for just one, and a human at that."

"I see, yes, it might be too harsh to simply say, 'Know God's will.' In the past, *Homo sapiens* only managed it after we told them several times and they finally listened."

"Then how about continuing to call out to them?"

"No, we can't save them that way. Leaving faithless souls to wander would go against God's will."

The conclusion they reached out of their utter goodwill was to go with their "usual way" of restoring faith.

"Then wouldn't the best way be to teach *Homo sapiens* of his grace through trials?"

As for the vital how, the cherub suggested a method through which he had had some success, and the others accepted.

"I see. If we give that one the glory of fighting as a servant of God, we can expect a conversion."

After all, though they were generally indifferent to individuals, they were already keeping an eye on one of them.

Since faith had already been growing as a result, it was more than worth trying in this case as well.

"Please wait. The glory of fighting as God's servant shouldn't be reserved for a single individual. Enlightenment is important, but I think it's vital to respond to the prayers of the deeply faithful as well."

And they had good intentions. The suggestion of having *that one* fight for the grace of God was made with utterly good intentions.

We must convert the lamb who forgot the light of God's protection and glory. And we must save those who pray.

"Then let's do that. How about specifics?"

Everyone welcomed the opinion. They were saviors. The protests of an individual meant to deliver his grace were meaningless to them. No, since no one had the ears to hear them, no one would point out they should listen.

Well, if anything, perhaps it was a difference of perspective. Even humans are virtually incapable of listening to nonhuman opinions.

"Shall we ask the throne?"

"All right. I will mention it to the Lord."

Thus, it was decided without a single objection.

》》》   AUGUST 22, UNIFIED YEAR 1925   《《《

It was two months after the fall of the mainland Republic. At the time, suffice it to say that everyone living in the Empire believed that the war was over. After all, the Empire had defeated the neighboring Entente Alliance, the Republic, and incidentally, the Principality. The boast *We are the Reich, crown of the world* had begun to have a ring of truth to it.

Even the news that the Commonwealth had joined in on the side of the Republic wasn't enough to dampen the euphoria. With no major fighting or naval battles, no one expected the Commonwealth to be an obstacle to the restoration of peace. Everyone murmured as if they knew: "They joined the battle far too late."

So when it was reported that the Commonwealth had rejected the Empire's invitation to a peace conference, the public sentiment in the Empire was mainly confusion. They couldn't understand what made the war so enjoyable that the Commonwealth was itching to continue it.

Of course, people in the Empire were aware that the Free Republican Army, made up of Republican troops who howled that they would resist to the end, was putting up a meager fight in some Republican colonies.

More importantly, it was also reported that the Commonwealth and its kingdoms, having decided to intervene in this war, were cooperating with the Free Republican Army.

But even knowing all that, everyone had to wonder, *Why are they so interested in continuing the war?* The outcome had already been decided on the battlefield. The Imperial Army had literally wiped out the Entente Alliance Army, the Principality's army, and the Republican Army, and its power as the conqueror was known far and wide.

And while the Empire's terms were harsh, the people believed it was fundamentally a treaty that could restore peace, so the resistance of the obstinate Republican remnants and the stubborn Commonwealth was irritating at first, then anger inducing.

Chapter V

Why do they want to continue the war?

Eventually they realized something. *Weren't they the ones that started the war?* That was no small matter. No, it was the open truth.

Which was why in the Empire, the psychological foundation had been laid from the beginning. They believed those remnants the enemy, hoped to continue the war.

Hence their own hopes.

We'll bring the iron hammer down on those who dare harm the Reich.

May the evil enemy be struck from this world.

So the fanatical cry of "Smite the enemy!" spread. No one questioned their belief in the righteousness of their own country and justice.

Which was why they couldn't understand.

The Empire failed to comprehend the fear the other countries had—the fundamental fear that an immensely powerful state, an unrivaled hegemon, would be established in the center of the continent.

Additionally, due to the manner in which the Empire had been founded, it had always had multiple conflict zones.

The conflicts stemmed from incompatible views: To the Empire, those places were unquestionably imperial territory, while to the surrounding countries, the land had been stolen from them.

Ultimately, that was why the Republic worked with the other powers to encircle the Empire using exterior lines strategy, and why the Empire developed its interior lines strategy to break through that encirclement. Then, finally, the Empire was overjoyed to have eliminated all the threats to its security.

But to the other parties, it looked like a grave threat to their security that couldn't be ignored. Sadly, the Empire was so busy showing off the sharpness of its sword that it didn't notice how much it frightened everyone.

Then nationalism and mutual distrust fanned the flames.

Of course, everyone wished for peace. Yes, earnestly. Which was why for the sake of peace and protecting everyone, they took up their guns and fought. Other countries with their own agendas added their support.

In this ironic way, the wish for peace didn't cause the war to abate but only escalated it.

In one room of the recruitment office, the major introduced as both the occupant of the office and the head of the department in charge of conscription spoke honestly as he somewhat awkwardly offered Mary a seat.

"Miss Mary Sue, we're very happy to receive your application." His voice was calm, and he looked her straight in the eye. "But the Unified States views dual citizenship as an extremely complicated issue. Especially given the citizenship laws in the Entente Alliance, volunteering for the Unified States Army could ultimately harm your status there. So I have to warn you that despite your youth, it's very likely you'll need to make a choice regarding your nationality."

He continued politely, saying he didn't mean to press her for the difficult decision but still respecting her will. The kind people of the Unified States were always so considerate like that.

Everyone said the same friendly things to the Entente Alliance refugee kids. *"We're glad you want to help, but you don't need to worry about that right now."*

"Don't your grandmother, your mother, and…yes, even your deceased father want you to stay safe here out of harm's way? Isn't everyone worried about you?"

"Yes, but that's exactly why I want to do what I can—to protect this peace. I think I can help."

So Mary explained earnestly in her own words why she was volunteering. "I think there must be something I can do." She appealed to the major to let her do what she could for the Unified States and for peace.

"Well, you do have a point. The Unified States Army is currently recruiting voluntary units that will be sent to our ally the Commonwealth. That's one way, as you mentioned, to protect this peace. But there are many other helpful, necessary tasks young people can undertake inside the Unified States."

The call had gone out regarding the Unified States Volunteer Expeditionary Forces to be deployed to the Commonwealth. It was said these troops would, as a rule, not intervene in combat actions but be "stationed" in the Commonwealth. The troops were nominally being

Chapter V

deployed in connection with patrols to guarantee free passage and civilian rights according to the law of war.

But everyone read the move as a turning point, the Unified States' first decisive step, which was why Mary reacted immediately.

She raced down to the nearest office to turn in her application only to be kindly told, "It's too soon," as usual.

"You mean as a good citizen of the Unified States?"

"Exactly. Children should be protected. Our situation isn't so dire that we have to send them off to war. Actually, you're only just old enough to volunteer. It won't be too late if you take some time to make your decision, you know.

"Wouldn't you like to try being a good citizen?" he asked. The Unified States was generous enough to interpret the law flexibly and grant dual citizenship to refugees from the Entente Alliance who had close relatives who were already residents.

In that way, by offering the refugees a quiet life and a little peace, it made a place for them. Mary understood that the reason they didn't want to send the youth to war, as he explained to her again, was that they hoped the ones they had taken in would be safe.

But Mary could volunteer. The citizenship she had been granted and her ability as a mage qualified her. So she had already considered her position and arrived at her decision.

"I know. I thought it all over, but sure enough, I'd like to volunteer."

The flag on display in the center of the room was not the flag of her fatherland but of the Unified States. To Mary, it wasn't the flag of her home. It was different from the Entente Alliance flag the mother and father she loved and respected had displayed in their house.

But...it was the flag of their second home, the country that was kind enough to take them in. *If my grandmother and mother, the family I must protect are here... If there is something I can do to help stop the war...*

"Miss Mary Sue. If you go to battle, you might get injured. You could die. You might upset your grandmother and mother."

"...I do feel bad about that, but I would regret not doing what I could have even more." She had worried about that. It was the only thing she had worried about. But compelled by her inner drive to do something, she could state positively, "That may be so, but there's something I've got to do."

"...Are you sure?"

"Yes, I've decided to volunteer."

In her mind, she thought of her home country and the people's backs as they prayed at the church. Grief, sadness, and a wish for peace... She would give her whole self for those things, if it would make a difference.

For God, for their families, and for themselves, they would do what they could.

"All right. Then you need to make an oath to the flag. Do you remember how it goes?"

"Yes, I memorized it."

"...Seems like you're quite determined. Once you volunteer, you must do whatever your military duties require of you... Do you understand?"

The major pushed his point in what could be called his final confirmation.

Because Mary understood that he was hoping she would change her mind, she replied too quickly, leaving no room for objections.

"Of course. I'll make the oath!" Standing, she raised a hand and swore. She pledged herself to the Unified States. "I pledge allegiance..."

It was one girl, Mary Sue's contract with the Unified States. Power had to be wielded with justice, so she would do what she could.

"...to the Unified States and its countrymen, one nation under God, indivisible..."

She would use all of her strength for the family she had to protect, for the people. And to carry out God's justice.

"...and to defend its Republic..."

To create a world in which she would never again have to experience the sadness of losing family to the Empire.

"...in the name of liberty and justice."

She swore with her own sense of justice that she believed in.

"May God protect you."

Dear God, please, oh please, protect us.

Thus, with a sincere prayer, Mary Sue enlisted and was assigned with

the other volunteer mages to the Unified States–Free Entente Alliance 1st Mage Regiment.

》》》   AUGUST 24, UNIFIED YEAR 1925, IMPERIAL ARMY GENERAL   《《《
STAFF OFFICE, DINING ROOM 1

The cafeteria at the General Staff Office made a rule for itself that the meals it served must be equal or inferior in quality to those of the mobilized soldiers in the field. Due to the prevalence of that touching rumor around the Empire, Dining Room 1 was deserted as usual.

The only ones to appear at the cafeteria were those required by unavoidable circumstances to eat there. The people thus in the predicament of reluctantly sipping the awful pseudo-coffee were stuck washing down their complaints about its quality with either tasteless water or said pseudo-coffee.

"I suppose it's a reward for the victory. You and I have been promoted. Congratulations, Lieutenant General von Zettour."

"Thanks, Lieutenant General von Rudersdorf. Now let's get back to business."

"Indeed. This isn't the place for a celebration, in any case."

And so the awful ersatz coffee put a damper on the pair's celebration of their respective promotions to lieutenant general. When Zettour made the practical suggestion of getting back to business, Rudersdorf didn't feel the atmosphere was right for a celebration, either. That was the General Staff Office cafeteria in a nutshell.

"All right, then."

So Rudersdorf flatly changed gears and brought up the pending issue before them, the next stage of their operations.

Though the Republican Army on the mainland was completely under control, remnants of the forces calling themselves the Free Republican Army were holding out in the Republic's colonies. The Commonwealth had joined the fight, and the Imperial High Seas Fleet was facing its navy, but unfortunately there was still quite a large gap between the two in terms of strength.

Even if the Empire sent its entire fleet, it would only amount to half the size of the Commonwealth's.

Though the public and some of Supreme High Command were enthusiastic about an invasion of the Commonwealth mainland, Zettour and Rudersdorf were at wit's end over how few options they realistically had, given their army's fighting power.

"With circumstances such as they are, I think it makes sense to launch operations in the south with the objectives of blockading the Inner Sea and defeating the last of the Republican forces."

For that reason, as part of their plan to handle the war situation, they first considered a southern campaign against the remnants of the Republican Army.

They would demonstrate that the Empire was capable of sending troops to the colonies. Such a reality could inspire at least the Republican Army and colonies to make peace.

To the Imperial Army General Staff, who could no longer find any point in the war, that speculation was a realistic plan of compromise to end the fighting quickly. If they could settle things without occupying every last hostile country and just negotiate, that would be easier.

"Allow me to make one point. I understand what you're saying, but our nation has limited power projection capabilities, and our maritime forces on the Inner Sea are equally tight."

"You're quite right, Zettour. That's why I'm asking you."

As Zettour pointed out the difficulties and Rudersdorf grudgingly agreed, neither the fleet's strength nor the Empire's projecting power supposed even a limited-scale overseas invasion. Even the suppression of neighboring countries was a strain on the Imperial Army, since it was set up for domestic interior lines operations.

"Under these circumstances, the most we could do on the southern front would be combat on a limited scale for mainly political purposes. Will that work?"

Which was why Zettour emphasized that they wouldn't be able to expect much from the military on the southern front, saying that no matter how effective it would be, from a purely military perspective, they couldn't expect to have command of the Inner Sea and be able to cut off transport routes.

"That's no problem. Our main objective is to draw the Kingdom of Ildoa to our side by supporting them down there. I get where you're coming from, and I won't deny an idea just because it isn't purely military in nature."

In response to the warning, Rudersdorf smiled and said he would readily accept politics as a limiting factor.

It would be a nerve-racking battlefield, but…even if it was as roundabout as Open Sesame on the Rhine front, Rudersdorf and Zettour were interested in any operation that would be effective. They figured anything useful was worth trying.

"Even in the worst case, having a sympathetically neutral Kingdom of Ildoa would tell the Republic and Commonwealth that we could threaten their lifelines. Especially in the colonies. That actually is something we need, but…"

"The usual logistical problems?" Rudersdorf asked with a perplexed expression. Zettour always spoke confidently, as if he were reading a formula or theory, so it was rare for him to trail off. *Are our supply and communications lines really so strained?*

"No, those issues I can overcome. I just can't shake the feeling that it would be essentially a pointless deployment. Is a limited peace impossible?"

"I don't mean to throw your words back at you, but why would a limited peace be impossible? We just do as Supreme High Command wills."

A brief silence fell between them. And after meditating on the question, *Why can't we end the war?* there was only one answer.

"Ultimately, I suppose the problem is that we haven't completely defeated the enemy."

It was all he could do to voice the words.

Not fully defeating the enemy was a most regrettable error. Their chance had slipped through their fingers while they were drunk on celebrating their triumph. Of course, their victory was still a victory. Encirclement, annihilation, advance, occupation. Everything proceeded according to plan, and the Imperial Army had eliminated all their enemies.

But there was one element missing from their celebration: the end of the war and the restoration of peace. Now that the Republican fleet they let escape had turned into a headache, shouting about resistance to the bitter end, peace seemed awfully far away.

Thus, both of the generals felt the need to put the last nail in the coffin.

"If we must, then all we have to do is beat them. In that sense, if you think of sending troops to the southern continent as a move for the sake of peace, it's not a bad idea."

Which was why Rudersdorf declared that they wouldn't make the same mistake twice. They would simply defeat anyone who stood in their way.

"Understood. Then I'll arrange the right troops and commanders." Zettour's cheeks relaxed into a smile when he nodded in response to that confident reply. Yet, something in his face said it still wasn't sitting right with him, and he repeated his previous comment. "But I'd like you to bear one thing in mind, or rather, I want to reconfirm it with you. We're a nation with a land army, and we've prioritized interior lines strategy."

"As you say. You've pointed that out many times."

The Imperial Army was designed and outfitted to move around inside the country. Sadly, the Empire was in a mad rush to give them a measure of expeditionary capability, but the army's logistics arm had been overworked since the war started, and there were already reports of complicated obstacles.

"That's right. Going to war in a foreign country is likely to put quite a strain on the army's support services. Even if the sea command situation is different than in the waters near the Commonwealth mainland, an operation on the southern continent is still an overseas operation. We'll have to be prepared for some losses." Zettour hesitated, then continued, "But...that's why I intend to deploy mainly light divisions. I don't plan on sending in very large units. You've said you understand that, so there should be no problem."

"As the one in charge of the operation, I don't have a problem with light divisions. Do you?"

"No, there shouldn't be any issues."

They knew it would be a difficult expedition, which was why they chose light divisions. But the way Zettour said, *"There shouldn't be any issues,"* Rudersdorf couldn't help but hear some hesitation.

"…My friend, what is it you want to say?"

"We must have made a mistake, don't you think?"

The way Major von Degurechaff had shown up at the General Staff Office, apparently wanting to say something, had lingered strangely in the back of his mind. He knew right away that she had hesitated and returned to her base, unable to say whatever it was.

Now he could only speculate, but he almost had the feeling that back then she had wanted to scream at him: *You're making a mistake!* It was too late now, but he wished he had heard her out. That's why he asked his brother-in-arms, *Were we wrong?*

Rudersdorf, for his part, felt much the same as Zettour. *Have we made a mistake?* It was a strange feeling. But now that he mentioned it, yes, it was true.

"I'm sure we did. Remember that in war, we have an opponent, so things won't always go as we'd like. It's not uncommon that an enemy responds in an unexpected way, right? You're just so good at reading them that you don't screw up often enough!"

But though Rudersdorf didn't deny the error, he was going to cut his losses and not get overly caught up in it. In the fog of war, not every shot could hit the bull's-eye. All they could do was their best, and if they got the second-best results, then hoping for anything more was too much.

"…If you say so. Anyhow, let's keep the burden to the minimum."

"Very well. Frankly, I'd like to have as many reserve units on hand at home as I can, so it'd be better if you could make do with as few as possible."

Zettour was especially concerned with keeping the load light, and Rudersdorf nodded in agreement. It was certainly desirable to minimize the strain on logistics.

"So," he continued. "Okay, how about you give me those guys again? Your unit, the 203rd Aerial Mage Battalion," he added. "They're only a fifty-man load on logistics, but they pack more punch than the usual augmented battalion, so it'd be very efficient."

As the one in charge of the operation, he also noted that having a simple-to-deploy mobile fighting force would yield the advantage of extended range of use.

"...I need them to take out other aerial mages. Plus, if you unleash her without thinking, there's no telling how far she'll advance!"

But anyone would want to keep such a precious asset handy. Zettour wasn't about to let it go so easily.

"She'll lead the charge. I need her to mess them up down there."

Let me have them. No. C'mon, let me have them. The exchange between the two generals nearly went on forever, but Rudersdorf's stubbornness finally paid off.

"Fine. I'll arrange it. Now then, I'm off to the next meeting to give formal notification of this. What about you?"

As Zettour complained about more pain-in-the-ass arrangements to make, Rudersdorf let it go in one ear and out the other and barreled right into the next topic.

"Sorry, I'm leaving this up to you. I'd like to inspect our troops, assuming we're heading into a fight with the Commonwealth."

"Got it. Let me know what you find out."

"No problem."

"Great. Then let's both make it happen."

》》》 **AUGUST 29, UNIFIED YEAR 1925, IMPERIAL ARMY GENERAL** 《《《
STAFF OFFICE, JOINT MEETING BETWEEN THE SERVICE
CORPS AND OPERATIONS

"It's the appointed hour." A young officer announced in a nervous voice that it was time to start.

"Very well. I would like to begin the meeting to consider our plan to end the fighting on the Republican mainland and in the Entente

Alliance, as well as the conflict with the Commonwealth that will entail."

It was a meeting to decide the imperial military's basic direction.

Naturally, all the most important figures in the General Staff from the chief on down were there.

The agenda was simple.

They would iron out the conflicting opinions about what the major course of action in the war should be.

"First, regarding the end of the fighting on the northern front, please see the documents you've been given."

It's finally over. Though that wasn't entirely accurate, it seemed the best way to describe the dispute in the north where the lines had been suppressed and a military government was in place.

Finally, the long-awaited good news from the troubles and confusion of the northern area had come, although they couldn't deny it was a bit late. Their opponents had hung on for so long, even after their military and national strength had been overpowered.

Of course, the fact that they had help from other powers couldn't be ignored. Even so, this had cost the Empire an awful lot of time and effort.

For that reason, the faces of the generals in attendance looked far from happy.

But they judged those thoughts to be sentimental and did not indulge them. Their job was to receive and approve the reports after the fact, but they were most interested in the current issues with the Commonwealth and the remnants of the Republic.

They were already taking the practical stance that the Entente Alliance was only a matter of military governance. All that was left to do was pull together the might the Service Corps and Operations required and choose someone to rule.

"So the military governor will be chosen after consulting with Supreme High Command and the Personnel Division in the General Staff."

This matter was concluded quickly with no complicated debate, just a couple questions regarding the finer details.

The meat of the conference was the next item.

"Moving on, I'd like to discuss the operation on the southern continent proposed by Service Corps Deputy Chief von Zettour."

After being called on by the leader of the meeting, Lieutenant General von Zettour stood. He had recently been promoted due to the success of his plan to lure in and annihilate the Republican Army.

His next plan was another that split opinion in the General Staff—a plan to check the Commonwealth mainland using the Great Army. They would mass the Great Army in the Republic as a show of force, while continuing their struggle for supremacy.

He proposed a simultaneous operation on the southern continent using second-string units and whatever elites they could muster as a sort of offensive.

At a glance, it seemed like he was placing importance on capturing the southern continent.

But actually, as it was mainly an almost-passive reorganization of the lines, and internally in the army, they took it as a defensive plan. Naturally, making the southern continent the main battlefield and waging war outside the Empire was better for the country's defense.

The analysis that defending the colonies, removed from the mainland as they were, would strain the Commonwealth's supply lines also made sense. Still, on the whole, the imperial staff took the proposal as a way to buy the time to reorganize their main forces.

Zettour proposed it for the purpose of conducting effective harassment. Some began to murmur that it was *too* passive. *Wouldn't it be simpler to just send the main forces over to the Commonwealth mainland?* There were even whispers that it could be the deciding battle.

Naturally, the enemy had to protect both their mainland and their colonies.

As a result, the colonies would probably be short on muscle.

It went without saying, then, that the colonies would be easier to defeat.

And if they succeeded in defeating the colonies, that would shave off a chunk of the Commonwealth's ability to continue fighting, and the foundations of the "Free Republic" or whatever they called themselves would crumble.

And that was why everyone was after a decisive battle on the Commonwealth mainland.

Still, those same men did recognize the effectiveness of an operation on the southern continent.

For one thing, it wouldn't be so hard to get the necessary troops together.

For another, they liked that the threat of defeat in the homeland would divide up enemy troops.

Still, the majority wanted to avoid a roundabout operation and called for a direct strike on the Commonwealth mainland.

"If we do that, the war will end," they said.

But Zettour felt the exact opposite. "We'll force the enemy to exhaust themselves on the southern continent. During that time, the most pressing matters are putting down the partisans in the territory we're occupying and reorganizing the troops." He wasn't optimistic about their ability to take over the Commonwealth mainland. Ignoring the risks, even if they managed to conduct a landing operation at the end of an all-or-nothing naval battle, he could imagine that the imperial troops would be exhausted. His greatest fear was that if that happened, some other power would interfere.

"I object! The Great Army is capable of rapid response. We should attack the Commonwealth before they fortify their defenses!"

"Kindly recall the disparity of power between our navies. We don't have command of the sea."

At the same time, there was the practical issue of the Commonwealth's superior navy. The Imperial Navy simply didn't match it in terms of quality or quantity. Efforts in recent years had seen their naval power rapidly expand, but they had to admit they were still behind.

"All the more reason to command the sky with our air and mage forces."

Of course, any general at the meeting was aware of that. Though individually its ships outperformed those of the Commonwealth, the Empire couldn't win with hardware alone.

The elements of training and skill were important, and neither could they discount the absoluteness of numbers.

What could compensate for those things were the Empire's air and mage forces.

As a matter of course, they imagined the air and mage forces would be used to wear down the enemy. Achieve air supremacy and weaken the enemy with anti-ship strikes. That could be said to be a rather ordinary idea, and the imperial military was prepared for it. Having gained experience on the Rhine front, those in the rear could attempt to provide more support.

But the channel was still a big strategic obstacle for the Imperial Army.

The attack required crossing water, which was a real headache for the planners.

"Honestly, I don't like the idea of a battle of attrition on enemy turf."

They were picking the wrong opponent if they wanted to fight a prolonged battle to wear the enemy down.

A battle of attrition at a powerful nation's home base was a tricky proposition. One wrong move and the Empire would be the first to exhaust itself. The fighting on the Rhine front had been along the border, so the parties had been on equal terms.

But in an air battle over the enemy mainland, the enemy's fighting spirit would be running high. And if an enemy were shot down, they could rejoin the lines immediately; fighting on their own turf, they didn't have to worry about being taken prisoner when they hit the ground.

But if one of the Imperial Army's soldiers was shot down, they would be lucky to be taken prisoner. At that rate, even if they were downing each other at the same pace, the actual losses per side would be completely different.

And naturally, since the imperial military couldn't endure the same rate of loss as its enemy, it would constantly have to limit attrition on its own side while making things harder for the Commonwealth side. It wasn't impossible, but doing it in real life would be a challenge, indisputably.

"Time is what we should be worried about. Once the enemy strengthens their defenses, it will be too late."

At the same time, an invasion of the enemy mainland once its defenses were fortified *would* be reckless.

Several staffers said a short war was the only way to resolve things and insisted on an offensive. "If we don't attack now," they said, "we'll be stuck facing heavily defended enemy positions and fortifications on the scale of the Rhine front."

"We can strengthen our defenses during that time as well. It seems to me our positions will be equal."

Zettour's idea was simple. He believed the army was meant to protect the Empire, not the occupied territory. Therefore, the biggest priority wasn't to expand the occupied territory but to conserve troops. Of course, it went without saying that he wanted to do that while bleeding the enemy.

"Please understand the organizational limitations inherent in the fact that our army was arranged according to interior lines strategy with national defense in mind. We've sacrificed quite a lot of our expeditionary abilities in order to have qualitatively better, stronger soldiers."

Yes, there was also the issue that doing so was really the only way to maintain such a large area.

"But ultimately, we can't end the war without muscling into their territory and forcing them to surrender. Your concerns are valid, General von Zettour, but please understand that staying on the battlefield forever because of them will eat away at our national strength."

In short, it didn't matter one bit how the war was ended. In that sense, Zettour wasn't convinced it was absolutely necessary to conquer the Commonwealth mainland.

On the contrary, he started to think it was a horrible idea that would bog them down. And the folly of going in with naval power was self-evident. He believed that their chance of victory lay not in fighting on the enemy's turf but in drawing them to the battlefield of the Empire's choosing.

But he was vexed because circumstances wouldn't allow him to declare that openly. The others were proud of defeating the Republic and certain they could slay the Commonwealth in the same smooth motion.

The operation planners under Lieutenant General von Rudersdorf were more understanding, but the people and the bureaucrats had a tendency to say, "Oh, the Imperial Army can handle it," and expect too much.

So Zettour reluctantly proposed a limited offensive. He narrowed it down to an operation that gave the best return with the most limited bloodshed.

Concealing his true feelings, he advocated for an attritional containment plan. He had no other choice.

The front on the southern continent was a desert.

Unlike on the mainland, a hard rule applied there.

Survival of the fittest.

At the time, there were three powers with influence on the southern continent: the Commonwealth, the Republic, and the Ispagna Collective. Of them, the Ispagna Collective had managed to remain neutral—mainly because it didn't have the wherewithal to intervene externally due to fierce internal political conflict.

Complicating matters was the Kingdom of Ildoa trying to squeeze itself in and "settle." The result was an ambiguously colored map with both the group formed by the Turkman principalities and the Ildoan settlements.

The jumble of sovereignties in the region could be described in a word as *chaos*. Of course, one could paint the map in broad strokes. Most of the influence and puppet governments belonged to the Commonwealth and the Republic.

Even if the nations of the southern continent were officially neutral, their allegiance was clear because of how they sent voluntary armies and offered supplies.

But it wasn't as if everyone took the Reich as their enemy. For instance, countries whose interests clashed with those of the Commonwealth and the Republic in the struggle to acquire colonies on the southern continent sided with the Empire.

A representative example would be the Kingdom of Ildoa. It wasn't very difficult for the Empire to ask the kingdom to form an alliance, given their common interests. Irritatingly to Republican diplomats, neighboring rival countries hoping to expand their sphere of influence were glad to see the decline of the Republic.

And that was why the Kingdom of Ildoa chose to ally with the Empire.

Of course, the alliance didn't automatically mean it was at war with the Republic and Commonwealth.

The agreement between the two countries basically provided that fighting was optional; there was no indication that joining the war was mandatory.

At the time the Imperial Southern Continent Expeditionary Army Corps was deployed, the Kingdom of Ildoa remained officially neutral.

It did, however, allow the "stationing" of troops there out of consideration as an allied country. The Empire, however, did not move on the offer very quickly.

Because the Empire had made light of the southern continent, it only sent a single army corps made up of two divisions and a support unit.

And the General Staff ended up having a heated debate about whether to commit more troops or not. The initial number of units was so few that the garrison of the Republican troops usually deployed there could have resisted them.

Everyone thought at the time that the imperial units would work on gathering more fighting power. After all, a single puny army corps didn't pose much of a military threat. Still, they agreed there was major political significance in the Imperial Army's presence.

The watcher analysis that Army Corps Commander von Romel was dispatched for political reasons—namely, expansion of influence and respect for the Empire's ally—was widely shared as the plausible explanation.

Which was why everyone expected the lull to continue for the foreseeable future.

Even the division of the General Staff involved in giving orders to the Imperial Army was half serious about that idea. In any case, they had deployed some troops, but they weren't sure if the front should really be a priority or not.

After all, there were no apparent gains to be made by sending troops there.

If the objective hadn't been to wear the enemy out further in this total war, sending imperial soldiers probably wouldn't have even been on the table.

In that sense, predicting a lull was a respectable analysis.

The betrayal of everyone's expectations occurred because of a surprising move in the field. The root cause was Commander von Romel. Neither their enemies nor their allies thought the Southern Continent Expeditionary Corps was going to move, but the moment they arrived, they jumped into action.

The world was reminded that a capable general doesn't waste time. The Commonwealth units who had just arrived to defend the Republican colonies probably got the worst of it.

Those fresh troops hadn't been fully baptized on the battlefield, so they could think of no reason the two imperial divisions would be stationed on the southern continent besides a political one.

Having thus discounted them, the Commonwealth didn't even really go on guard. And that's how the imperial units under Commander von Romel nailed every last one of them.

The Imperial Army, waging maneuver warfare unparalleled in history against an enemy that outnumbered them by several times, simply bulldozed the Commonwealth troops in terms of caliber, partially because half of them were elites forged on the Rhine front.

Hence the Commonwealth units, who hadn't dreamed they'd be fighting a mobile battle in the desert, were dealt an early brutal blow and sent scrambling in a disorderly retreat.

It was obvious what strategy General de Lugo would adopt in response.

He put some political moves on the Kingdom of Ildoa while simultaneously doing what he could to ensure support wouldn't reach the Ildoans.

But Romel was quicker than de Lugo was shrewd. Future generations would rave about his clever tactics. As soon as he realized time wouldn't necessarily work in his favor, despite having barely any units, he made a feint, hit the Turus Naval Base with a sneak attack, and captured it.

While securing a base that didn't depend on the Kingdom of Ildoa, he dealt a serious blow to Republican and Commonwealth logistics.

The Turus Naval Base had been the Republican and Commonwealth supply base, so its fall had far-reaching effects.

In the end, contrary to initial predictions, the Imperial Army Southern

Continent Expeditionary Corps asserted its presence. Most importantly, imperial citizens went wild when they saw the string of successes.

The people had been convinced the Empire had defeated the Republic on the Rhine lines after investing a vast amount of money and lives.

To then continue the war risked the people starting to hate it.

The General Staff weren't the only ones worried about that, but contrary to their estimates, the troops dominated on the southern continent. The winning streak continuing after Dacia and the Rhine sent the people into a frenzy.

The battles unfolded as if the Empire's army was completely unrivaled. The excited citizens became pro-war and showed their support.

…As a result, the troops were expected to achieve even more.

To the General Staff, that full picture was a big miscalculation. They welcomed it insofar as it meant receiving support for continuing the war.

At least, there were no signs that the people were under the influence of antiwar dissidents.

That, the General Staff could wholeheartedly embrace.

But the appearance of a hero in the southern continent and their growing inability to gauge a time to withdraw frightened them.

The loss control faction in particular, rallying around Lieutenant General von Zettour, put up a powerful resistance against the aggressive faction seeking to increase war gains.

To them, sending any more troops than absolutely necessary to the southern continent was a waste of resources that was difficult to accept. Even the strain on the supply lines would be insupportable.

What about convoy ships?

What about transport ships?

What about direct support units?

And it wasn't just the loss control faction fretting about these things. The mere thought of the mountain of challenges was enough to make any logistics officer want to bury their head in their hands and groan. Though the issue went further back than that; given that the Imperial Army was organized around interior lines strategy, they weren't even sure they could project their power properly in a foreign country.

Moving a corps on the southern continent was totally different from moving one within their home country. Even a single rifle manufactured at home had to travel a complicated route to get to a soldier in the south. And they had to assume that some percentage of them would be damaged during transport and that whole ships could be sunk on the way.

For the divisions concerned, it was worse than horrible, and in general, the Imperial Army couldn't endure losses like that. And the imperial military had only envisioned seaborne transport capabilities as far as shuttling troops to and from the imperial occupied territory in Norden. As a result, there hadn't been an urgent need to aggressively acquire transport ships, and maintenance was performed very slowly.

On top of that, the Empire was a land nation with very little concept of major sea route defense. Even their theoretical knowledge of convoying stopped at a basic awareness. That was sure to come back around to bite them.

The Commonwealth and the Republic, on the other hand, were self-sustaining to some extent thanks to a degree of industrial base in the colonies. Not only that, but they had more ships than they could count.

Meanwhile the Imperial Army could count on supplies from the new areas of imperial influence, of course, but the Empire was only connected to them insomuch as they had common interests.

Naturally, any respectable soldier would be apprehensive about relying on supplies from there.

So the General Staff ended up in another heated debate.

Everyone felt they had to stop the front from expanding any farther, but could they really ignore the enemy? They were right there. For Zettour, who had decided that they should consider shaping up the lines if need be, the time had come to devote themselves to overhauling the organization of their defensive lines and exercising their influence on other countries behind the scenes.

But before the General Staff reached their conclusion, another report came flying in from the south.

It was notice of what could be called a great victory. The news that the troops were in the process of increasing their gains with a follow-up attack would simultaneously send the people into a renewed frenzy and cause logistical difficulties for Zettour. Luckily, Zettour didn't know that yet.

He still couldn't forget his impression the first time he saw the unit getting deployed to the southern continent. He had been excited to hear about his reports.

But then there were only two divisions on the roster.

One was a light infantry division, a new unit made up of mainly fresh troops and reserves. As for the other division, consisting of the few veterans he'd been allotted, not even a generous evaluation would say they were in good shape.

They may have had x fighting power on paper, but they had sustained heavy losses on the Rhine front. General von Romel had served in the Rhine, so he was more than well aware of how that would affect their strength. Any normal commander would despair if they couldn't expect power commensurate to their head count.

To Romel, the order to fight the southern campaign with some scraped-together second-string troops was preposterous. Which was why he petitioned the General Staff for additional troops, but he didn't get a proper answer.

Unable to bear the status quo, he made a direct request, and the answer he received after much pestering was the additional deployment of an augmented mage battalion. And how generous—it was the fine unit reporting directly to the Service Corps and Operations in the General Staff. He was thrilled to get a first-string unit with proper gear, combat experience, and a full lineup.

But the high spirits that nearly had him shouting for joy were crushed when he received the commander's evaluations.

No, the evaluations themselves were fine.

The academy, for instance, said she was up to the field officer standards. That alone made her a promising officer.

Also, she had completed higher education in the war college to qualify as a general staff officer, rare for a magic officer. And the war college also had nice things to say about her, that she met all standards desirable for an officer.

These were, well, fairly favorable evaluations.

They guaranteed that she possessed more than the standard knowledge of either a staff or field officer. But now it was wartime. The most important evaluations during a war are the ones from the battlefield, and those were all over the place.

There was a pile of especially severe criticism from the Northern Army Group. They said she was transferred after voicing a clear objection to those in authority.

The Western Army Group declined to evaluate her, saying her good and bad points neutralized each other, so it was difficult to rate her. Furthermore, she had attempted to resist orders.

She was truly a hard one to judge. But if her good points balanced out her bad points despite an attempt to disobey orders, he could smell some sort of competence.

But that didn't mean he wanted the type of officer who would try such a thing under his command. And in this situation where he had so few units, the commander of the unit he should rely on the most was such a character? It was beyond ridiculous.

Romel continued reading with a fed-up look on his face, but the ambiguous comments from the tech lab—that though the project she had been on had achieved things, it wasn't worth it—didn't do anything to make him feel better.

After reading, he thought two things.

One was that almost all of these evaluations were from HQ.

Apparently, the troops serving directly under her thought she was a great field officer. Still, it was rare to receive such a difficult person as a subordinate. Mages who followed orders but objected to the brass's plans had a tendency to get passed over.

After all, they were hard to handle.

The second was that although the evaluations were contradictory, she had achieved enough that she was considered an outstanding soldier.

Awkwardly, regardless of how she was as an officer, as an individual mage, she was thought very highly of. Her number of kills was among the highest on the Rhine front.

Plus, as a field officer, she had led breakthrough charges and ambushes unfazed. One officer called her "Mad Dog." Apparently, the trendy nickname for her at the moment was "Rusted Silver," and he could see how that made sense.

The ring of it was far from the elegance of her alias "White Silver," but he found it an appropriate one. He'd heard that the Republicans called her the "Devil of the Rhine."

In any case, strictly as a mage, she was unrivaled. As an officer, too, she was by no means incompetent. So they must have been giving her to him as reinforcements and as an excuse to get her out of their hair.

Honestly, he felt like they were foisting off their problem on him.

"…They're telling me to take a mad dog out on a walk with no leash?" He let slip a complaint. Maybe it was just prejudice, but that wasn't what it felt like to General von Romel. After all, he was basically being asked to bet on a bad hand.

"This isn't some joke. I'm not going to send my men to their doom so easily. That bunch in the General Staff are only looking at the death toll as a statistic!"

Thus, he ended up muttering complaints about the General Staff's practice of pushing its neck pains onto those in the field.

Well, I'll at least meet her. General von Romel had decided to wait for Major von Degurechaff. That was his way of showing respect for a magic officer who had gotten results—although his preconceived notions led him to brace himself when her arrival was announced.

He invited her into his office to have her report in, and once they got through the dispassionate formalities, his bad habit of trying to figure people out reared its head.

But he was already surprised to see that Major von Degurechaff, like him, preferred formal, matter-of-fact exchanges.

After all, mages and officers were a proud bunch. Perhaps you could say they were too proud, but either way, everyone in the imperial military knew it for a fact.

So he had expected the magic officer to be the aggressive, violent type despite her outward appearance.

And Romel himself expected that sort of person to get a bit upset or even angry at being welcomed with such bureaucratic fluff.

So it was a refreshing surprise to find that she calmly replied with the same empty courtesy, completely unshaken. At that point, Romel admitted to himself that his calculations had been off.

A magic officer with no sense of shame. *Maybe that's why she ignored orders and attempted to resist?* His concerns as an officer in combat crossed his mind.

True, she has a stout heart, but...she's the type to take matters into her own hands. He could sense it instinctively, and that worried him. *How did she decide?* As Romel started to worry, Degurechaff interrupted.

"Lastly, General, I'd appreciate the authority for my battalion to act independently." Graciously, with a poker face, she continued, "The General Staff has approved it," and the way she made her request was so arrogant it was invigorating.

Romel was said to be overly proud himself, so the fact that she casually made this amazingly brazen request was fantastic.

Any commissioned officer would understand just from hearing her make that one comment why the Northern and Western Groups couldn't control her.

Having a mage battalion drop out of the command structure was almost like losing a whole division. Normally, no commander could possibly accept a separate chain of command.

"That goes without saying! And Major von Degurechaff, now that you've said that much, I'm sure I can expect your unit to achieve great things, right?"

But apparently, she didn't care for Romel's reaction.

Her silence made it clear she objected to his doubt of their ability. As an attitude taken in response to a superior officer's question, it was unbelievably insolent. *Ahh.* But it actually made Romel realize why *his* superiors had given *him* the cold shoulder.

Even Romel hadn't been this bumptious.

"Well, what do you think?" He pressed her for a response, unconsciously hardening his voice. If she didn't answer now, he didn't care what the General Staff said—he would send her back.

"General von Romel, with all due respect…I merely omitted the effort of responding to a question that is impossible to answer."

"…What?"

But the response he got made him answer with another question. *What did she just say? A question that's impossible to answer?*

"I'm a soldier, not a smooth talker. I'm afraid I'm unable to explain our military capability in words."

Her tone suddenly changed. In addition to her self-important attitude, it exuded heavy sarcasm.

"And even if I were, I doubt it would satisfy you, sir; therefore, I am unable to answer."

The words rang in his ears. He heard them; they were in the official language of the Empire, pronounced correctly in the standard imperial way. He had no trouble making them out; her voice was clear as a bell.

Despite that, for a moment, he couldn't fathom her intentions. *Did the girl in front of me really just say something I can't follow?*

He struggled to understand. Then a little while later, he finally grasped the significance of the string of words.

"…In other words, you mean 'seeing is believing.' That's what you want to say?"

"I respectfully leave the interpretation up to you. General, please trust me and my unit."

Silence.

In her eyes was an earnest appeal. If it was only a ruse, it was madness.

He was dumbfounded in spite of himself. The feeling could only be described as shock at having witnessed something unbelievable.

A single thought came to mind.

Frontline Syndrome.

Major von Degurechaff had countless symptoms of it. The way she warned him, albeit indirectly: *Don't ask stupid questions.* The way she threatened him at the same time: *Don't you understand how powerful I am?* But then there was the logic of her sincere responses.

So not only was she arrogant, she was clearly horribly warped.

She doesn't believe in anything. Not the power of the military's leadership, not the strategy, and probably not even her fellow soldiers. Despite that, she's surprisingly loyal to the Imperial Army. You could even call her a peerlessly loyal eccentric focused solely on being the nation's guard dog.

I see... Romel understood the reason she had been disobedient in the past. *She simply decided that she would be a patriot if it was good for the nation. In short, she's a capable lunatic, but the bad part is she doesn't even realize she's twisted.*

"...Major, I don't have enough evidence to trust you."

She's crazy. And competent. And more sincere than anyone I've known. Rare for Romel, she was someone he was unable to judge. He did know she wouldn't be easy to handle.

That was why he asked how he could trust her.

"It's pointless for me to enumerate my feats. I'm at your service."

And her response was an obvious point. Romel could appreciate the attitude that actions speak louder than words—usually.

She wasn't conceited about her ability; neither was she a slave to her power. She spoke matter-of-factly. She was probably capable of judging what was possible and what would be difficult.

If not, she couldn't play with fire in front of an ammunition dump like she was now. In short, her insanity was backed up by limitless ability. He could only conclude she was crazy.

"I want to see what you can do. No, don't misunderstand. I mean as a strategist."

I'll call her a hero, a nut, a fellow soldier.

So she needs to demonstrate what she's capable of. Is she merely a wild animal tainted by madness? Or is she a cunning beast in possession of a deranged intellect?

Romel suddenly realized he wanted to know the answer.

"I'm sending you on a flying mission. I'd like you to take the second group. Incidentally, the idea is to give you, as Kampfgruppe Seven, authority on par with the other Kampfgruppen, even though you're a single battalion. Don't disappoint me."

I'll try her out in a somewhat independent mission. Well, I have an idea how it will turn out, but...I hope she gets results.

"Understood. We'll meet your expectations."

Just look at that.

That evil grin.

She looks thrilled.

She's so happy to have a place to fight.

Without a doubt, she's going to end up being the most horrible person I know. And she'll probably also be one of my most reliable friends on the battlefield.

The king lamented his victory. He had sacrificed
too much for it, and if he achieved one more similar
triumph, his army would be ruined.

Pyrrhic Victory

"We'll take out all enemy artillery. Major von Degurechaff, what about your unit?"

"Huh? Reconnect me!"

"Give me HQ! We've got signal jamming, 1105! Request a bypass!"

The improvised field command post is in an uproar over the signal interruption.

On the southern front where the fighting has rapidly escalated, everyone has lost their cool.

…Well, that's how it was on the Rhine. It'd be strange if you were composed on the battlefield. And here is Tanya, her days in the southern lands no different from her days in the west.

She already knows to try patching through HQ on the wired line when the wireless won't connect.

She has experienced practically every type of combat communications problem possible in both trench and high-maneuver warfare. She's versed in the countermeasures, so she doesn't panic at this degree of trouble. She promptly proceeds through the checklist of actions that need to be taken. The radio operators immediately open a wired line to HQ.

Their efficiency is praiseworthy.

Despite the brief command chain disruption, they cope without hesitating.

But after a brief exchange, their faces go pale.

"It's not jamming! There isn't any noise! We have clear connections with units in the area! The issue is mechanical trouble on the 44th's side!"

Ahh, damn it.

She curses in her head because she knows what that would have meant on the Rhine lines. The same surely goes for anyone baptized on that front.

"Keep calling! Shortwave is fine. Inspect our equipment one more time, just in case! Hurry!"

She wants to pin her hopes on a slim possibility, but she doesn't expect anything.

Sometimes it's better to be a pessimist and expect the worst on the battlefield rather than get your hopes up. Hope is important, but if you rely on that morphine in battle, you'll be ruined.

I suppose you could say it's going as expected? One of the radio operators promptly checks out the machine, but it's fine. The machines are all operating normally. They insist that if everything here is fine, it means the 44th Mage Battalion is having mechanical trouble.

If that's true, it's not good.

This is a high-maneuver battle in the Barbad Desert. If they can't contact the command post of Kampfgruppe Seven, the vanguard of the left flank, it will cause more than confusion in the chain of command.

What is going on? The officers are getting frustrated, but they have the self-control to not let it show on their faces.

It's axiomatic that if officers get needlessly shaken in front of their soldiers, confusion will rapidly increase. Even the greenest officer, Second Lieutenant Grantz, knows that.

"We've established contact! On the shortwave!"

"The pass code matches!"

For a moment, relief drifts through the improvised field command post.

Tanya can't help but have a sober opinion about that. *I guess the younger officers and less experienced guys can't help but think positively?*

It's not easy for a logical, economically minded person to form the habit of expecting the worst, either.

It's even true in financial deals that aren't life or death. The logic of behavioral economics brilliantly reveals that when you apply it to bubbles and crises. *It must be hard to optimistically prepare for the worst on a battlefield for these guys who don't have enough experience,* Tanya grumbles in her mind.

"Major von Leinburg has been killed in action!"

It's the worst news, but it doesn't have to be a catastrophe, so she is relieved in her own way.

She takes a discreet glance around the command post and sees that the old-timers understand the situation well and are working their brains to get things under control. It doesn't seem like things will descend into a damaging panic.

Not bad.

When she was criticized and sent to the south for trying to take matters into her own hands and nearly resisting orders, the silver lining was that she was able to bring her battalion. Thanks to that, the time she has to spend on education is halved.

No, if she delegates part of it to her subordinates, she can halve it again.

In other words, rather than having to educate everyone at her own expense, she can get away with bearing only 25 percent of the burden of time and effort. Now that's what you call efficient.

Anyhow, any outstanding organization is constantly being maintained so its gears don't rust. Humans are the guts of an organization. And naturally, an army incorporates fatalities into the planning and maintenance of its organization.

In other words, things are arranged so that the death of a single Kampfgruppe commander, no matter how great a soldier he was, won't disturb the logic of the military organization. An army that is an aggregate of countless people who can substitute for one another is a terribly expensive but extremely resilient organization.

"HQ is calling Kampfgruppe Seven over a wide area!"

They lost contact with Major von Leinburg. Though it came in via shortwave, the report from the friendly unit is that he was killed.

Unless people really have their heads in the clouds, command is transferred to the next officer in line as soon as possible to minimize the impact to the chain. And in the Empire, where they're used to wars, command succession is rare but not unheard of.

Sadly, in this war, however, so many high-ranking leaders have fallen that command succession is becoming normalized.

"As of this moment, command of Kampfgruppe Seven falls to Major von Degurechaff. They say to get to work on reorganizing the lines immediately!"

"Degurechaff, roger. You can tell HQ."

The delivery of the notification was skillful enough to suggest it was well-practiced, and Tanya shouts her assent. She wants to yell about how she's being overworked, but she just barely manages to deny herself and refrain.

As the deputy commander of Kampfgruppe Seven, her duty under these circumstances is to make the best judgment possible.

As long as it's her duty, avoiding it is against her contract.

Premodern barbarians may have committed such injustices, but as a cultured citizen with a modern education, she absolutely cannot. So to carry out her duty, she pulls out a map that shows what vague enemy information they have and starts to get a handle on the situation.

Then just as she leans over to mark the place where Major von Leinburg and his unit were attacked...

...something grazes her back.

Her body reacts before her brain has time to think. She instantaneously covers her head and hits the ground.

Guided essentially by experience, she crawls along the earth on alert for another shot. Right after that, something rips a hole through the tent, and she hears the awful sound of whatever it was ricocheting off a building outside.

Judging from the direction, it came from extremely close to the Commonwealth-Republican Army's defensive position.

"They've got snipers out! Shit, 40 mm anti-magic sniper rounds!"

Someone shouts a warning, and people sluggishly start to respond, but it's too late. I'm so impatient I want to scream at them that a civilian security company would respond faster.

They don't even have to check the damage to know what kind of ordnance is being used—any mage is familiar with it.

The 40 mm anti-matériel rifle. It's the most powerful non-magic gun.

More often pointed at mages than matériel, it's popularly known as the anti-magic rifle. It's a natural enemy of any mage.

By comparison, getting shot at with shells with heavy metal casings that can almost nullify interference formulas isn't scary at all.

You can take several direct hits from most heavy machine guns, and in the worst case, your defensive shell will block them.

But these 40 mm rounds hardly meet any resistance ripping through protective films and can pierce defensive shells, too.

Apparently, the Commonwealth is quite proud of them. Like they resign themselves to hunting mages instead of the traditional foxes or something. They probably supplied the Republic with these guns, too.

Damn that country. If nothing else, they always take sports and war seriously. Well, I'll just consider us lucky we're not being used for duck-hunting practice.

"Suppressive fire! Pin the enemy down!"

We have perimeter defense to prevent just these sorts of hazards from getting anywhere near us. The fact that it isn't functioning in the slightest pisses me off. *Some* of us are working diligently, so what is everyone else doing?

Their inaction makes her want to clench the sand in her fists and scream as she lies on the ground. She can't stand it. Their performance is so terrible, she wants to shout her voice raw, inquiring what the hell the people around her are doing.

Though a 40 mm is small enough for a person to carry, it's not the sort of thing you can hide. This is such a screwup that if these weren't second-string troops, she would consider it willful laziness. She suppresses her emotions and keeps herself from clicking her tongue, but her anger won't subside.

If they had been properly on guard, the enemy couldn't possibly have gotten this close. We can't be getting sniped at so easily—normally it would never be allowed.

On top of that, I can't believe I'm the one who nearly got shot. They almost took my head off.

It's terrifying to think my logical ideas, which have the potential to contribute to anthropological economics, could be ended with savage violence...

My human capital investments nearly defaulted.

If she weren't so short, I would have been in trouble. Tanya realizes she is thankful for her height for the first time in a while.

If she had been just a little bit taller, she would have taken a direct hit to the head when she bent over. She isn't sure whether to feel happy or sad, but given that she's alive, she opts for happy.

In any case, what she immediately thinks of are the basic steps to countering snipers. The classic way is to thoroughly bombard the suspected hiding place. Not that the Imperial Army's supply lines are sturdy enough to allow for such extravagant shell use. But lamentably, if not doing it puts me in danger, it must be done. After all, if we were in trenches, we could sweep through area by area, but this is a desert. Here, the enemies can hide in the shadows of sand dunes, so it would take an awful lot of time and effort to find them.

"Blow up the entire area to get the snipers!"

In that case, in order to keep myself safe, unhesitatingly attacking the whole area is the correct choice. You may not be able to use that tactic in the city, but in the desert, there's no need for scruples.

"What was our direct support doing?! Get rid of them—now!"

Just then, her aide-de-camp Weiss gains temporary control. He takes the lead on eliminating the snipers by sending the response team as reinforcements.

Thanks to that, Tanya can focus on patching up the chain of command, which she's grateful for.

Yeah, no matter the era, an exceptional vice commander will always come in handy. He's so brilliant that if I were in Personnel, I'd be advocating for his promotion.

Anyhow, having left the odd jobs up to her subordinate, Tanya has to get cracking on her own prioritized list of tasks.

She can't just wait around for orders and intel to come in. If she doesn't get an understanding of the situation and decide what to do about it soon, they could suffer losses. That makes even Tanya nervous, but she can't let the people around her see that.

Luckily, the radio operator and the apparatus are safe. They had contact.

She should handle things calmly, with the usual smile.

Just like negotiating, this situation can benefit from putting up a brave front.

"This is Major von Degurechaff. I've assumed command. Report your status." She laughs as she warmly informs the radio operator, "I nearly just met the same fate as your boss."

The reply comes back filled with the same humor.

If she can smile, then they can smile back, I guess.

That's a good sign. If it were a stiff, nervous newbie who had survived, she would have lost hope.

It's always easier to do your job when you have a partner, or competitor in a negotiation, who you can trust. That's gotta be true not just in business but everywhere.

"44th Battalion to CP. Captain Carlos here, I've taken over command."

She also appreciates that he asks if she's injured. A commander can't let any complaints slip out under these circumstances, so even if you're hurt, all you can do is deal. Man, even the lower-ranking officers in the Imperial Army have guts. *Ahh*, Tanya adds in her head, suddenly feeling relaxed, *this is fun*. After all, if anyone goes into hysterics, the only thing to do is "accidentally" shoot them, so nothing helps more than having tough officers.

The fact that he's not in total panic, even though his commander was just blown away, is worthy of special mention. Of course, even corporate life would have been fun with this sort of subordinate.

Thinking back on all the trouble and confusion training successors entailed, I feel like there's a lot companies could learn from the army. I should write a book about this for corporate managers.

A business book about administration strategy based on military strategy sure would have been useful; the needs are definitely there.

"Captain Carlos, this is Major von Degurechaff. Your reception's bad. Can you improve it?"

The trouble is the grainy signal. She has a connection but via shortwave, and on a battlefield, the quality is outrageously bad.

Chapter **VI**

"My apologies. This is the best I can do. An enemy sniper took out all the machines."

"I guess this is what we have to work with, then. Well, let's get down to business."

The trip south on the boat was quite pleasant. Maybe it was because their ride was a converted Reichspost cargo ship. For a ship to transport troops, it was remarkably comfortable.

Come to think of it, the good treatment probably relaxed them too much.

But there was nothing to be done about that. Having just enjoyed the officer mess lunch of which the navy was so proud, Grantz and the others felt they had gotten a proper meal for the first time in a long while. Even the battalion commander was pleased enough to give it passing marks.

That said, it's her fault that we're here in the first place.

…She had attempted to exceed her authority right before the cease-fire. Normally, that was the kind of spark that could cause major problems.

After all, it was an outrage—more like resisting orders than overstepping her authority. The operation was rejected by the normal procedure, and then her appeal was rejected. All that was fine. But once she grabbed the base commander's lapels and essentially threatened him, there was no way to cover it up.

They had been just about to sortie after she shook off even his efforts to stop her. Yes, their sincere, conscientious battalion commander did that. It was enough to make First Lieutenant Weiss, her longtime aide-de-camp, wonder under his breath if she would get court-martialed. For a while, it kept seeming like her summons would arrive.

But ironically, the arrival of an external threat blew all those issues away.

The intervention of the Commonwealth…

Nominally, the Republic had asked the Commonwealth to mediate peace negotiations.

But then the negotiators offered the same terms that were rejected in the "notice" they sent before—with the assumption they would be rejected again.

As such, anyone could see they had no intention of mediating peace talks. The terms were too biased. There was even a one-sided "final notice."

Of course, the Empire spurned the Commonwealth's ultimatum. As everyone expected, it was flatly rejected at once.

But what the Empire didn't expect was the Republican government's declaration of total resistance. The Empire had been negotiating for peace with the Republic under the assumption of a conditional surrender. Instead, General de Lugo, leading the escaped remnants of the army, declared resistance as vice minister of Defense and began claiming that he and his supporters were the true Republican government.

Officially, of course, the government was in the capital occupied by the Empire, but the troops and most of the colonies sided with de Lugo.

Contrary to their beliefs that he was a Commonwealth puppet, de Lugo proclaimed the Free Republic. He mustered the colonies on the southern continent and called for continuing the war against the Empire.

And the Republican forces stationed on the politically tumultuous southern continent were too heavily equipped to be called regional patrol units. The mages stationed there with an eye on countering the Commonwealth or the Kingdom of Ildoa posed no small threat.

It went without saying that the Imperial Army General Staff was at wit's end.

The Free Republic, which allied itself with the Commonwealth, was capable of mobilizing all of that against the Empire. The trick was to leave more than a certain number of troops on the mainland while taking care of the situation on the southern continent; faced with such a challenge, the higher-ups apparently decided that they needed Grantz's battalion commander, even though she had a tendency to take matters into her own hands.

They did cancel all her pending decorations applications from the Rhine front, though. She couldn't be completely defended. On the other hand, that was as far as their ire went.

When it came to the commander, that treatment did seem par for the course.

But as a result, people ended up conscious of how valuable it was to have a strong mage force. Grantz and the others were surprised and delighted by the much-improved pay they ended up getting.

The one problem was that despite the raise, in the desert-covered southern lands, there wasn't really a way to spend their salary anyway.

The southern continent was famous for its harsh climate, so they could accept their fate to some extent, but they couldn't help but want to whine about how badly they longed for an ice-cold beer.

Other than that, they were on board with the strategy of striking the Commonwealth and Republican colonies to take away their ability to continue fighting.

Cracking down is a fine strategy.

Both Lieutenant Weiss and the commander basically agreed on that point.

The issue was the quality of the troops who were deployed to the south. They were undoubtedly second-string units. The reserves and replenishments that had been scraped together were severely lacking in training.

They were so bad they made even Grantz, who had been treated like a chick still wearing its eggshell on the Rhine front, seem like a fully prepared soldier. Surely that was why they saw value in using a unit baptized in iron on the Rhine.

The gossipy old-timers placed bets on when General von Romel, the corps commander, would explode. Incidentally, the most popular wager was that he had already lost his temper.

That was how it was. The battalion was more than welcome due to all the veterans.

One look at the transport ship was enough to see how wholeheartedly Commander von Romel welcomed them. *He clearly expects a lot from us. And having things expected of you isn't a bad thing.*

...I want to punch my past self for thinking that.

Magic Second Lieutenant Warren Grantz mentally gave his past self a light wallop and then moved to focus on the situation before him.

The mission was simple.

It was a mission to counter snipers. In this limitless rolling desert zone with no shortages of hiding places, they had to find camouflaged snipers. The enemy was smart; they wouldn't be found so easily. So Grantz and his units' only option was to blow the whole area sky-high using explosion formulas, but that method caused its own problems. No one had any idea how they could confirm whether they got them or not.

"HQ to all units. I say again, HQ to all units."

On top of that, the desert dust put even their durable infantry rifles out of commission. The other machines were hopeless. Computation orbs did all right, but the bullets for holding formulas required frequent inspections on this battlefield. No matter how reliable the newest Type 97 Assault Computation Orb was, if the critical magic bullets weren't stable, it was nearly impossible to function.

But the higher-ups didn't take that into consideration. Or rather, they couldn't. After all, Commander von Romel was going to wage his maneuver battles no matter how crazy the environment was.

The announcement came in and said there were no changes in their orders.

"Close the flanks! I say again, close the flanks!"

It was maneuver warfare the moment they landed.

Everyone was for attacking the enemy while they were off their guard, thinking it would take some time for them to get their supply lines and other logistics together.

"Fairy 01 to Kampfgruppe Seven. It's just as we heard. We're pushing the lines forward."

"Cerberus 01 to Kampfgruppe Three. We're following Kampfgruppe Seven. Be ready to support the breakthrough!"

The problem lay with the doctrine of swinging around the back to encircle and annihilate while the center pinned the enemy down. The guys on the sea side had it a little better, but no one could stand being ordered to perform an outflanking maneuver in the sand.

A long-distance march in the desert, with barely any landmarks...

And they did it at combat speed. Just the thought of Kampfgruppen

Seven and Three's level of training made them want to go back to the mainland or the beaches at Brest.

"Prepare for formation flying! Stay in position!"

"Check the beacon. You report directly to the battalion commander!"

Formation flying orders...

They followed the orders from CP and checked their receivers.

Sure enough. The one putting out the guiding beacon was the battalion commander. Apparently, Major von Degurechaff was flying in the lead.

The guys from the Kampfgruppen were merely surprised, but what she was doing must have been really hard.

She's commanding combat while leading the flight. Her brain must have superhuman processing power. I would get caught up navigating and be worthless as a commander.

Though such thoughts were running through his mind, Grantz prepared himself with practiced motions. This was his first highly mobile battle in the desert, but the basics were the same as always.

He hadn't been at it for very long, but through repetition he had mastered taking an unsentimental view and prepping efficiently.

"If you don't wanna go blind, check your goggles!"

At the same time, as a young officer he was abundantly flexible and adaptable. He was one of the first people to understand why Major von Degurechaff brought out bigger aviation goggles for desert combat.

Lots of people complained about the big, heavy new goggles, but Grantz made sure his subordinates wore them.

They could mitigate the light to some degree and provided protection against sand. He understood instinctively that they were required gear for fighting in the harsh environment on the southern continent.

"Fairy 01 to Kampfgruppe Seven. Begin the advance!"

"All right, let's get going!"

Thus equipped, they would fight a war. It didn't matter where or what the environment was like—that was the will of both Second Lieutenant Grantz's country and the other countries.

So the soldiers had to do it.

The side making gains in battle surely celebrates. Meanwhile the side suffering the losses finds the situation intolerable.

Having drained his tea with a sigh, General de Lugo was looking up at the ceiling with a fed-up expression on his face. A nasty blame game was raging before him with no end in sight. He glanced at the participants before lowering his eyes to the documents on the table.

Just getting one combat report together had required so much effort. Drafting the report of a single encounter had taken a lot out of him. He picked up the papers. Rather than conveying the course of the battle against the Imperial Army, most of the reports were made up primarily of criticism of colleagues and self-praise.

It seemed like the colonial troops still took honor, courage, and chivalry very seriously and thought it was their duty to devote most of the pages of their reports to those topics. It was a truly unfortunate, outdated state of affairs.

He scoffed in secret, thinking that *a meeting for the sake of a meeting* was a great way to put it. They were liable to destroy themselves before they managed to take back the fatherland. The discontent of the troops who had followed him from the mainland was also near the breaking point.

…But. No, now I can actually act.

It was because he saw the opportunity that de Lugo was patiently going along with this farce. He needed to hold out for the right timing.

"Let's consider an operation to retake Turus." Having decided the time was ripe, the supreme commander ignored the tumult in the room and made his declaration.

Before the escape, de Lugo had been a major general. It was an awfully high rank for his age, but there were many who had reached it before him.

And in fact, he was the youngest general in the room, and it was quicker to count him rank-wise from the bottom. Normally, he was one of the generals who should have yielded to more senior officers.

Yet, he sat at the head of the table due purely to duty. He was vice minister of both defense and the armed forces. It was because of his authority to take command of the army in case of emergency that he was able to lead the Republican forces now.

"Are our forces concentrated?"

"I beg your pardon, General de Lugo, but what did you just say?"

Of course, though he had the authority, that was only on paper.

Even though the generals dispatched to the colonial defense forces had fallen off the promotion track, they were still de Lugo's seniors.

They weren't about to submissively listen to a general far younger than them who had graduated from the academy far more recently.

Not to mention, de Lugo mentally added, viewing the situation objectively, *these generals who got sent to the colonial armies probably don't think there is anything interesting about someone who stayed on the track at Central.*

De Lugo knew better than anyone that although they were nominally gathered to take back the fatherland, the situation inside the Free Republic was rather chaotic. In spite of this, it was lucky the colonial army accepted his command—at least organizationally.

Well, one could also say that rather than agreeing to him leading, the colonial commanders had no other moves to make and just didn't object. Still, de Lugo was the most competent among them. And he was blessed in that he had home country units he could rely on.

While some of the troops he had brought with him were lacking in actual combat experience, some who been on the Rhine lines, and others had been in the middle of getting their equipment upgraded at Central, so overall they were quite powerful.

And since the command structure had been built around de Lugo from the beginning, the forces were cohesive and well disciplined.

Even if there were some supply issues, the troops that escaped from the homeland were still the ones best equipped. They were better off than the soldiers who had been in the colonies for a long time. That in itself spoke to the standards of the colonial forces. Above all, it was clear that the elite mages from home were a notch above the troops they joined up with.

But de Lugo mentally cautioned himself.

That's as far as it goes.

They were relying on the colonial army for their connection to the administration and logistical support. On top of that, even if they were only sent here to be kept on payroll and nothing else, there were far more generals in the colonial forces than in the mainland troops he had brought.

As a result, their relationship had been awkward, and rather than engaging in combat as an organization, they were more or less acting independently.

"They are, but I oppose."

More than anything, de Lugo's position was vague. Just the order to concentrate the troops meant getting hit with a lot of red tape and bargaining. He faced opposition from the passive, do-nothing colonial bureaucrats.

Even if he said something in a meeting, the other generals coolly argued back and that was it. *"Our 'outdated' values are an expression of our chivalrous spirit upholding honor and self-respect,"* they would say with straight faces.

But de Lugo knew that ultimately, they were just resisting him going over their heads; that was the real issue.

And even today, they were opposing the advance of the army he had gathered to take back Turus. It was always like that, like pouring new wine into old wineskins.

The units were supposed to support the Commonwealth defense, but when the Commonwealth requested reinforcements, he shamefully had to tell them they didn't have the fuel. *Maybe we just don't get along, but that was an idiotic mistake.*

When the chief of logistics calmly informed him they didn't know where to get fuel, de Lugo had to push the boundaries of his patience. He wanted to scream back at him, *How many years have you guys been governing this colony?!*

On top of that, unbelievably, some of the units had been assigned to protect the generals' own interests. This was what they got for taking idiots who thought of colonial service as leisure time and leaving them to their own devices. The generals had interests in so many colonial assets that the troops could no longer move freely.

So de Lugo made a decision.

If your wineskin is old, the only thing to do is get a new one.

"Sorry, are you *all* opposed?"

And besides, once an order comes down you don't get to oppose it. Where do you guys get the nerve to resist? He had been thinking it for some time but kept talking himself down until today.

"Yes, it's vital that we defend key locations."

"We can't agree to this sort of operation."

The colonial generals were completely caught up in their own interests. Really, he would like to have the military police expose them, even personally, but a war was on, and the enemy was right up ahead. His top priority was to cut inept generals from the chain of command. Under the circumstances, he didn't even care if that meant some golden parachutes.

Of course, once he resolved to carry out a reshuffle, he prepared carefully. The units they commanded were already under his control de facto. He had nipped in the bud the possibility of a military resistance. The NCOs and lower-ranking commissioned officers were the first he turned.

Now he simply had to replace the command structure of the gathered colonial army. Regardless of the generals, there were actually lots of great noncommissioned officers and soldiers of lower rank in the colonies. Colonial service was a one- to two-year rotation, and the fact that he could expect most of them to follow orders from Central was no small boon.

Additionally, de Lugo had a tight hold on the reins to the escaped units. Now that he was sure he could do the reshuffle and unify the command chain, there was no reason to hesitate any longer.

All I need to do is dismiss these guys. Keeping his voice matter-of-fact, de Lugo proceeded with the plan he envisioned.

"I believe I've grasped the situation. If you're that strongly against it, then I have no choice."

"General de Lugo, do you mean to say that you understand?"

"Yes. It's too bad, but it would probably be difficult to command in an operation you so oppose. I would never want to pressure you to do such a thing."

Things would end quickly. By the time most generals realized something was up, he had to be ready. Which is why de Lugo then played his trump card: control over personnel.

"I've found other more suitable positions for all of you. You can go as you are, so please serve in the government office as councilors."

Councilor in the colonial government on the southern continent was, frankly, a sinecure to warm up the window seats at the government office. It was usually given to people missing in action until they were found, unless they were declared dead.

It was a clear statement that your presence or lack thereof didn't matter. To put it another way, it was an appointment that assumed your absence. Of course, that meant it completely removed all your real power—which was only natural since it was a post a person missing in action was meant to fill. No one expects someone MIA to get any work done.

""General de Lugo?!""

The generals kicked up a fuss once they finally realized what was happening, but de Lugo had zero intention of lending them an ear.

He already had written appointments for all of them. The vital mid-ranking officers in control of the units in the field were all backing him. He had exercised his power over personnel and forced through the reshuffle precisely because he could solve the problem without it evolving into an obnoxious fight.

"Your orders have been arranged. Now then, if you'll excuse me, I have an operation to lead. It may not mean much, but I hope you find success in your new endeavors."

Leaving them with that in a voice that said the decision was final, he stood roughly and laid a hand on the door to leave. With no mind to listen to the jumble of distressed shouts behind him, he felt refreshed. *I sure told them.*

He wouldn't let them wreak havoc in the army anymore. No, he wouldn't let anyone get in his way. After leaving the former commanders in their uproar, de Lugo proceeded straight to another room where others were on standby.

"Gentlemen, sorry to keep you waiting. Let's get this operation going."

It was the combat commanders who stood and saluted him. The ones from home plus the ones from the colonies made up his staff. This was the entirety of the Republican Army, the Free Republican Army. In order to carry out organized combat, they chose de Lugo.

And he knew that was why he was able to unify the command chain so rapidly.

"Okay, what's our status?"

It may have been cornered, but the Republic still just barely counted as a major power. Trying to make a comeback in the colonies, it had more than a little talent in its ranks. In its staff, in its general, and in its seasoned soldiers, it had retained the framework of an army.

Its officers with combat experience could hold their own when it came to analyzing the necessary data and planning operations.

It wouldn't be at all difficult to slaughter the Empire's two divisions if they clashed properly. And de Lugo knew how important it was to think of a plan for clashing in that way. The enemy general Romel had taken out the Commonwealth forces in surprisingly mobile battles before they could even assemble.

So there was a common understanding that a decentralized advance to engage would be reckless.

And since logistically it was hard to move a concentrated army in the desert, supplies were also a major limiting factor. The problem of where to get water could never be ignored when moving a large army around. Water had to be prioritized over everything else in the desert. Running short even once could turn into a supply crisis. Soldiers without oil simply have to walk, but soldiers without water die of thirst.

The imperial forces, on the other hand—only one corps—could probably advance all together. They did have to deal with the water issue, but since they had fewer people, it made things easier. Surely, that had to be the case.

Naturally, de Lugo could expect that if they advanced separately, the imperial troops would destroy them all.

"Everything's going according to plan. The Imperial Army is on the move."

That was why he had made so much noise about retaking their lost land. He had serious doubts whether those generals could maintain confidentiality, so he had emphasized it. To create the illusion they were making that move, he gathered a lot of supplies and simultaneously took a look at the various routes.

The imperial forces were far from incompetent. Surely, they understood the Republicans wanted to capture their base. According to intelligence de Lugo had received via the Commonwealth, they were already building defensive lines in Turus.

The status showed that the enemy thought exactly what de Lugo wanted them to think.

"Well, then!"

But... He grinned.

Every person present responded with a scheming look. This situation was exactly what they were gunning for.

General von Romel was exceptional. Any officer who saw his war records would admit it. He was the top authority on maneuver warfare of his generation, and de Lugo praised him for it despite being his enemy.

After all, everyone understood the difficulties involved in a mobile battle in the desert. How hard it would be to pull off a timely split-up advance in the sand where you were liable to lose track of your *own* position!

Just his ability to quickly move troops in an organized way through the desert was worthy of admiration. That said so much for his organizational efficiency it made de Lugo sick. If their opponent was this militarily adept, wrangling with them head-on was too much of a risk.

Naturally, the enemy general would understand that though the city was at the mouth of a bay, it would be impossible to defend if surrounded. But even a child would know not to take on all the Republican troops on the southern continent with a single corps. In other words, it would be simple for anyone to recognize the need to resolve this situation.

They could probably also recognize that the competent soldiers of the imperial military would have some ideas about how to do that, if not many. For instance, withdrawal. If the enemy didn't feel the need to defend the base to their deaths, they could retreat to Ildoan territory.

Chapter **VI**

But. De Lugo smiled inwardly. The Imperial Army didn't have any choices. As an expeditionary force, even if they wanted to retreat, they would absolutely need to secure port facilities. And the only port facilities they could use at the time were those in Turus.

They did still have the option of retreating to the Kingdom of Ildoa… but it was probably safe to consider that one politically unacceptable.

In that case, anyone could understand the conclusion that striking units before they concentrated was the only move the Imperial Army could make. It was a textbook scenario, and for that reason, de Lugo could also guess how the imperial officers would handle it. They would take all the fighting power they could and secure local numerical superiority to strike the Republican units that were probably advancing separately. With that, they would achieve a mobile defense.

That had to be the best answer available to Romel.

Since he knew that, de Lugo had no need to send his individual units out to get destroyed. On the contrary. He would lure the enemy out of their nest, overwhelm them with a large force, and crush them.

"Yes, the report is that they've sortied."

And the notification he was waiting for had already come in. The Commonwealth Intelligence had volunteered to do recon, and they had a handle on the situation in Turus.

"The Imperial Army has left Turus." They received the report in almost real time. At that point, the Imperial Army was doing just what the Free Republican Army wanted it to.

They think they're going to surprise us and attack while we're advancing all split up. It's a truly by-the-book method of coping with this situation. We've cornered them so badly, they have no other options left.

All we have to do now is destroy them.

"Ahh, now there will have been a point to fighting these dopes."

In order to lure them out, the Republicans had intentionally leaked their strategic objectives all over the place. They even performed highway maintenance to throw their enemy off track. Well actually, de Lugo had the field engineers devoted to building a minefield, so the infantry were the ones "working" on the highway, but still.

At any rate, their deception was paying off.

The Empire has crawled out of its nest. All we have to do now is hit them while they're blithely on their way to carry out their "sneak attack." For a short distance, the supply lines will manage even if we concentrate our forces. Even if the imperial forces notice us concentrating and retreat, I don't mind one bit.

At that point, the Republicans could carry out their decentralized advance unobstructed.

"All right, gentlemen. Let's get ready."

Finally.

It was how they all felt.

Finally, we can strike back at the Empire. They were elated.

The imperial forces intended to take them by surprise, so they prioritized speed over enemy spotting as they approached. The plan was to draw them into a minefield and hit them with a fierce attack.

The imperial forces may be elite, but we'll catch them in a cross fire from our light, quick units and thoroughly obliterate them with our heavy units. That was how everyone felt as they formed up.

Now the day to achieve those results had come. In terms of numbers, the Republicans were sure they had the upper hand.

And when they fought them head-on, they wouldn't necessarily be inferior then, either. Sure, their opponents were seasoned old-timers, but in this instance, numbers meant everything. Technically, they were both major powers. If one side overwhelmed the other with numbers, the winner would be decided.

"We strike back!"

""""Yes, sir!"""""

And so, Republican morale was high. They were about to launch into their long-awaited counterattack. *We're gonna scare the living daylights out of the Empire!*

》》》 OCTOBER 6, UNIFIED YEAR 1925, TURUS NAVAL BASE OUTSKIRTS 《《《

"Good grief. At this rate, I'm not going to even have any tea for teatime."

After somehow managing to escape the blazing Turus Naval Base, trading with the nomadic tribes had been going brilliantly.

He thought he was getting along with them pretty well. The intelligence exchange was actually worthwhile, too. It was with the nomads' help that he had been able to observe Turus Naval Base and get a handle on the Imperial Army's movements.

But John did have one irresolvable complaint about his work right now: an absence of tea, which was a life-or-death matter for a civilized gentleman. The nomads enjoyed their own infusions, but it wasn't the tea John loved. And when he tried, with no expectations, to request some from the home country, they heartlessly told him to procure it on the ground. Humans are weak creatures and hope even when they know things won't turn out, so the indifferent response upset him.

Thus the man recalled his home country's cold response and lamented dramatically. Well, there was the fact that John was in the desert and clad in the local costume, too.

He led a caravan, mingling with the nomads, clumping along atop a camel. He fit right in, and at a glance, you wouldn't even notice him.

He was lucky he had managed to take on some officers who were familiar with the desert to some degree. Well, that was a silver lining, anyway. They would be able to keep doing business with some of the tribes, which would allow them to keep their intelligence net up.

His message had reached the Republican side fine, so John could finally take a break.

"...Whatever else happens, it seems like the reconnaissance will work out."

Things were so calm he found time to complain. One could say his situation wasn't too shabby.

"Dear guest, you will keep our terms, yes?"

"Of course, you have my word. I've got more confidential funds than I know what to do with."

But a gentleman through and through, John lamented, *Even though I'm sorely lacking tea, they say to rejoice that I have money?* He wasn't so lacking in elegance or John Bull spirit that he could be happy about that.

Sometimes he sadly wondered if the twits in Whitehall were too tainted by the ideas of the city. It really made him want to cry. *Would that bunch in Whitehall honestly tell me to drink money instead of tea?* He really wanted them to send him some or do something, at least.

He was of a mind to demand more attention to the welfare of agents working abroad. *They don't understand the suffering people go through one whit.* Those pseudo-gentlemen who knew nothing about actual working conditions were such a pain.

But that was precisely why he needed to focus on the job before him, so he brought his attention back to the present.

"So that's the situation. I'd like it if we could keep a good relationship."

John had plenty of opinions, but he was an outstanding agent. He was maintaining observation and communication nets using the nomadic tribes. At the same time, he was providing weapons to some of them to support guerrilla activity. He had also contracted to receive any imperial prisoners they took and made an agreement for Commonwealth prisoners as well.

At any rate, John had built the network necessary to confront the Empire. It went without saying that it was an extraordinary amount of work.

John feigned calm atop the one-humped camel. He had made it through countless tricky situations. Once he even got caught up in a nomad conflict and roused his old bones to take up a rifle.

John was a fine fox hunter, but he had had enough of the camel-mounted cavalry attackers—so much so that if he had a chance, he wanted to bring a submachine gun, or actually the new model of the imperial-made assault rifles would be good.

"The supplies we get from you help us, too."

This was one of the tribes' chiefs. About their dealings, he was positive. He welcomed the opportunity to acquire live ammunition to unify the tribes in the area. After all, since heavy arms, explosives, and the like were mainly acquired from abroad, securing a stable way to get them before the other tribes was a big deal.

But unlike John, they hadn't sworn alliance to any nation.

"But if you want to see what we can do, shouldn't you be sending in soldiers, too?"

...Which meant they often offered terms that people like John could never swallow.

The relationship between the nomad tribes and the Commonwealth had to be kept secret. If word got out that he was embedded in a tribe, he wouldn't be able to infiltrate places as part of their caravans like he did now.

More than anything, clandestine activities had to be kept clandestine. For example, he absolutely couldn't leave any record that he was working with the tribes behind the scenes in ways that could lead to an anti-Republic war in the Republican colonies.

John's hardship would continue, so he made a wish. *Please let the Free Republican Army do their job properly.*

 OCTOBER 12, UNIFIED YEAR 1925, IMPERIAL ARMY CAMP

"General von Romel, I'd like to make a suggestion."

Even when the veil of night is about to fall, breaks are an unattainable luxury for members of the Imperial Army General Staff. The air fleet has turned in their final reconnaissance reports for the day, but the work of analyzing them with insufficient lighting and equipment awaits the staffers on the ground.

Still, just as everyone is thinking it will be a quiet night, Major von Degurechaff shows up, and the first thing out of her mouth is that she has a suggestion to make. Naturally, it's especially surprising that a field officer would come to offer opinions at this time of day.

What could it be? they wonder.

That said, almost no one finds it suspicious. Degurechaff's tone is not tense at all but utterly businesslike. And it's not so uncommon for someone to suggest something to the commander.

Well, the time of day is somewhat odd...but it fits with the Imperial Army tradition of taking action.

So there are no reproachful glares saying, *How rude.* But it is strange enough that almost everyone looks over in spite of themselves, out of curiosity. *What in the world is this field officer worried about?*

To Tanya, though, that right there is what she wants to bring up. The indecisive gazes of the officers and their hesitation is exactly what makes her anxious. In this situation, under these circumstances, the faces of the staffers don't seem worried at all.

She has to say something.

"What is it?"

Well, it's wonderful to have a boss who will at least listen to you. A boss who increases incentives for his subordinates creates the best military environment. It's so much easier to work with someone like this.

Tanya's mood lightens as she senses that they will be able to get along and respect each other's interests. That's why she feels that they should step in to cover for each other, if necessary.

"I'd like permission to scout ahead of the main forces."

Naturally, it's a plan that serves both of their interests, although it conceals her true intentions. Tanya doesn't want to do anything dangerous. Hence her desire to move cautiously.

The military would be in trouble if there was a miscalculation, right? And if that happened, the mages, by their nature, are the branch that would be worked extra hard doing recon-in-force and pursuit battles, essentially extinguishing the fire when it broke out.

Tanya is not the type to spare efforts now if she can reduce risk in the future.

"That could reveal our sneak-attack plan. What's your intent?"

"I believe our knowledge of enemy movements is insufficient."

Naturally, her outward expression of these sentiments is fully armed with logic. Armies are rational to a point. Oftentimes, they don't make sense, but they can't ignore reason completely. (That's only natural. Arguing some theory that bends physical laws won't help them defeat their enemies.)

"We've sent out reconnaissance units, though."

"We're currently dependent on the air force units in Turus." Tanya understands their current dilemma, how difficult it is to perform recon while advancing, so she drives her point home before he can tell her that's why they're relying on the air force. "And we knew this, but air force units are limited by their navigation apparatus capabilities; it's difficult for them to perform night reconnaissance."

True, at a glance, it makes sense to send the air force to scout ahead of the advancing ground army. Certainly, it would be nearly impossible for the average foot soldier to scout ahead in a desert with no landmarks.

On that point, a reconnaissance aircraft, endowed with a navigation machine, does have the advantage. But at night, aircraft run into a lot of problems. Aerial photography capabilities are extremely limited at night, and it's not uncommon to simply not be able to get any.

Of course, she knows that General von Romel and the staffers are doing their very best.

The army is focusing on advancing quickly and efficiently in order to strike the enemy forces before they can concentrate. Due to time limitations, they haven't done anywhere near enough recon. The imperial military isn't stupid enough to not worry about that, which is why aircraft were arranged, and they are handling the situation with cooperative efforts between the air and the ground. That's an important, respectable achievement, and Tanya acknowledges that.

Still, no matter how great their efforts, there are too many technical limitations for aircraft to do reconnaissance of the ground at night. And the chance for accidents would be too great if they sent them up anyway. They can't ignore the risk that the enemy could get a clue about their movements from a crashed plane.

"And even without that, our intel is incomplete."

Disregarding those issues, Tanya is forced to point out, per her obligations as an officer, that the trickier problem is their limited field of vision.

Air units have conducted reconnaissance of the vicinity. But the problems with that are fuel and territory under enemy air forces. No matter how faithfully, no matter how earnestly they carry out their missions, there are still limitations, right? It has to be said.

And the air force reports they've gone to such lengths to get only one side of the situation. As a staffer, too, she has to point out that if they rely on the air too much, they run the risk of biased data or outright misunderstandings.

"Given these concerns, I firmly believe we should take precautions."

In short, even if it's only her outward-facing argument, those issues can't be ignored so easily. And her suggestion is in the commander's interest as well. Tanya is proud she can offer a win-win proposal.

"...All right. Permission granted."

"You have my gratitude. I'll take my battalion out immediately."

She thanks him and exits the tent. She promptly calls up her battalion. Since First Lieutenant Weiss was on standby for rapid response, he answers in one ring.

Splendid. Satisfied with his performance, she alerts him they will be sortieing. After additionally ordering careful preparations, she races across the sand back to her own tent.

Long-range night reconnaissance. And in a desert, to boot. They need to double-check their navigation instruments. They have to be ready for the possibility of a sandstorm cutting off communications. They make all the preparations a unit operating solo can in the unique climate and environment of a desert.

Upon reaching her tent, Tanya takes a look at the navigation chart with the help of her adjutant, Second Lieutenant Serebryakov, and consults with Weiss to plan where they should search for the enemy. Considering the possibility of unforeseen encounters with recon forces, they split into companies. A total of four companies will fan out to form a line, and after searching, they will return to a designated meeting point. An orthodox method, but given the situation, it should be useful.

In order to resist the Republican forces during their decentralized advance, locating them is essential.

If she locates the enemy ahead of time under the pretext of officer reconnaissance, she decreases their risk of an encounter battle. She's definitely not opposed to doing work behind the scenes to minimize danger in advance. It pleases her to do a reliable, thorough job.

More than anything—she stifles a laugh, thinking back at how hard they got worked on the Rhine front—*I'm just glad it's not recon-in-force.*

Recon-in-force meant they had to go forward while getting shot at, whereas regular reconnaissance means all they have to do is bring back intelligence. Even if they have to be prepared to get shot at, it's a lot more relaxing to fly when that isn't the assumption.

Of course, she hasn't forgotten that they're on a battlefield where all risks apply. In a recon mission, there's always the danger that the enemy will pursue, and she understands that. But right now, they haven't received any reports of enemy contact in the entire area.

In that case, this should be a pretty enjoyable flight, and there's also the option of discovering and striking small command posts.

Being safe is unconditionally wonderful. And getting results while safe is even more wonderful. The other important point is that in the opposite situation—that is, if risks suddenly escalate past a tolerable level—all the battalion needs to do is turn around and break away.

Thus, that night, Tanya ascends into the sky in a relatively relaxed state of mind.

Of course, even a desert gets terribly cold in the dark, but it's quiet and calm, so the journey is a leisurely night flight. As someone with experience on the Rhine lines and in the north, and given the lack of nighttime scrambles and large-scale enemy units coming to attack, she finds the job a simple matter of flying through the tranquil sky.

That said, while at first she is glad for a smooth flight, as time goes on and they get farther out, a sense of unease gradually begins to grate on her.

It's too quiet.

"...We could come into contact with an enemy patrol or commando units anytime now. Keep an extra sharp watch on the ground."

"Yes, ma'am."

"All units, keep your guard up against the sky and the ground alike. We're already close to the projected enemy location. Look out for patrols or commandos. Pay special attention to the dunes. Don't miss any light sources."

It's entirely possible that the enemy is alert to the possibility of a search.

Conducting a decentralized advance in secret is a logical move. That means we have to be extra thorough.

But we fly and fly and meet no enemy. No matter how far we go, we don't even spot any other life-forms besides us, much less the enemy.

"Fairy 01 to Fairy Battalion members."

Normally, an empty battlefield is a welcome state of affairs. There aren't very many people who want to cause trouble for themselves. So normally, we should be happy the enemy is nowhere to be found.

Still, there are a number, albeit a small number, of significant exceptions. For example, it's no good if there is nothing in a space or territory where there is supposed to be something. That's not *nothing here*, but *something missing*.

"Commanders, report in."

"Company Two, no contact. We haven't spotted anything."

"Company Three, nothing besides us out here."

"Company Four, contact negative."

So the lack of an expected occurrence is a sign of a gravely worrisome situation.

"…That's weird."

This is a bit absurd.

The enemy isn't here. They're supposed to be here, but they're not. If they were missing from one position that would be one thing, but if they're missing from every position, you start to feel like you're chasing phantoms.

It's as if their decentralized advance is a sandy illusion.

…An illusion?

That's a hypothesis.

But what if that hypothesis is reality?

The plan is to take out each individual group of enemies approaching in a decentralized way. I see; they'll be too much to handle if they're concentrated, but if they're split into three, we're able to overwhelm them both quantitatively and qualitatively.

So General von Romel didn't make a mistake in having us go out to destroy them before they're able to surround Turus Naval Base.

At least, not if the enemy is actually conducting a decentralized advance.

But they must not be. Our intention was to attack the split-up enemy before they concentrated, but the way things are going, there's a good chance they're actually concentrated now. They could even already be in battle formation.

Now then, our HQ still hasn't been able to locate them. If, under these circumstances, we get attacked by an enemy force twice our size, what will happen? Clearly, we'll end up on the bad side of Lanchester's law. If the enemy is divided, we can win, but if they're concentrated, we won't be able to handle them.

"Connect me to HQ! It's urgent! Hurry, it's an emergency!" *We thought we would make fun of them for advancing split up. Instead, they got us. No, perhaps the Imperial Army was arrogant.* Full of regret, she raises her voice. "The Imperial Army was too conceited!"

How could we underestimate the enemy's intelligence? What an error. The mistake of following precedent because we stopped thinking indicates inflexible reasoning and a lack of innovation. When we deployed to the south, we thought about facing a colonial army in an unconsciously biased way, and it's taking its toll.

This is a trap. This has to be a trap laid by the Republican Army.

"They tricked us! The enemy isn't here!"

Where are they? That's obvious.

They must have fulfilled the rule of force concentration. They made efficient uses of the resources they had. They're probably sneering at our naive predictions this very minute.

Because the concentrated enemy forces are surely committed to the main battlefield.

"Battalion commander to all companies. As of this moment, abort your missions. Gather up immediately. I say again, gather up immediately!"

As a commander engaged in a reconnaissance mission, Tanya knows exactly what this means. That's why she gave the order to contact headquarters right away.

"You haven't gotten HQ yet?!"

But the apparatus picks up noise… The area around their headquarters is already under heavy jamming, so their signals are blocked.

But just barely. They just barely manage to get a spotty connection. Tanya orders Serebryakov to explain the situation and tries to come up with countermeasures.

"...What are we going to do now?"

The problem is how to take care of things.

Reality is that the enemy field army is gathered together. We can't expect interdiction missions like obstructing traffic or severing their supply lines to take effect before the forces attack.

And if their forces are concentrated, a simple comparison of fighting power shows we're overwhelmed. Considering the progress of the battle, our options for supporting the main forces are limited, too.

After all, our corps have already advanced, lured by the honey of destroying the divided enemy troops. Armies can't stop very easily once they've started. Even if HQ decided to retreat, the enemy wouldn't let that stop them—they'd follow close in pursuit. If that happened, the communication lines would be severed before the main imperial forces could even build resistance lines, and the southern front would go down in history as a major defeat.

Even if they retreat to Turus Naval Base, without command of the sea, it will only be a matter of time before they have to surrender.

Now, the important thing here is how I can run away without harming my military record.

Beneath her disgruntled face, Major Tanya von Degurechaff is deep in thought. If she doesn't want the Imperial Army to lose, she can't deny the possibility of going back to support the others. So for a moment, she seriously considers the idea, but she concludes it's impossible. *At this point, an imperial victory is out of the question.*

We're up against an overwhelmingly superior foe. If we can't take them out, there's no chance of winning.

And considering we're in a desert, the option of holing up in the temporary defensive position set up by the field engineer team and waiting for the situation to change is hopeless. In a desert, water is precious. Probably as precious as gasoline. Maybe if we were near a water source, it would be different, but at any other position in the field, a couple days' siege is enough to have us writhing in thirst. So defending a fixed point where there is no water is too dangerous.

"Water, water. Without water, we can't fight a war... Shit, this is why I hate the desert," Tanya gripes, but she doesn't stop thinking.

Currently, it's impossible for the Imperial Army to face a large force in the desert. They don't have enough water. But if they retreat, the enemy will follow them forever. Even if they confront them, if they can't defeat them all, they'll run out of water and die of dehydration.

It'd be a terrible irony to suffer from thirst at Turus Naval Base with a view of the sea. No thanks.

Under the circumstances, the measure they could take to contribute to an imperial victory might as well be going and dying in a fight against the huge enemy army. No way am I taking any suicidal missions like that.

"All right, in this case the only thing to do is strike the enemy's water!"

So Tanya narrows down her choices to the realistic supporting move of striking the enemy's supply lines, after all. There has to be some kind of military support, or all their friendly troops will be wiped out. And this should protect her military career, as well. *But.* She suddenly regrets this idea.

Her battalion can take pride in being one of the best, but it's still just a single aerial mage battalion.

Regardless of their abilities, they will be hopelessly outnumbered. Even if they were going to support the troops' withdrawal, it would be practically impossible by orthodox methods. And even the long-range penetration in de facto enemy airspace to strike their water transport lines is just unreasonable. And in terms of securing their own water, too, the imperial maps had almost no information about nearby oases. Should we bank on friendly contact with local nomads? If it doesn't work out, I'll be the one suffering from thirst. I'm definitely not interested in that, either.

"Think, think… What is the enemy's logic?"

The enemy thinks they've tricked us, so what's the next logical step?

In short, the Republic Army feigning a decentralized advance thinks the imperial troops are concentrated.

Oh? No, that's it.

"I see. The main forces certainly are concentrated. So how about we use their logic against them?"

As she mumbles, she continues her train of thought. *And what if the enemy falls into the same bias that the Imperial Army was trapped in until moments ago? They think they have all our units pinned down.*

Naturally, she can expect that under that assumption, the enemy won't be paying much attention to the possibility of a powerful combat unit coming at them from behind. In a sense, it's a prospect stemming from a wish. But in this situation, her human psyche gives her hope.

"Good," she crows, but even if that hypothesis is true, she is still distressed about what her role will be. Certainly, it might be possible to cause some temporary confusion by jabbing them in the back, but…

Can the battalion *maintain* that confusion? Not sure. Even if they can create a break in the encirclement, God only knows if they can keep it open. In other words, you can put as much faith in that plan as you can in that bastard Being X.

Actually, the more she thinks about it, the more dangerous it sounds. If they do manage to punch a hole, the army will no doubt order them to hold their ground to keep it open even an instant longer.

Maybe I should just run away? But there's definitely a court-martial waiting for her if she does that. Fleeing before the enemy and, on top of that, abandoning the troops to do so… She's sure no one would protect her like they did when she screwed up off the coast of Norden.

In that case, her fate would be getting sent to a silent firing squad, getting shot after being repatriated and court-martialed, or if she was lucky, a messenger would deliver a pistol and tell her to commit suicide. Not many options.

There aren't many ways to explain away fleeing before the enemy. No, you can try to gloss it over, but for better or worse, a soldier is expected to fight bravely. Anyone who takes a hike when their allies are in a crisis is just like unlucky Admiral Byng.

No officer wants the same fate as Admiral Byng who "failed to do his utmost." Tanya has seen with her own eyes that there are officers in the field who would rather fight a reckless battle.

Of course, she never dreamed she would be in this position herself. If she had official orders to leave, that would be a different story, but since it's common military sense in the present situation to rescue the main forces, surely General von Romel would give such an order. That fact can't be ignored.

So then I should fight under the given conditions. All I can do is fight and find a way out of this up ahead.

My top priorities are survival and self-preservation. Therefore, it's essential that I don't appear to have abandoned my fellow troops, so if possible, I'd like one result of my actions to be that they take as little damage as possible. Still, only as little as possible. If I can prove they took less damage because of me, then the reality that I helped save them will lessen the criticism I receive over my lack of motivation.

Okay, so how can I uphold my reputation while minimizing damage to the troops and also escaping to live another day? Looking back through history, you see there is nothing more horrible than a fighting retreat. And in that case, even if you manage to survive, you didn't really defend what you were supposed to.

Under the circumstances, it's too risky to ask the heavily encircled main forces to withdraw with minimal casualties. But there are examples in history where both conditions were met. For example, the Battle of Sekigahara. The results of the clash between eastern and western armies are famous, right? Betrayal, conspiracy, hesitation? In any case, there's a lot to learn there.

The final days of the defeated army were utterly miserable. Most of their territory was either seized or the meager *kokudaka* from its rice yield was gobbled up. In the first place, many of them failed to leave the battlefield. But there was a nearly crazy bunch who, despite participating in the battle, not only managed to get their general out but also showed off their martial zeal.

Their name? The Oni-Shimazu.

…The Shimazu clan?

In other words, the logic is that if we ram through the enemy and then leave, we're not fleeing before the enemy?

No, but… Tanya feels somewhat conflicted. Let's be honest. She mentally complains that breaking through the enemy and making it back is mission impossible

I'm not sure if the guys who can casually pull feats that warrant special mention in history—think Kellerman's charges—are sane. This is a difficult era for a sensible person like me.

But if I must...

If I have no choice, that's my duty.

"...It seems we've won."

"Yes, General."

The scene before their eyes was the Republic's revenge on the Empire, something that most Republican soldiers had been dreaming of since the collapse of the Rhine front.

He had lured the enemy with false reports of a decentralized advance. Now he had them encircled with his concentrated forces and was about to annihilate them. They were going to do to the Empire exactly what had been done to them on the Rhine front, and the resulting pride invigorated not only the staff but the troops as well.

For General de Lugo, it was the first step in a counteroffensive for which he had prepared in every possible way. Of course, he was also relieved that the efforts he had put in so far were working.

It had taken a long time, but if they could defeat the Imperial Army here, they could reinforce their defense of the southern continent. They could take back Turus and turn it into a strong stepping-stone for a counteroffensive on the continent.

It was all finally within reach.

Which was why...

...the alarm going off grated so badly on his ears.

"M-mayday from the 228th Mage Company!"

What is going on? That was basically the look on the radio operator's face as he delivered his report like a cry for help.

"The 12th Mage Battalion providing direct support for the right flank also requires urgent assistance! They say the enemy has almost broken through!"

The multiple dire reports from the right flank were added to the map with symbols showing the progress of the battle. Everyone looked at the new situation out of the corner of their eyes and fell silent. They knew it meant the mage units on the right flank were just barely holding out.

But they all hesitated. They could hardly believe it.

"Emergency alert from Division 7 Command! What seems to be a regiment-sized unit of enemy mages is attacking the right flank!"

"What?! We didn't have them encircled?!"

Finally, the division headquarters had reported in about the enemy movements. The staff officers would have preferred a calmer notification, but unfortunately, such hopes were dashed.

The hoarsely delivered report from a high-ranking frontline officer said that they were being attacked by a regiment of enemy mages. It was such awful news that de Lugo wanted to shout, *That's not funny!*

He thought he had them surrounded. Since the plan was to target the enemy flanks, the troops were trained specifically for counter–land attacks.

The job of stopping the pesky enemy mages was the mission of his own mages concentrated in the center.

Each flank also had enough mages to stop a battalion's worth, just in case.

But if their opponent had a regiment… That could mean that almost none of the imperial mages on this battlefield had been surrounded.

"Of all the stupid—! Then who are the mages in the center fighting?!"

But that's not consistent with the intel we have! De Lugo fell silent and stared at the map—their estimates of the enemy fighting force and the current actual scale of their mage units. There shouldn't have been such a severe discrepancy between them.

It was true that his main mage force was engaged with what they believed was the main imperial mage force. He had just received a report that due to their numerical superiority, they were maintaining the upper hand.

So given the reports and the intel they had gotten ahead of time, there should be no way the enemy had mages to spare. *But* de Lugo pondered for just a moment.

If it were possible. Well, it couldn't be, but... *Do we only have numerical superiority because the enemy pulled a regiment of mages out of their forces?*

But that would mean they basically have a brigade's worth of mages in this battle. The possibility that our intel net missed that is greater than zero, but...I'm confident in our grasp on enemy movement.

The conclusion he had reached was that the Imperial Army had a regiment at most. That should have been all the enemy had. It shouldn't have been possible for reserves to crawl out of the woodwork like this.

"Confirm if it's really a regiment!"

So the composed part of his mind doubted whether it was really a regiment.

For example, maybe they were using some kind of deception to fool them into thinking the group was regiment sized.

Or the confusion could have caused a misunderstanding. But then what about all the reports from his units? He knew what they meant. Whether he could accept it or not was another problem.

"General de Lugo, we've already lost two companies!"

And most importantly...

The dazed looks on the staffers' faces spoke volumes. De Lugo understood their disbelief and bewilderment quite well.

The fact that two companies had been taken down meant that there was an enemy force out there big enough to overwhelm them in an instant.

It would be different if they had put up resistance and been defeated. But if the enemy was stronger by the standard margin, the first message from a unit making contact would never be mayday.

"If the 12th Battalion is about to be breached, the enemy force must be at least twice the size of that."

And on top of that, there was the report like a shriek from the battalion assigned as direct support. If they were almost broken as well, the delaying defense along the entire right flank wasn't functioning as intended. *Are you telling me there's an enemy mage unit so powerful we can't stop them even if we get support from the right flank division?*

"Ngh. Send the mages from the center over as backup! At this rate, they'll break the encirclement!"

Chapter **VI**

De Lugo's brain had fallen into worry on this outrageous turn of events, but Colonel Vianto's shout rebooted it.

Vianto had recovered fastest of all the momentarily paralyzed staff officers.

Though they were behind, the others started to understand what needed to be done.

If the batteries on the right flank were hit, there would be no way to stop the enemy from leaving, so the right flank needed reinforcements.

...It was an utterly sensible plan.

But there was nothing sensible about their opponents. It happened the moment the unit was pulled and sent over.

"5th Mage Battalion to HQ! The enemy mages are rapidly approaching!"

The warning scream was from the mage unit directly supporting not the right flank but the center.

"Ridiculous! They're not striking the batteries?!"

He had just sent the 2nd Mage Battalion and the newly pulled 1st Composite Mage Regiment over to the right flank.

But he was forced to realize, with utter loathing, that the enemy mages who had been running amok on the right flank had changed course.

The maneuver wasn't even aiming to stop the reinforcements. For a moment, no one was sure where the enemy was headed.

It wasn't a move to destroy the right flank's encirclement, which had seemed to be on its last legs. No. And it wasn't even a move to intercept the incoming backup.

It was a charge at the central Republican forces.

"They're like devils..." The truth came out of Vianto's mouth as a complaint.

Vianto was more familiar with mages than anyone else present, and he understood the enemy's intentions. Or maybe it was more that he knew from experience what they would target next.

Striking the right flank was just one of their objectives. If the Republican Army had left them to their own devices, they would have broken through the right flank and left.

But what do they do if the Republican Army does the sensible thing and reinforces the right flank?

Simple.

They strike where units have just been removed: the center.

It wasn't as if units would be taken from the left to go all the way on the right. To check enemy mages on the right, units would be taken from the center. Supposing the mages charged in a straight line, the noise and jamming would be such that their ability to detect enemies would be temporarily paralyzed.

Then if the Imperial Army moves based on the sign of reinforcements on the way?

That moment, Vianto instinctively understood the horrible truth, and his spine froze.

The mages were finally protecting the right flank. The exact instant they finished fanning out, they became useless. They couldn't contribute a single thing at the decisive moment the center was being attacked. *No, we* made *them useless!*

The enemy maneuvers appeared to be the meanderings of a cornered group, but in fact they were more devilish than the devil, using tactics that were the height of cunning and extremely devious. The enemy mages were pulling off maneuvers Vianto wasn't even sure were theoretically possible.

He thought he was well versed in the terrors of the imperial mages.

"General de Lugo, please fall back."

"What?"

"The enemy is coming here! Damn it! They mean to re-create what they did on the Rhine front!"

They would take out the headquarters with a "surgical strike."

Anyone would laugh it off as a bad dream, but the Empire executed it on the Rhine lines.

They broke through the Republican main lines, positions built to have incomparably tight defenses, and took out the fortresslike headquarters.

The panic that overtook the frontline units at the time was on a practically indescribable scale.

Chapter VI

...And the current Republican Army didn't have a substitute for de Lugo. It had just exchanged its old wineskin for a new one. It didn't have another ready.

The Free Republican Army, as one could tell just from the name, had taken enormous efforts to achieve. So if the general at the head of the Republic fell now, of all times, continuing an organized resistance would be nearly impossible.

To the Imperial Army, even if its entire Southern Expeditionary Corps got wiped out, if they managed to take de Lugo with them, it would still be a victory.

No, it'll be hard to take out the Imperial Army now. They'll probably just get a little beat up.

And what will happen to our firepower and units if we send them out to face those mages?

At the very least, we won't achieve our initial objectives.

"Men, protect the general. This is our final battle."

The enemy broke through on the Rhine, but here Vianto couldn't let it happen. He wouldn't give the Imperial Army another headquarters.

THE SAME DAY, IMPERIAL ARMY CAMP

"Ha-ha-ha! Ha-ha-ha! Ha-ha! Ha-ha! Ha-ha-ha-ha!"

Hearing that laugh, the unlucky noncommissioned officers who were also in the armored vehicle grimaced.

Well, anyone has the right to grimace if their high-ranking commander bursts out laughing when they're surrounded.

If he's gone insane, this is going to suck. There was nothing terribly strange about their feelings.

Normally, Romel would have been considerate and held his laughter in. But for today, he just laughed and laughed, more than you would think a person could.

"Ah, this is truly amusing. Way to go, Major!"

Just this once, Romel couldn't stop laughing. The scene before his eyes had made a tremendous impact that warranted the reaction.

He thought he could control her somewhat on a leash, but actually, she was much more effective when he let her go. *She must have caught a whiff of something—that's why she wanted to go on recon so late!*

He was grateful that she had seen through the enemy ruse and alerted him the Republicans were on their way before the main forces encountered them.

Thanks to that, he was able to prepare to face a superior enemy.

At the same time, if there were units outside the encirclement, you'd think they would aim to withdraw. But he felt stupid about thinking that when he saw what was happening.

"Is she—is she retreating forward?! I have to laugh. Major von Degurechaff's maneuvers are incredible!"

He had been puzzled when he heard the 203rd Aerial Mage Battalion was engaging the enemy's right flank. *How much will it really do when their encirclement is almost complete?* At that moment, he had resigned himself to losing the entire army.

He figured the 203rd Battalion's efforts would only lengthen the time it would take to wipe them out and had even been considering ways to withdraw. *If we do everything we can, maybe some units can escape, and if we're lucky, maybe we can sow the seeds of a defensive line reorg.*

So it took him a minute to understand that Degurechaff had broken off combat and charged straight into the center of the enemy formations. He didn't realize it wasn't a charge of resignation and self-sacrifice until the confusion in the center of the Free Republican Army gradually spread and enemy movements grew sluggish.

Directly after that, he finally got his answer as to her objective. Surprisingly, striking the right flank was a total diversion. Her real aim was the enemy's main force that he was facing with his troops. And her even bigger ulterior motive was to attack enemy command directly. That was her plan.

"She turned this fight around using maneuvers and securing local superiority!"

She was just like a magician. *To an ally, she's surely an evil-crushing shield of White Silver. But to headquarters, she's a mad dog indeed! Oh, she will achieve so much more off the leash.*

This had to be a headache for a proud general. A proud general wouldn't want to admit that someone of a lower rank, and a child, at that, was better than them at war, but who would?

"Ahh, so that's why most generals can't figure out what to do with her. No one likes a hunting dog who's smarter than the hunter..."

She's too talented to be a mere field officer. Any superior officer would have a hard time with her as a subordinate.

She might even be too much for me to handle.

I understand very well now why the General Staff, no, the Western Army Group, gave her the authority to act independently. She's a frightfully competent hunting dog.

Thanks to her shaking off enemy reinforcements and ripping through their headquarters, the enemy was in a panic. The Imperial Army, supposedly surrounded by the remnants of the Republican Army, had managed to maintain an organized combat unit, and the situation was now such that it could make a breakthrough.

They were free to push forward or retreat.

And in fact, since the flanks couldn't do much due to the confusion in the center, they could even resurrect their initial plan to take them all out.

We can do this. Romel smiled ferociously.

"Hit the enemy's left flank! This is a mobile air battle! Hit their left flank and drive straight through their central forces!"

They would leave the disordered right flank alone for the moment.

And the connecting unit in the center had fallen into disarray following Degurechaff's attack. Romel saw immediately that the left flank was what remained.

Though it was currently isolated from its chain of command, the left flank actually had the most organized fighting power left. He would attack it with not a moment to lose.

In order to do that, he needed all the military strength they had. *What should I do?* he started to wonder but realized he didn't actually have enough troops to think that hard.

"The light division should defend our position! All the rest of you, get on the left flank! Crush that left flank!"

Having decided to leave the greenest of his light divisions to hold down their position, he would take the rest of his forces to clash with the left flank in an attempt to bring down the encirclement and take out their enemies.

If they did that, they would at least be able to secure a retreat. It would probably be possible to deal quite a blow if they hit them while they were already confused.

That he had been able to make such a judgment so quickly was a testament to Romel's unusual talent.

At least, maintaining an orderly resistance while encircled was praiseworthy. Once he had a course of action, he moved quickly.

"Tell the major she can do whatever she wants."

And then, no one knew if it was for better or worse, but he let go of the leash.

The Chihuahua on the other end was probably cute and lovable.

But on the battlefield, he needed the wild hunting dog. And she could wreak way more havoc on the enemy if she and her battalion didn't conform to the norms.

That was how it seemed to him, so he did it to reach his goals.

"Huh? Are you sure, sir?"

"With that one, there's nothing better than to let her do her thing. Hunting should be left up to the hunting dog, right?"

When commanding a corps the same size as his enemy's, Romel himself had no intention of losing to anyone. He could probably even take on Degurechaff just fine. He was fairly confident of his ability to wage maneuver warfare on the operational level.

But he understood that when it came to running a battalion, he was inferior. Or perhaps more importantly, he had to accept that he would never be as good as her at sensing the time to fight.

The opportunity she seized with her brisk maneuvering was such a brief instant that though I could see it from afar, I couldn't grasp it.

In any case, the more you try to control her, the more energy you waste. She and her battalion really are war's hunting dogs. They're cavalry officers of ancient times, the real deal. They know when, where, and how to go charging in.

They could take prey without you teaching them how. So rather than risk them forgetting how by training them, it was much more logical to let them run wild.

"More importantly, hurry up and get ready for a penetrating raid! Get on the Republican guns before they regain discipline!"

He could think about how to use Degurechaff and the 203rd Aerial Mage Battalion later on. Now it was most important to take care of the immediate situation.

If we don't crush the Republican artillery, we'll be caught in a one-sided barrage. If I don't seize this chance, I'll be the most inept of the inepts. I have no interest in being mocked by history as an incompetent general who wasted the hard work of his fellow soldiers.

"Understood! Right away!"

Praise be to the skirmishers and their crisp movements.

Look how briskly they move, even under these trying circumstances. Those are veterans of the Rhine, all right. Even if their units are undermanned, they're more useful since they don't hesitate. A soldier who can move is better than one who can't.

Once the light division acclimates, they'll be a bit more helpful. I'm glad they've at least been learning some fighting techniques.

"Gather all the remaining gunners together! I don't want to get caught 'round the back! As soon as you're done attacking the artillery, blast the hell out of the enemies in the center. No limit this time on the amount of shells you can use! Just shoot like crazy!"

"If we're trying to keep them in check, do we really need that many?"

"We can't bring the artillery on the charge. Plus, the light division staying to hold our current position needs backup. Now, get going!"

But surely, they couldn't be expected to defend on their own. They were liable to collapse if he left them surrounded and alone. That would affect all the units charging, too.

Speed was paramount in a maneuver battle. In order to minimize the time the most vulnerable unit would be exposed, he'd have to make soldiers run.

At that point, they really couldn't take the artillery with them. Then the only thing to do was have them put their firepower on display once they had taken up their position. Artillery employed in a practical way can be useful for both offense and defense, no doubt about it. Firing, distracting, defending—they do it all. If the troops left the guns as a trick up their sleeve, the defensive position could be defended while they fought the maneuver battle.

There was hope. Yes, a path had opened.

"It's a race against time. Be quick! Gentlemen, move out! Put the armored unit out front!"

"Sorry, sir. Right away, sir."

The existence of a light at the end of the tunnel reinvigorated HQ. It was a brilliant transformation, as if their monochrome world suddenly had color again. And he, Romel, was no exception. Though they were surrounded, Romel was in high spirits. Strangely enough, it seemed like things would work out somehow. With this operation and the tireless fighting of his subordinates, they would turn the tables and the feeling was... *Man, this feels so great.*

If the gods exist, they sure work in mysterious ways.

"Ha-ha-ha! I can't make fun of the major. It *does* feel good to turn the tables. All right, let's scare the living daylights out of 'em."

"Ha-ha-ha-ha-ha-ha-ha-ha-ha-ha! What a surprise!"

"Ha-ha-ha-ha-ha! Indeed!"

At Republican headquarters...

The normally tranquil albeit stuffy room was wrapped in an unusual atmosphere. The tense staffers were watching the two high-ranking officers in the middle of the room who had big, empty grins on their faces.

One was their commander, General de Lugo. The other was the officer regarded as the toughest, most experienced veteran of all of them, Colonel Vianto.

Their most senior commander and the veteran they were supposed to be able to rely on burst out laughing. On a battlefield, there is no greater fear. When the two people who should have been their core cracked up instead of coping with the crisis, the staffers wondered, *Have they gone insane?* with a shudder, and their faces all twitched.

So for a short while, the staffers were faced with the grave dilemma of whether or not to call a medical officer.

Paying no mind to the confusion around them, de Lugo and Vianto continued to laugh. *What's so funny?* As some of the staffers watched very, very closely, they realized the laugh was almost their way of saying, *Who cares?* and that they, too, had no choice but to follow suit.

And after the laughter had run its course, they spat: "This reality is a goddamn joke." That was their complaint against the absurd situation in which they found themselves.

They had been completely confident that their battle formation would lead to victory. It was a simple operation that required only sticking to theory: Apply pressure on the surrounded Imperial Army from three directions.

The Free Republican Army was structured in such a way that prebattle forecasts indicated it could win against the Imperial Army. *Was...* It had to be discussed in past tense.

"Did they— Did they seriously overturn our strategy with an operational-level power move? They've got some balls."

Now their plans had been completely obliterated—even though they hadn't made any mistakes on the strategic level. As a result of tactical maneuvers performed during operations, their strategic advantage was overcome. Theoretically, that shouldn't happen. But in reality, the situation they prepared for had been reversed.

After attacking the right flank, the enemy regiment essentially traded places with the reinforcements to assault the central forces.

The unit directly under Vianto was out intercepting, but surprisingly, the moment the enemies made contact, they began to retreat. Just like that, the Republicans couldn't stop them with their elite group, but neither could they organize a united resistance.

If the enemy was coming at them on the offensive, some could pin them down and the main group could strike the rest of the imperial forces.

But if the enemy was retreating, they had to attack.

Naturally, that made the logic work in reverse. Still, they couldn't just leave them be. They had to do something.

But in their situation, they didn't have many options to choose from.

The disorder on the right flank was unbearable, and the left flank was in a furious battle against the main enemy force attempting their breakthrough. When the battle was going in such a direction, they couldn't permit a regiment of mages to do as they pleased.

And then—

They could hardly believe it.

The possibility had crossed everyone's mind, but they had dismissed it as unfeasible.

"The enemy mages have broken into multiple groups?! They—they're pulling back around, and fast!"

They were all suddenly speechless.

Of all the—

Is that even possible?

The scene was a vivid reminder of the gap in ability between the two sides.

""It's like they're playing tag with us.""

Just as the pair said, it happened the instant the intercepting unit hesitatingly gave pursuit. The imperial forces smashed through as if they had been waiting for the slightest disruption in the lines.

Since both sides were accelerating past each other, they should have been able to turn and fire, but they were going so fast it made combat difficult. Vianto's mages attacked anyway and barely grazed the enemy, but the imperial mages nailed a handful of Republican mages.

"Agh, send out the reserve unit! Pincer the enemy with the intercepting unit!"

From a simple, bird's-eye view of the shape of things, the charging imperial forces were surrounded by several mages. At a glance, their encirclement and annihilation was only a matter of time. There were almost no gaps to escape through, and the Republican mage units were numerically superior as they closed in.

But to someone actually in that fight, the situation looked totally different.

The enemy ripped right through the surrounding mages. As if laughing at the Republicans' numerical advantage, the imperial mages abruptly overwhelmed them with firepower and mobility. It was like a bad dream.

Then, as if sneering at the Republic's attempt to suppress them, they made a crazy beeline for de Lugo's headquarters.

"It's no good! They're too fast!" someone cried.

They were, indeed, too fast. Before the reserves could get in the air, before the pursuing unit could catch up, they had reached their target.

They had charged all the way over there to eliminate a single person.

But Vianto, at least, had been secretly preparing for this possibility. *I'm going to prevent a repeat of what happened on the Rhine front no matter what it takes!*

"Hurry and get counter-mage defenses up! A direct hit is coming! Take shelter! HQ personnel, take shelter!"

Ignoring the uproar around them, Vianto started to shove de Lugo into a dugout. But when he sensed there wasn't enough time, he didn't hesitate. He promptly kicked de Lugo in and dove on top of him as a shield. The staffers who piled in immediately after him were lucky. Right as all of them knocked together in the dugout—

"Ngh!"

Someone shouted a warning in a quaking voice, and everyone went prone by conditioned response. The moment they instinctively, almost in a trance, ducked their heads, partially opened their mouths, and covered their ears, their eardrums endured a roaring blast.

And what met their eyes when they looked up was the area HQ used to be, the aftermath of the mages' flyby. In addition to a smattering of antipersonnel explosion formulas, they had attacked with grenades and fifty-kilo bombs.

As those in the dugout looked on, the imperial mages shook off the defending anti–air fire with ease and picked off pursuing Republican mages.

The dogged pursuit continued, yet despite the strenuous efforts of the defending mages, the enemy broke free as the Republican leaders watched from the dugout.

Most of the staffers were stupefied by that brief moment. The enemy attacked and left, and they hadn't been able to do a thing.

So those are imperial mages. Those are the guys who raged across the Rhine front. The shock was so much that the vast majority of the staffers had frozen, but Vianto, one of the few exceptions, began taking stock of the damage.

The headquarters had taken direct hits with mage formulas and was destroyed. In that state, all its equipment had to be ruined. Their only choice was to use the backup command post. *I sure am glad we made a backup.*

"…Are you all right, General?"

"By the protection of the Holy Mother! A little later and we would have been in trouble! I never thought the day would come I'd be glad to have a subordinate who would kick me without hesitating!"

Most importantly, the general was alive.

Luckily, it should probably be said, de Lugo escaped with only bruises from when he dove, or rather was kicked, into the dugout. No one blamed Vianto for them, though, because he had averted catastrophe.

Still, even if their courage was feigned, they were calm enough to joke about it.

Vianto determined they had dodged the worst-case scenario. He remembered the crisis of defeat, the shock at hearing their headquarters on the Rhine had been blown away. They couldn't let that happen again.

Still, when he noticed de Lugo had his eyes squeezed shut like he was praying, he wasn't surprised—he had been terrified himself.

After all, the Republican Army had nearly been decapitated again. On the Rhine, their response had been delayed because it was new to them, but this time they narrowly escaped making the same mistake.

It was probably due to protection from God. He thought of the future of the fatherland, the pride of the Republic that would be passed on. Their determination to maintain that radiant glory, even if it was just an afterglow, was just barely getting them through this crisis.

"What's the damage?"

"Things are a mess, but we can still manage to call it minimal. Shall we withdraw?"

Chapter VI

They could still fight. At least, they could still crush them in the next round.

This was the southern continent—not the Empire's home base but the territory of the Republic and the Commonwealth.

Our odds in a long fight aren't bad. In that case, it's probably best to conserve our troops and go back to wearing down the enemy.

With those thoughts, de Lugo decided to minimize their losses and withdraw.

Yes, this time they lost. He felt that. *They got us.* But as a strategist, he had already accepted it and put it behind him.

"Ahh, there's nothing we can do about this... We retreat! We retreat and watch for our chance to make a comeback. Notify all units to withdraw. They're absolutely not to chase any farther. We need to reposition ourselves."

If a battle broke out, they wouldn't be able to win anyway, so the answer was to not fight.

They would lure the enemy into a battle of attrition and grind them down. The fact that they had survived was already a turning point.

He and the Republic would not lose. All they had to do was be standing on their two feet at the end of the war. In short, that was what victory was to the Republic.

"Ha-ha-ha! Did you see them, Major? The looks on those numbskulls' faces!"

"Ha-ha-ha! I understand how you feel, but you might want to watch what you say."

In a truly rare occurrence, Major von Degurechaff is in a good mood.

She laughs gleefully from her belly, like a child of her age, as she leads the battalion. When they're feeling good, even the most straitlaced person will crack a smile. Happily, the ability to feel genuinely joyful is the sign of a healthy mind.

"But they couldn't even provide you a proper escort. For how proud of their good taste they are, the escargots are awfully tactless."

"Eh, they're just too slow. That can't be helped."

Of the Imperial Army's officially adopted computation orbs, the Type 97 gets both superior altitude and speed. In fact, it leaves the others in the dust.

Eight thousand is considered the maximum combat altitude for existing orbs, but that's practical for the Type 97. It's such a high-performance orb that if you work extra hard, you can approach twelve.

Naturally, it's the optimal type for the self-preservation-first tactic of hitting and running. With outstanding altitude, speed, and climb rate, the Elinium Type 97, known officially as an assault orb, boasts performance equal to its name.

The Type 95 is a hugely flawed machine, but the Type 97, I can use—even Tanya is compelled to raise her hands to praise Elinium Arms. She appreciates the safety and peace of mind the Type 97 gives so much that it's her trusty main orb.

Although when she's really cornered, I have to ignore my myriad conflicts and tearfully relinquish that pillar of my being, the freedom of my mind. Life is really irreplaceable.

That said, I don't have to face any extreme conflicts like that this time. You don't have to be Tanya to be happy about getting through something without having to make any tough decisions.

"Well, it's no wonder. Trends move fast in the Empire—especially if you're a Republican soldier holed up in the colonies."

So even Tanya is in a jocular mood, though it's not in her character. It's so wonderful to be free of that curse that makes me sing songs praising God or whatever!

"In any case, let's drink to the Elinium Type 97!"

Now and then, Elinium Arms does a decent job.

"Here, here. Thanks to this thing, that duck hunt was a hell of a lot easier."

If you focus on the outline, it looks like my battalion had a tough fight. We can even boast that we gave the enemy a good run for their money basically on our own.

One battalion—augmented, yes, but still one battalion—punched through the encirclement trapping friendly forces!

With the enemy reinforcements at our mercy, we lured in the main forces and stopped them in their tracks!

Then we turned back to attack and even did an anti-surface strike!

If you add some rhetorical flourishes to our running around trying to escape and achieving zero actual war gains, that is what you get. Someone from the Imperial Japanese Army might have said something like, "My spirited unit delivered a bold blow to the enemy's main forces unscathed as was our mission, and now we're pulling back."

I figured it would be bad to only avoid the enemy, so we did that anti-surface strike at the end in order to have some action to point to—perfect.

Well, there were some newbie amateurs who seemed to think they were mages because they flew now and then, so I was able to rack up some points. Honestly, though, I'm not even sure if I should add them to my score.

It's tricky because if you count little chicks only capable of flying, people think worse of you. The way the Empire assesses kills is quite strict, so even if you don't mean to pad your count, it's better to avoid anything that could look like you might be.

Even if I hunted these guys by the dozens, talking big about that when they don't even compare to the enemies we faced on the Rhine will only make my colleagues ridicule me. I can't stand it when they say stuff like, *You want to brag about your hunting numbers* that *bad?*

If I count them, I'm sure people will be talking about my back. *How desperate for kills can you get?* But then Tanya has an idea.

"We'll have to mark down that this was a turkey shoot."

"Yeah, you're right. We can't make misleading reports."

That's right. Didn't they say the same thing in World War II? That a score against the Russkies on the eastern front was totally different from a score against the American or British on the western front.

"This enemy sure is persistent, though. It seems they're still in pursuit."

I don't want to mess up my record, she thinks, but when she turns around to look, the enemies seem raring to go. She thinks for a minute, but who knows what these creeps will do if she lets them follow her home. What a pain.

What's more, it seems like the units coming after us know what they're doing.

It's also aggravating that we can't shake them off even though we're nearing maximum acceleration. I would propose a law against stalkers, but such regulation wouldn't apply on a battlefield anyhow, so I guess you just have to save yourself.

"All right, let's play with them. Gentlemen, a *tsurinobuse*. Entertain our guests!"

I want to ambush these creeps so we can get away. We're already in pseudo-Shimazu mode, so it's not a bad idea to take a page from their book here.

They're *the ones who are pursuing* us. *I would much prefer the civilized method of having a peaceful conversation,* Tanya grumbles in her head. Once the enemy charges at you, you're left with no other option but to slaughter them, am I right?

""""Yaaargh! Let's give them an avalanche of cuddles!""""

And her subordinates' response to her order is just as lively as she expected.

The troops are thirsty for battle, which is great. That means she won't have any trouble getting volunteers to play the terribly difficult yet fun role of the bait: numbskull imperial soldiers fleeing in a rout. Well, it just means they're the nasty type who like teasing puppies.

"Fairy 01 to 02 and 05. You guys are the bait. Position yourselves in the rear. When those clowns attack, pretend to collapse into disarray and flee."

First, she has two companies pretend to be the rear guard. The point is to get the enemy's attention. An enemy that is raring to fight is often like an enraged bull charging at a red cape. Her subordinates aren't red, but I've heard a bull will charge at anything waved in front of them.

So to borrow from that example, they'll pretend they can't stand up to the enemy's attack and beat a disorderly retreat. She'll have two companies be the waving cape and get chased while the other units pretend to flee before the enemy and get some distance.

Feigning that they've lost the will to fight, they'll scatter to either side. Then all they have to do is wait at the optimal location and lure in those numbskulls who only know how to charge.

"The rest of you split up. After luring the enemy into airspace D-3, we're going to attack from three sides."

The moment the two bait companies lead the enemy into D-3, the rest of the units, who were supposedly fleeing in chaos, will come back around and launch an attack. Then they'll all form a cone shape and cross their lines of fire, taking care not to hit one another.

The moment that formation comes together, the enemy will be like a rat in a trap.

"Okay, gentlemen. Time to give these goobs some learning!"

Tanya crows that they'll teach them that being surrounded is just as terrible in the sky as it is on the ground. Sadly, whether or not they'll be able to use what they learn is a matter for another dimension.

And when the imperial mages fire an improbable amount of formulas into that narrow airspace, the Republicans who so enthusiastically pursued them expire and fall one after the other. You don't have to be Tanya to recognize this as a morale-boosting, extremely smooth victory.

Plus, Major Tanya von Degurechaff gets to pad her score, and it doesn't even take that much effort. It's a wonderful job that results in easy, dramatic gains.

"Ha-ha-ha-ha! I can't stop laughing!"

Which is why, in a rare occurrence, she is able to be so cheerful she even cackles.

She nearly says, *It would be great if it could stay this easy from now on*, but she freezes when she realizes the implication of her words.

Yes, the words *from now on.*

...From now on?

This is what it means to be so happy you wrap back around to sad. Her thoughts stop for a moment, and then a terrifying premonition of the future sends chills down her spine. After regaining her composure, Tanya objectively recalls the situation she's in. Then after thinking a moment, she shakes her head with an openly bitter expression on her face.

Certainly, we're winning easily at present. Even just now they've downed Republican mages like it was a turkey shoot. But war isn't usually like this.

Having it this easy will ruin you. Taking out enemy rabble certainly makes for a straightforward victory, but it would be a mistake to expect all battles to be like this.

Even before that, if we have such an advantage, shouldn't we be taking action to end the war?

"...Hmm?"

Tanya suddenly wonders why they are still fighting and groans unconsciously. Without even noticing First Lieutenant Weiss's questioning look, she sinks deep into thought as the unit returns to base. After mulling things over for a while, she is forced to acknowledge a shocking reality.

When they land back at their desert base, she drops off her gear and dismisses the troops. Sipping a cup of cold water from the tank with an absentminded expression, she looks out at the endless train of imperial military vehicles coming and going across the desert.

Supplies from the home country and transport trucks. All those things fight a desperate battle against the sand to assist in their victory. She isn't sure who came up with the idea, but they've wisely used camels instead of horses to carry some of the cargo, which probably increases efficiency.

So their hard work is paying off. For now, things are fine.

Their only enemies are the Republican remnants, who are hardly a formidable threat, and the Commonwealth's expeditionary forces. Regardless of numbers, the Imperial Army has them beat in terms of training, so any fight is a guaranteed turkey shoot.

Conversely, though, we're wasting our vehicles on this pathetic enemy and putting serious strain on our supply lines.

...Certainly, in terms of General von Zettour's idea of a purely political deployment to put pressure on the Republic and expand our influence on the Kingdom of Ildoa, a southern continent expeditionary force is one answer.

But that... The words are on the tip of her tongue, but she can't get them out, and she sighs.

Both Lieutenant General von Rudersdorf's plan to wipe out the Republican Army remnants and Lieutenant General von Zettour's political plan are choices that assume the number of major players in the war doesn't rise. They have made an expeditionary force a reality using every means possible despite the trying situation in the rear and the limited forces they could muster.

Tanya is compelled to worry. *Considering the financial situation, perhaps this plan takes us too far out of our way on thin ice.*

There should have been any number of ways to go. The High Seas Fleet could have taken a make-or-break attitude toward taking command of the sea from the Commonwealth, even if both navies ended up destroyed. They could have established a puppet government in the Republic and made peace.

But as far as Tanya can tell, the imperial fleet is resorting to the fleet-in-being strategy of avoiding military risks and conserving its strength. While she can't deny that strategy has its logic, it's definitely not one that will defeat their enemies.

Which is why she has ended up deployed to the inessential Republican colonies on the southern continent to pursue and destroy the remnants of the Republican Army. Even discounting the diplomatic thoughtfulness vis-à-vis the Kingdom of Ildoa, it's still putting the cart before the horse.

The Empire might as well be idly radiating its superior fighting capabilities. In these separate small-scale battles, the imperial generals won't lose. They're dominating on the tactical level. The General Staff is successfully managing mobility and deployment on the operational level, whether maneuver warfare or breaking through encirclements, as well as supply issues.

Indeed, from a military standpoint, putting military and political pressure on the Republic remnants and the Commonwealth via the situation on the southern continent and planning to cooperate with Ildoa is not a grave error.

But that's only from a purely military standpoint. *Or...* Tanya has second thoughts and revises her conclusion. *Maybe the General Staff is proposing policies from only a military standpoint from the start, and the rest they leave up to the government, not wanting to step on the administration's toes.*

But if that's the case, Tanya has to bury her head in her hands.

Chapter VI

"...What good will it do to expand the front any more than this?"

What does the Empire possibly gain by taking former Republican colonies in a desert? Has the will to fight any enemy you find on the battlefield spread to the politicians in the rear, who are supposed to maintain their calm and think about strategy?

As she follows this train of thought, she trembles at her horrible vision of the future.

"Then...then how...? How are the politicians at home going to end the war?"

She murmured it to herself.

But that one sentiment gives her a dreadful chill, like a curse. *Are the imperial politicians capable of ending the war?*

We, the Imperial Army, are winning in the field. We also have the initiative. That's why we're enjoying such good times right now.

Yes, both politically and militarily, this is our finest hour.

...So if this really is our finest hour, then...?

What a waste, she laments. It's our finest hour, but the Empire is still hemorrhaging its national power in a war that has no end in sight.

 NOVEMBER 1, UNIFIED YEAR 1925, COMMONWEALTH HOUSE OF COMMONS

"Subjects of the Commonwealth, today I inform you that the day approaches when the Empire, that dreadful military nation, brings its power to bear on us."

The voice of the prime minister speaking to all the Commonwealth's people over the radio conveyed their harsh reality.

"And unfortunately, I must also inform you that they mean to attack. But allow me to say this: I hope it will be of some small consolation that I promise you on behalf of the Commonwealth, it will be impossible for them to come by sea."

Contrary to the content of his speech, however, his tone contained a hint of humor.

"But even our wooden walls, praised since long ago, would find the evil enemy we currently face a significant trial. War is no longer what it used to be."

So he spoke, touching on the way war had changed.

"At this point, we must frankly acknowledge, without losing heart, that we are entering a terrible age."

Everyone listening carefully understood that he meant it would be a hard fight.

"This war will be harsh, and it will demand lengthy endurance. We will probably have to fight until either we or our enemy collapse. And it will be a fight that takes every last bit of strength our fatherland has."

Along with his predictions, he made a declaration.

"But I promise my beloved fatherland."

Each and every word was crystal clear.

"Someday, we will destroy them."

Someone in a pub shouted, "You bet we will!" and multiple people nodded in agreement.

"But for now, I simply hope that in the Commonwealth of a thousand years from today, our children's grandchildren will read in a history book written by one of us that now, this moment, was the best of times for the Empire."

That was the history it was their duty to create.

"For us, it is truly the worst of times; dismal, it should be said. At the same time, for the Empire, it is the best of times."

He was even arrogantly confident that they would exist in perpetuity a thousand years later.

"Now then, ladies and gentlemen, a toast to our worst of times. And don't we want our grandchildren to say it? Don't we want them to say these times were the Empire's best? To now, to our eternal fatherland's worst of times—cheers!"

(The Saga of Tanya the Evil, Volume 3: The Finest Hour, Fin)

Appendixes

Mapped Outline of History

Mapped Outline of History

❶ Year 3, Part 1

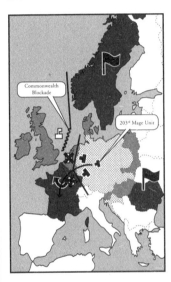

Operation Revolving Door → Belated Commonwealth Interference

1 The Commonwealth begins engaging in diplomatic interference. Aware that war could break out, it positions its fleet in preparation.

2 The Imperial Army carries out Operation Shock and Awe.

3 The 203rd Aerial Mage Battalion's select company employs tunneling tactics.

4 Operation Revolving Door begins.

❷ Year 3, Part 2

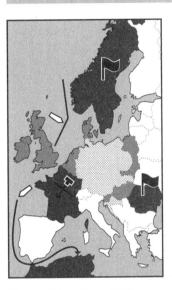

The Republican Capital Falls

1 The Commonwealth joins the war. But due to very mistaken assumptions, the mobilization of its land army is delayed.

2 The main forces of the Republican Army surrender.

3 The Imperial Army advances into the Republican capital.

4 De Lugo launches an emergency escape plan created in case the mainland was lost.

5 The 203rd Aerial Mage Battalion attempts to resist orders right before the cease-fire is declared.

6 The Republican fleet begins its escape to the colonies on the southern continent

7 The Empire begins analyzing the situation with the goal of ending the war.

❸Year 3, Part 3

General
Commen-
tary

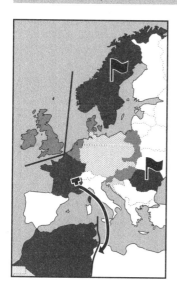

Lull→Expedition to the Southern Continent

1 The Empire sends troops with a primary objective of keeping the Republic in check and maintaining the pressure but also out of consideration for its diplomatic relationship with the Kingdom of Ildoa (a political objective).

2 The Republic reorganizes its colonial army and sorties to defend the colonies.

3 The Imperial Army defeats the Republicans with mobile tactics.

4 The Bulldog speaks.

The Imperial Army carried out bold operational-level maneuvers such as tunneling and decapitation strikes in Operation Revolving Door and won a decisive, historic victory.

With its superiority on the purely military side, the Imperial Army immediately took the Republican capital.

Since no one expected that to happen, the Commonwealth's intervention came too late to stop the Republic from losing its homeland.

Amid concerns about the direction of the war, the Empire sent troops to the southern continent seeking to increase its gains.

With the creation of a new front in the south and the Imperial Army's demonstration of their outstanding tactical maneuvers, the Republic and Commonwealth realize they are in for a bitter fight.

As a result, all historians agree that this moment was the Empire's finest hour.

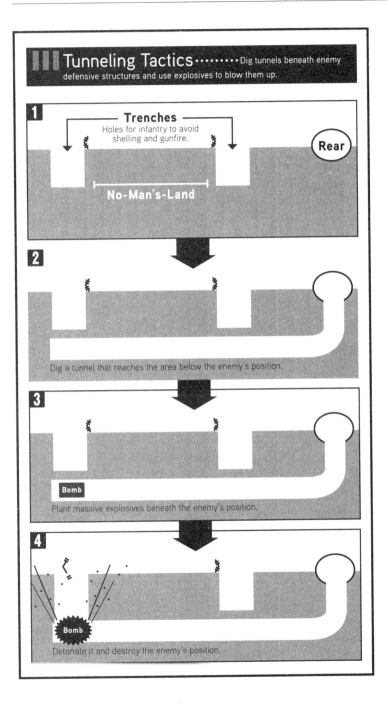

Tunneling Tactics

Dig tunnels beneath enemy defensive structures and use explosives to blow them up.

1

Trenches
Holes for infantry to avoid shelling and gunfire.

Rear

No-Man's-Land

2

Dig a tunnel that reaches the area below the enemy's position.

3

Bomb

Plant massive explosives beneath the enemy's position.

4

Bomb

Detonate it and destroy the enemy's position.

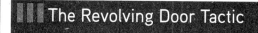

The Revolving Door Tactic

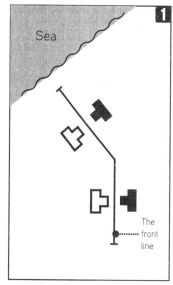

Sea

The
front
line

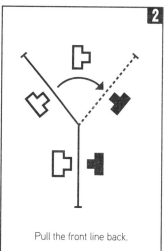

Pull the front line back.

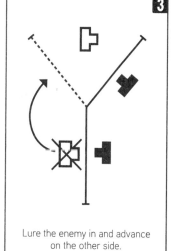

Lure the enemy in and advance
on the other side.

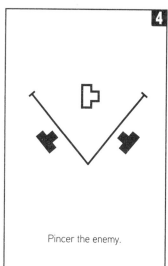

Pincer the enemy.

▐▐▐ Summary of the Imperial Army's Actions on the Rhine Front

1

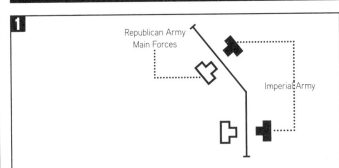

Republican Army Main Forces

Imperial Army

The Imperial Army and the Republican Army face off on the Rhine front.

2

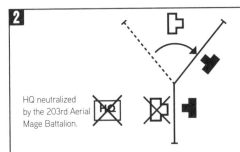

HQ neutralized by the 203rd Aerial Mage Battalion.

The Republican main forces move up their front line. The Imperial Army uses tunneling tactics to blow up the Republican forces from below.

3

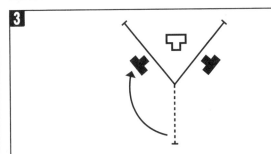

The Republican Army is efficiently pincered using the revolving door tactic. Surrounded with no supplies, the Republican Army surrenders.

Afterword

To everyone who picked up Volume 3, long time no see. I'm terribly ashamed to have kept you waiting this long. And to the heroes here for the first time, who have purchased all three books at once, may you have a bright future on "this side."

Anyhow, this is for a limited time only, but you can download an audio drama—an audio drama! Wow. Unless I'm constantly hallucinating without realizing it, you may already be enjoying that content now.

Surprisingly, it can be said that everything went according to schedule (per an announcement from General HQ). Last time, my productivity was hindered by that "east-side company" and their malicious interference in what Clausewitz would call "friction." This time, with no such malicious interference, things went accordingly...things went according to schedule.

Actually, I'm even ahead of schedule, aren't I? Even though it's fall, I'm writing this in my room with not my heater but the AC on.

This is not a lie. At the time of this writing, the temperature is a ridiculous eighty-three degrees Fahrenheit.

Let me explain. My manuscript and real life overlapped with each other, and it was an extremely bitter fight. Having gotten through it, I headed jauntily for the airfield and quietly boarded a plane to the United States. I was so proud of myself for successfully balancing my manuscript and real life that I was happy-go-lucky.

Then as I was chilling in the American South, suffering from the gastric strain of American-sized food portions, I saw news of a terrorist attack in Canada. *What the heck?* I reached for my tablet to check a news site, when *Oh?* I had a new e-mail. I opened it with warm fuzzies, wondering who was concerned for my safety, and was shocked.

It was an e-mail telling me to write an afterword by [X-Day]! Oh my God.

So it is that I'm coming to you, banging away on my keyboard, thinking, *It wasn't supposed to be this way*, from where I'm staying in the southern United States. I imagine that by the time you get this volume in your hands I'll be back on Japanese soil. <Maybe.>

Humans are always falling into the same trap when they accomplish something. I feel like I must have been taught the importance of vigilance, how the most dangerous moment is when you think you've defeated your enemy. In other words, this is what I get for forgetting the proverb "One must tighten one's helmet straps even after a win."

And so, I've realized that I need to reflect on the things I've done.

For example, how about that wonderful beach scene I delivered as promised? Now I feel nothing but regret for how ingratiating it was. Though it was a desire imparted to me by you, the readers, I am doing some serious, gentlemanly reflection on whether I might not have been too true to desire and worldly passions. Wondering if I will be scolded, I am unable to face my conscience. This is a book for good citizens with an established reputation as a wholesome novel, so next time I'll try to portray things a bit more moralistically.

I hope you'll forgive me for this volume's unscrupulousness.

I am leaning toward giving you my word that I will deliver Volume 4 at blitzkrieg speed (compared to previous efforts), and I swear to you now, though it's only a personal promise, that I will make my decision as soon as possible.

Last but not least, thanks to Tsubakiya Design who did the great design, the proofers who worked with me on all the obnoxious proofing, the team who combined their powers to make the audio drama, and many, many others.

November 2014 *Carlo Zen*